**This book is to be returned on or before the last date stamped below.**

St James voluntary
library.

16 11 AUG 1997

LIBREX

Gorman, Ed

Blood Red Moon.

# BLOOD RED MOON

# BLOOD RED MOON

Ed Gorman

**HEADLINE**

First published in Great Britain in 1994
by HEADLINE BOOK PUBLISHING

10 9 8 7 6 5 4 3 2 1

British Library Cataloguing in Publication Data

Gorman, Ed
Blood Red Moon
I. Title
813.54 [F]

ISBN 0-7472-1124-8

Typeset by
Letterpart Limited, Reigate, Surrey

Printed and bound in Great Britain by
Mackays of Chatham PLC, Chatham, Kent

HEADLINE BOOK PUBLISHING
A division of Hodder Headline PLC
338 Euston Road
London NW1 3BH

To Matt Bialer

*Time is the fire in which we burn.*
Delmore Schwartz

I would like to thank Marlys Brunsting for all her help with this manuscript, and Robert W. Walker for his assistance with the process of 'profiling.'

I would also like to thank my friend and editor, Bob Gleason, for supplying key material for this book.

E. G.

# One

# 1

First day of incarceration, there's a killing.

Big black guy named Blade gets stabbed thirty-seven times with his own knife.

According to the inmates, of course, nobody saw shit.

Blade got killed? Hmmm. Surprise to me.

Did I hear anything? You mean like screams or somethin'? Nah, man, I didn't hear squat.

Did I see anything? Not a thing, man. Not one thing.

He realizes, after hearing about Blade's death, that he is never going to make it out of this prison alive.

All the shit that turned women on, the almost pretty face, the almost wasted poetic body, the air of suffering . . . that same shit is going to get him killed in this place.

Very first thing another inmate said to him was, 'Hey, white dude, they gonna love that ass of yours in he-ah.' Black guy giggling all over the place. Crazed animal eyes like so many in here.

But—

Is not gay. Does not want to be touched by another man under any circumstances. And certainly does not want to be harmed.

And—

Is not stupid, either.

First three days in the joint all he does is watch and listen. (And try to get used to his cellmate sitting down on the john every hour or so, creating a kind of intimacy that is totally repugnant.)

Not hard in a jungle like this to figure out who has power and who doesn't.

Four days in the joint, on the yard, decides to risk his life by going up to the inmate obviously in charge of this cell block.

3

*Servic, his name is. Big muscle-bound Bohunk from Milwaukee. Shaved head. Enough tattoos to start an art museum. Brown teeth.*

*Courtiers are in session, maybe eight guys standing around Servic brown-nosing him shamelessly.*

*His little army.*

*He goes right up to Servic. 'Like to talk to you.'*

*'Yeah?' Smirks to the courtiers so that they know he knows what a little faggot this new guy really is.*

*'Yeah. Want to tell you how you can make two thousand dollars a month.'*

*Smile goes. 'You wouldn't be fuckin' with me, would you, fairy boy?'*

*'One I'm not a fairy boy. Two I wouldn't be stupid enough to fuck with you.'*

*Servic looks around. His merry band looks every bit as confused as he does.*

*Maybe this fairy boy has gone nuts. That happens here, usually right off the top. Just can't adjust and so they go crazy.*

*But Servic has no reason to be afraid of him, crazy or not, so he says to his boys, 'I'll see you guys in a few minutes.'*

*'You want us to split?' says a con.*

*'No,' Service says, 'I want you to bake me a fuckin' cake. Of course I want you to split, asshole.'*

*They split.*

*'You ain't gonna last here very long, fairy boy,' Servic says. 'Not pushin' your luck like this.'*

*'That's what I wanted to talk to you about. About lasting here. Surviving.'*

*'What about it?'*

*'I want to pay you two thousand dollars a month – deposited on the first of every month in any bank account you choose, anywhere in the world – to be my bodyguard.'*

*'You're shittin' me.'*

*'Two thousand a month. Tax free.'*

*'I'll be goddamned. You're serious, aren't you, fairy boy?'*

*'One other thing, Mr Servic. Quit calling me fairy boy, all right?'*

*Servic looks at him a long moment and then breaks into laughter that echoes off the steep walls surrounding the yard.*

4

*'I'll be a sonofabitch,' Servic says finally. And then grins. 'Kid, for two thousand bucks a month, you got yourself a bodyguard.'*

*Then Servic puts out his hand and they shake and then Servic calls his boys over and introduces them to his first client.*

*His first two-thousand-dollar-a-month-client.*

*Who said America ain't the land of opportunity?*

# 2

The day it all started, I'd spent most of the morning on the phone with the National Center for the Analysis of Violent Crime (NCAVC). As a former FBI man who'd worked fifteen years in the behavioral science unit, I could still be a help on certain difficult cases – and they could help me on some of my own investigations as well. These days I was a consultant to various small-town police departments and to trial lawyers who wanted me to prove that their clients were men and women of unimpeachable integrity and unfaltering love for stray puppies.

The particular case my old friend Gif wanted help with concerned a serial killer operating in the area of Huntsville, Alabama. One of the local TV stations had begun receiving letters supposedly written by the killer. As a trained psychologist, I had spent most of my days in the unit working on the profiles of various killers. Gif wanted to know if a man who dismembered bodies and buried the various parts around the city would also be the type of man who would send letters about himself to TV stations. I said that I guessed not. The killer's M.O. indicated a disorganized, secretive man, a man who killed out of passion rather than some grand scheme . . . one not likely to want this particular kind of attention. Gif thanked me, we talked a bit about the old days, he said he was sorry about my wife and how was I doing these days, and was I still flying the biplane?

As indeed I was. Ten minutes after hanging up, I headed for the hangar.

There's one particular problem with these old biplanes. When you're running them too slow, they sometimes take you into a sudden descent that's tough to get out of.

That's what happened to Mac Thompson, the man who taught me how to fly my crate: he had a little trouble with his fuel valve and got caught in a spin. He met the beautiful green Midwestern earth at maybe 150 mph. Head on.

I was the first one to reach him and it's not likely I'll ever forget the crushed and broken look of him, the quick red gleam of blood, the blanch-white jut of bone through flesh.

That was a year ago.

This year the Civil Air Patrol of Charlesville, Iowa had a new daredevil, Robert Payne by name. That would be me.

I'd done forty-five minutes for the kids on this chilly but sunny April afternoon out in pastureland next to the airport. All the usual showboating you might expect, too, loops and rolls and flying far lower than I should have. But I enjoyed it even more than the kids did because all the time I was up there I was one with wind and sky and cloud, the same kind of pilgrim the earliest aviators were, when flying was still a romance and not just another means of transportation. I was born too late to see the old barnstormers first-hand, but my uncle had been one and we had hours of scratchy old family film of him playing eagle. He was a rangy man whom I resembled, with shaggy blond hair and one of those small-town Midwestern faces that appear simple and happy and trusting, till you looked more closely at the blue eyes and noted the wariness that too many years of city life had put there.

Problem was, even with my leather jacket, leather flying helmet, leather gloves and goggles, the open cockpit tended to get a little nippy on days like this, when the temperature was still only running about 42 degrees. My nose was running pretty bad. That wasn't supposed to happen to daring young men in Snoopy helmets.

Right now all I could think of was some brandy warmed by the fireplace in the venerable old house where I live, and the opportunity to smoke my one allotted bowl of Captain Black for the day and to pick up where I'd left off in Robert Louis Stevenson's *The Master of Ballantrae*. Or to do some more reading for an anecdotal history of Iowa I'm planning to write – a task that requires a great deal of research.

I put the handsome red barnstormer down in a field of reedy

green buffalo grass, the tall wheels bouncing merrily over the bumps, the engine expelling war clouds of thin blue smoke.

No Saturday afternoon cowboy hero had ever been better treated to the adulation of young people than I was that afternoon; there were twenty-six of them in all, a few more girls than boys to reflect our modern age, each nattily gussied up in the Patrol uniform.

'You ever going to take anybody else up in that, Robert?' a ferociously freckled girl asked.

'If I can ever get the right kind of insurance,' I said.

'Oh, shoot,' she sighed, disgusted. A small choir of groaners joined her.

'You ever get scared in an old bucket like this?' one of the boys asked. 'I mean, after what happened to Mac and all last year?'

I grinned, the dashing hero to the end. 'I can't think of a better way to go than in old *Liberty* here.'

'Did you name her *Liberty*?' another boy asked.

'Nope. That was the name she came with.'

A girl beamed. 'I'm glad she's a she.'

I looked out over the faces and said, 'I need six bodies to help me push *Liberty* into the hangar over there. Any volunteers?'

They all joined in, of course, resembling a noisy mob in a movie, *Liberty* regal in her stubborn way as she was pushed through grass almost tall enough to brush the engine. Flat Midwestern prairie rolled to distant blue hills, and a pale gold scimitar of moon could be seen now that four o'clock was here.

'Thanks, everybody,' I said, starting to tie her down once we were in the hangar, and now that their adult leader had begun to hustle them into the three waiting vans.

He was named Neely. He was a nice guy who'd been under the spell of aviation his entire life.

'Gosh,' he said, sounding awfully young for someone well into his sixties, 'the kids sure did love the exhibition.'

'Well, I loved putting it on for them.'

'You're a great guy, Mr Payne, and I'd like to thank you.'

He took my hand and pumped it like a well handle he was having some trouble with. Even at his age he was gangly and a little awkward with the social graces. But he was honest and decent and industrious, and our country needed a whole hell of a lot more people like him.

Then he was gone, his footsteps echoing out of the small hangar, leaving me to a chill wind and the smell of fuel and oil and the cold spring day itself. I had goosebumps and my nose was still running.

I was finishing up, pulling the tarp over the double cockpit, when I heard a voice say, 'You sure do all right with the ladies, Mr Payne.'

'I do?' I said, turning around now that I was done.

It was Peterson from the adjacent airport.

He leered, his thick horn-rimmed glasses raising up on his pudgy cheeks. Peterson was the successful nerd all grown up, a beeper clipped to the waist of his wash pants, a formidable ring of keys dangling from his belt, a walkie-talkie filling his left hand and half a dozen pens lining his shirt pocket. His shoes were scuffed brown Hush Puppies with black shoestrings broken so many times their knots resembled tassels.

The tiny airport Peterson manages has a coffee shop where one afternoon a female cousin of one of the local pilots was bold enough to ask me if I'd like to have dinner with her that night. 'You're a very interesting man, Mr Payne,' she'd said. 'My cousin even seems to believe that you might have been in the FBI at one time.'

Ever since then, Peterson has taken the opportunity to tell anybody who would listen that I am a 'lady-killer'. Indeed, I had recently overheard him employing a phrase I don't believe I've come across since 1962. 'Ole Payne here,' he told a mutual friend in front of me, 'gets more ass than a toilet seat.'

Whoever said that we live in a coarse and vulgar age has never met the eloquent Harold J. Peterson.

'I'm not sure what you're talking about, Harold.'

'This woman. Real high-class stuff. She just stopped by the coffee shop. Wanted me to give you this.'

He handed me a heavy number ten manilla envelope sealed carefully with long strips of fiber tape.

I hefted it, felt a familiar shape inside.

'She give you her name?'

'Nope. And she wasn't the kind of gal you ask questions of,

9

neither. Pulls up in this fancy dark blue Caddy four-door that looked like it had just rolled right off the dealer floor. Hell, when she opened the door, I could smell the new leather seats. Even had a driver – a guy in a suit and mirror sunglasses. Looked like an FBI agent, actually. You know – like you used to be.'

'She say anything else?'

He shook his head. 'Nope, just asked if I knew you and would I give you this envelope.'

'Thanks, Harold. I appreciate it.'

'Got time for some coffee?'

'Afraid not. Want to get home and lay out some things for tomorrow. Try some new tackle on some carp.'

'Hell, my pa always said that there was no tackle or no man that a carp ever feared under any circumstances. And he was right. My cousin used to say they were demonically possessed, was how they could chew up tackle that way.'

I smiled. Fish lore dies hard up near the Mississippi. Marquette and Joliet, who were among the first white men to see the vast river, were warned by Indians that it was inhabited by monsters and giant fish that would devour them. This was back in 1673, about the time they reached the mouth of the Wisconsin river. Some of those Indian tales are still being told today.

I thanked him again and walked over to my Jeep in the tall grass, fired her up and let her idle a few minutes. She was born Army green in late 1944, just about the time we put the hammerlock on the Germans, and since then she had been passed down from my grandfather to my father to me. Whenever my mother wanted to gently nudge me toward getting married and settling down, she'd say, 'Wouldn't it be nice if you had a son to give the old Jeep to? It would've made your father so happy.'

While the Jeep was gaining strength, I slit the envelope open with a thumbnail and looked inside.

There was a half-inch of good green currency. Thumbing it, I guessed somewhere in the vicinity of 10,000 Yankee dollars.

I sat there in the soughing Midwestern wind for a time and watched a hawk splay its wings in silhouette against the soft blue prairie sky.

I wondered who the woman was and why she wanted to give me so much money.

# 3

In this part of the state, the soil is rich and dark and loamy. I helped dig the grave for Katherine Louise Payne so I know about the soil first-hand. We went down six feet as mandated by law.

We dug on a hot August morning, deep into earth cool with moisture and entangled with plant roots. It took two hours, even with their ravenous machinery, and when we were done I went over to the wide oak and sat under its leafy awning and looked out at the land she'd loved so much, river and forest and limestone cliffs, and thought all the way back to our First Communion in 1957, the day we'd first met, all the way up to two years ago when, standing in our kitchen, she'd complained of a headache and had then suddenly fallen into my arms.

Aneurism, the doctor explained later.

She'd been dead by the time I got her to the hospital, my friend for twenty-four years, my wife for eight.

On the way back to my house, I passed the graveyard, looking through the black iron fence to the hill where the oak waited. Sometimes I sat up there and smoked my pipe and talked to Kathy – not in the awkward and imprecise words of the tongue but rather the simple poetry of the heart. I wanted to stop there now, see her gravestone and say a prayer and tell her I loved her, but there wasn't time.

I needed to find out who wanted to give me 10,000 dollars – and why.

The house, in case you're interested, is what they call a 'Colonial farmhouse,' meaning a one-and-a-half-story Colonial with a porch running the length of the main section and a group of narrow gabled dormers and four floor-to-ceiling bays lending the

11

place a feel of old Williamsburg in George Washington's time. It sits on five fertile acres, three of which are farmed by a CPA from Cedar Rapids who secretly fancies himself a pioneer, and the remaining two make a nice island of grass and hardwoods and privacy for the house. It had been a wet spring so the forsythias were an especially vivid gold, and the daffodils weren't doing so badly either. Kathy had taught me patience first, and then gardening.

Our kids were going to be raised out here, but given the nature of my work for the government, we never quite got around to kids. We had to settle for three cats who were still with me, fortunately, their names being Tasha, Crystal and Tess, tiny Eloise having died at six months following a freak reaction to one of her booster shots.

The inside is just as Kathy had left it, an eclectic mix of Colonial, suburban shopping mall, and what I call post-hippie. You know, water pipes that have been converted into flower pots, and authentic fake Indian wall coverings that look great in the basement covering up cracks in the plaster.

In the kitchen is a framed blow-up of a segment of a 1901 teacher's contract that Kathy, a teacher once herself, had found in a dusty box in an antique shop. The blow-up lists five rules that the undersigned teacher had to obey absolutely:

The teacher shall not go out with any man except her brothers or father.

The teacher shall not dress in bright colors.

The teacher shall not use face powder or paint her lips.

The teacher shall not loiter in an ice-cream parlor.

The teacher shall wear at least three petticoats under her skirts.

Dusk was gray and grainy in the den window as I stoked up my pipe. The beer I poured, nothing special, whatever brand I'd found on sale, tasted cold and clean and good. The cats were lined up on the couch next to me, sleeping.

The heavy envelope was on my lap.

Who would want to give me 10,000 dollars? Nobody who had anything legal in mind, certainly.

With the remote, I snapped on the local TV news. The lead story was about the upcoming May Day celebration at a nearby mall. A slow newsday, apparently. This was followed by a thirty-second commercial for hog-raisers whose animals suffered from diarrhea. I was glad I didn't happen to be eating supper at that moment.

A few minutes later, me instantly clicking off the TV set, I heard a heavy car crunch up the gravel driveway. I kept picturing the big Caddy that Harold Peterson had told me about. The engine was shut off. Just dusk birds loud and frantic on the fading day – then a car door opening and chunking shut. Footsteps on the porch. Knock on the door. My mother having raised no idiots, I picked up my trusty Ruger Speed Six .357 Magnum and went to open it.

The mysteries of the envelope were about to be revealed.

I saw what Peterson had meant about the driver looking like an FBI agent. He managed to look tough even in an expensive suit, which was the first requirement; and you could feel the contempt of his gaze even through the mirror sunglasses, which was the second. He was probably forty and bulky in the strong way of somebody who religiously works off the gin at the gym. He could probably afford to buy a little better shoulder rig, though. His weapon was obvious. But then maybe he wanted it obvious.

'Mr Payne?'

'Yes.'

'I'm here about the envelope.'

I smiled. 'I figured somebody would show up to take it back.'

But men who wear mirror sunglasses after dark rarely smile. Ruins their image.

'My employer's name is Nora Conners. She'd like to come in and talk to you. Is that all right?'

I shrugged. 'Why not?'

'She'll be in momentarily.'

That's another thing guys who wear mirror shades after sundown never do. Never say goodbye.

He just turned, went down the stairs and out to the Caddy,

which was every inch as impressive as Harold Peterson had said. And, at least in the faint porch light, it did look as if it had just rolled off the dealer floor.

I went inside, picked up some newspapers from the past two days, folded them neatly by the firewood to the right of the fireplace, and when I stood up and turned around, there she was.

I had been expecting a young woman, for some reason I'd imagined she would be in her late twenties, but Nora Conners was at least forty. And quite lovely, her quietly beautiful face suggesting vulnerability, intelligence and a very private but exciting sensuality. She wore a gray designer suit that flattered the lines of her tall, slender body and lent her blonde chignon a prim but erotic quality that most chignons don't convey. She clutched a tiny black purse with a kind of endearing desperation. Perhaps she had another envelope containing 10,000 dollars in there.

'I know you prefer to be called Robert rather than Bob,' she said, as I took her extended hand. 'May I call you Robert?'

'Of course.'

'And this is Vic Baker. He rarely introduces himself.' She smiled like a mother introducing a mischievous son. 'He flunked out of finishing school.'

Not even their little private joke evoked a smile on the stone face of Mr Vic Baker.

'Listen,' I said, 'why don't we all get comfortable and take off our sunglasses?'

She laughed. 'Vic gets kidded a lot about his glasses at night but actually he suffers from an eye inflammation called uveitis. Supposedly the medication he's taking will clear it up in the next sixty days or so.'

'If you say so,' I said.

We all sat down. She took the couch, sitting in the center of it and on the very edge where her nice knees went white behind her hose, while Vic the Vampire chose the austere straight-backed chair by the fireplace. I made for the over-stuffed chair beneath our best Chagall print.

'Well,' I said, 'you certainly leave memorable calling cards.'

'I wanted to convince you that I'm serious,' Nora Conners said.

'About what?'

14

'About tracking down the man who murdered my daughter.'
She paused, giving me a moment to deal with what she'd said.
'Three weeks ago, a friend of yours, Mike Peary, was killed in
a hit-and-run accident. I believe you worked with him sometimes.'

I nodded. 'They just arrested a teenager for killing him.'

'Very bad detective work, Robert. They arrested the wrong
man. Mike Peary had been working for me for the past seven
months. He had tracked the man who killed Maryanne – my
daughter; she was twelve years old – to a small town up near the
Minnesota border. The man murdered him before Mike could get
back to me. Fortunately, Mike had mailed me a long letter before
it happened. I have that letter in the car.'

'Why not take it to the police?'

'Because they wouldn't listen to me.' The pause again. 'Do you
know who Richard Tolliver is?'

'Sure. Guy who lives in Des Moines. One of the richest men in
the state.'

'He's my father.'

'I see.'

'No, you don't. He's not only my father but he's also my jailer.
I've been married twice and both times he managed to put me in
mental hospitals.'

'You can't just put people in mental hospitals. There's a whole
legal process you have to follow. It's not all that easy.'

'It is if you're my father and three of your best friends happen
to be on the state supreme court.' She sighed. 'My father has
convinced most people that I'm not a very stable woman, never
have been, and that, since the death of my daughter, I'm even
crazier than before. If I took Mike's material to the police, the
first thing they'd do is smile patronizingly at me and then turn all
the material over to my father.'

She looked at me steadily. 'Mike said some very flattering
things about you and convinced me you could help us if anything
ever happened to him. He said the two of you had helped the
police on three cases involving missing children and that you
found two of them. He talked about you both being in the FBI
together and said you were probably going into business together,
assisting small-town police departments. He told me you'd both

15

obtained private investigator licenses.'

I grinned. 'You make me sound like one hell of a guy.'

'You are one hell of a guy, Robert. That's why I want you to pick up where Mike Peary left off. You're not the old gumshoe sort, but you are a detective – a very modern one. Mike told us all about "profiling" and how you both use it.'

'That still doesn't make me a wizard.' Whenever anybody turned her life – and all her hopes – over to me, I get nervous. I looked at her, which wasn't a real unpleasant task. 'You really think Mike was murdered?'

She nodded. 'I'm sure of it. So's Vic. He was just about to start the second part of his investigation. Then he was killed.' She paused. 'If I can be blunt, I know you need some work. I happen to be aware that your finances aren't in terribly good shape. You're three payments behind on your mortgage and you haven't paid your hangar fee for your biplane in six months.'

'Vic's been a busy boy, checking me out that way.'

Nora opened her small black purse and did a magician's trick, taking from it another manilla envelope that looked far too big to have fitted inside.

She stood up, walked over to me and set it on the arm of my chair, then went back and sat down again, primly smoothing her skirt before she did so.

'I'd cry and plead with you if I thought it would do any good, Robert, but I don't think it will. But I would like to say that I loved my daughter just as much as you loved your wife, and I want her killer found.'

'The police don't have any leads?'

'No leads at all.'

'And it's been how long?'

'Eight years.'

'Where was she killed?'

'The parking lot of a shopping mall. I was living in a town in Illinois. It was Christmas-time. She'd gone to the mall with one of her friends and the friend's mother. One minute Maryanne was with them, the next she was gone, just vanished. They found her much later that night, in a dumpster. He'd cut her up with a butcher knife. I don't want to tell you any more than that. It's not good for me to talk about.'

16

I looked at the envelope she'd just given me. 'Another ten thousand?'

'Fifteen.'

'Ah.'

'Making twenty-five altogether. One half down. Even if you aren't able to catch him, you'll make twenty-five thousand dollars for trying. Your banker would be very happy to hear about that.'

'You have Mike's letter?'

'Vic can get it.'

'How about if I read it tonight and call you in the morning?'

'I'd appreciate you doing that.'

'I'm not making any promises, understand.'

'Of course.' She looked at Vic. 'Would you get the letter, please?'

Vic left.

'That guy could get on my nerves,' I said. 'Doesn't he ever shut up?'

'Everybody's curious about Vic – especially my father. Actually, it's very simple. We had a pretty mediocre affair several years ago, but in the course of it I found out how good Vic was at managing my life. When I came into some money at the age of twenty-one, I hired Vic as my personal assistant. I pay him a lot of money and he's well worth it.'

He sure was. He was back before she could say another word.

He walked over to me and handed me a plain white envelope. The letter seemed sizeable. FBI agents are very good at writing coherent, detailed reports. That would have come in handy if we'd ever gotten around to starting that private investigations outfit we'd talked about so many times.

Vic went over and sat back down.

'We're staying in Cedar Rapids,' she said. 'The Collins Plaza.'

'I'll call you tomorrow.'

'I'd appreciate that.'

She stood up. So did Vic.

She came over and shook my hand. 'Mike said you were one of the best trackers he'd ever known. He swore you could find practically anybody.'

'I used to pay him to say that.'

She smiled. 'You don't take compliments very well, do you?'

17

'No,' I said, 'I guess I don't.'

I walked them out to the Caddy and stood in the drive as they pulled away, their headlights sweeping over me as Vic turned toward Cedar Rapids thirty-five miles away.

By now, it was full night, and my friend the barn owl was calling out from his crook at the top of the hardwood down by the creek.

It was a lonely sound, a perfect complement to the look in Nora Conners's eyes.

I went back inside, fed the cats, fed myself, opened another beer and started in on Mike Peary's letter.

Dear Nora,

I'm mailing this to you on the night before I go back to New Hope, Iowa and see which of my three suspects falls into the trap I set. More about this later.

I wanted to review everything with you in case something should happen to me and you need corroboration for the County Attorney when you finally turn everything over to him and he then brings in the police. I think you're right. From what I know of Haldeman he's a good and honest public official and I think he'll resist your father's interference.

So, for the record, here's my official statement:

On 9 October, 1992, I, Michael John Peary, was hired by Nora Conners to find the murderer of her twelve-year-old daughter Maryanne. She had been killed eight years earlier, in Illinois. No arrests had ever been made. Local police led Nora to believe that no serious suspects had ever been turned up in their investigation. Recent murders here in Iowa suggested that Maryanne's murderer may have left Illinois and come to Iowa.

I was hired because my last five years with the Federal Bureau of Investigation were largely spent working out of the FBI Academy. I helped local law enforcement agencies do 'profiling' of killers, which simply means looking for patterns in crimes and speculating on the nature and characteristics of the offender. This kind of profiling led to the FBI's capture of several infamous serial killers.

I took early retirement because I'd always wanted to write

18

suspense novels and I figured that age fifty-three was not too early to start.

The novel wasn't going so well when Nora Conners showed up at my apartment in Ames, Iowa that afternoon. She told me about Maryanne and about her own determination to find the killer.

She said that, given my background, and given the fact that this was the only case I'd be working on, I would likely do a better job than the police had. She offered me a generous amount of money to lead her search.

The first sixty days were spent at various computers. The circumstances of Maryanne's murder suggested that she had possibly met up with a serial killer. I say 'suggested.' I was operating on hunch and instinct as much as anything. There was always the possibility that a local child molester had grabbed her, then become panic-stricken and killed her, as frequently happens.

I started by going through the national computer files searching for all similar cases. When I had those categorized, I sub-categorized them again by A) similarities B) differences.

I found that four murders with a heavy percentage of similarities had taken place in Iowa over the past three years.

1. Victims were all girls 12-14 years of age.
2. The victims' necks had been broken.
3. The victims' bodies were severely mutilated with some weapon on the order of a butcher knife.
4. The victims' genitalia were cut up and pieces of them placed on their lips.

During the ensuing seven months, I studied the case history of each girl, still looking for similarities.

Because serial killers sometimes tend to murder the same 'type' over again – girls with blonde hair, black girls, crippled girls, etc. – I wanted to find one special element that the girls had in common.

One was Jewish, one was Catholic, one was Methodist, one belonged to no particular church. One was involved in sports, one was involved in theater, one was starting her own rock band, one collected dolls. None of them had ever seen the same doctor, dentist, hairdresser. Two wore glasses, two did not. One had been a Dairy Princess contestant, three had not. Three had enjoyed playing video games, one had not.

Then I started making notes on various trips the girls had made over their lives and that was how I learned about New Hope, Iowa.

For different reasons, each girl had visited New Hope shortly before her death.

MONICA KOSTNER had visited there on 6 January 1990 on an excursion to the Midwestern Pioneer Museum. She was accompanied by her mother.

SUSAN DOUGHERTY had visited there on 17 November 1991 to see her aunt, a Mrs Charles DeWitt. She was accompanied by her father.

MICHÈLE ROYCE had visited there on 3 July 1992 and again on 16 August of the same year to see her grandfather, who was dying of throat cancer. She was accompanied by both her parents.

BETTY NOLAN had visited there on 8 August 1992 to stay overnight with a former classmate, Donna Simpson, who had recently moved there with her parents. Betty took a Greyhound bus from Marion, Iowa to New Hope. She was unaccompanied both up and back.

After compiling all this data, I spent the next three weeks in New Hope, Iowa looking for a man who would fit my profile.

He sounds very organized to me and so I'd say that he is in all likelihood a firstborn son. His father's work would be stable, but his parental discipline has always been unstable and inconsistent. He has an average or above average intelligence, but he usually works at jobs below his ability. The FBI profile would show that he'd probably be fascinated with news coverage about himself – his 'secret other self' –

and might keep a scrapbook of clippings or even a photo album showing his mutilated victims. He is probably between twenty and forty years of age.

There is a lot more, of course, which I'll share with you at a later date.

During the course of my investigation in New Hope, Iowa, I met three men who qualify as serious suspects per the profile. They are:

CAL ROBERTS, 36, Caucasian, married, no children. Heavy travel schedule part of his 'mission' for the True Light Church, a TV ministry that is always trying to line up new cable outlets. Roberts travels a six-state area calling on local cable companies.

RICHARD MCNALLY, 38, Caucasian, father of one daughter. Sells gourmet honey for local beekeeper. Travels the Midwest mostly talking to upscale restaurants. Has been in Des Moines many times.

SAMUEL LODGE, 38, Caucasian, married, no children. Used to teach art at the U. of Iowa. Now gives private lessons and helps his wife run an antique shop. Lectures throughout the Midwest.

This is my report up to date. Tomorrow, I'm going to rent a room at the River's Edge Lodge and get into some serious investigation.

I have to say that I don't have any particular reason to suspect any of the three men I've named here. They simply, in broad terms, fit the profile.

As per agreement, I will call you at least twice a week with updates.

Talk to you soon,
Mike Peary.

Peary had attached several pages of forms and notes that went into his findings in clinical detail.

What surprises most people about such reports is that they aren't much concerned with the crime scene itself – the way a detective's report would be – but with the mind of the killer itself. Most folks on the behavioral science unit hold degrees in psychology and psychiatry. They speculate on the killer rather than his deeds.

The profiling was identical: you collected and evaluated data, you reconstructed the murders, and you began interpreting the data to give yourself a rough draft profile, which you then began refining. You needed not only a good, intuitive police mind, you also needed a strong stomach. You learned a great deal from studying autopsy and crime-scene photos, and most of them were tough to deal with, no matter how long you'd been at it. After that, you did your profile of the killer and looked at how it fit previous patterns.

Peary and I had talked about applying for a Small Business Administration loan and setting up shop some time. If we could have agreed where to put it – he wanted to stay in Des Moines, I voted for Cedar Rapids – we might have even had a chance.

But no longer. All that remained of Peary was a large stack of papers from his very first, unfinished case.

# 4

After reading Mike Peary's letter, I sat in my den with Tasha in my lap and the other two cats next to me. Tash was a tabby, the others of very mixed but very cute heritage.

I sensed that this was going to be the same kind of claustrophobic assignment our own friendly government had often given me: Undercover work with people who were either indifferent to my investigation and therefore uncooperative, or who were downright hostile. Small towns were the same the world over. People tended to be suspicious the moment you started asking questions.

I also thought about Mike Peary. He'd won most of the citations and awards the Bureau gave its agents. He belonged on the front of a Wheaties box – a smart, cautious, fair-minded and brave agent who was determined to help rebuild the Agency's reputation following the last sad years of J. Edgar Hoover's time.

Then Mike's life took an unexpected turn. He'd hinted for years that his marriage was less than wonderful but over our last lunch he told me that his wife had fallen in love with one of the men she worked with. The man was getting a divorce; so was Mike's wife.

I started hearing rumors of Mike spending an undue amount of time in Cedar Rapids bars. I phoned him once late last year to see if he wanted to go to an egg-nog party some people we knew were throwing. He declined, saying he was pretty busy. Now I knew that he'd been busy working for Nora. I asked him about his novel. He said that he was temporarily stalled but would be getting back to it when this job was over. He actually sounded reasonably happy. 'It's getting my juices flowing again, Robert. I really may be on to something here.'

'You going to tell me about it?' I asked.

He laughed. 'You know better than that. I can't discuss an on-going investigation with a guy who won't move to Des Moines. But when it's all over we'll have a steak dinner and I'll give you every gory detail. And believe me, they really are gory.'

So now here I was all these months later, sitting with his letter in my den, a chill rain starting to pummel the roof and windows, Mike dead and me about to get involved in the same case that, at least as Nora told it, may well have taken his life.

I picked up a Xerox copy of an article I was going to use in my book about Iowa. The article was about granny medicine in the Midwest, granny medicine being a kind of radical folk medicine practiced on the very early frontier. Next time you think that going to the doctor is so bad, consider some granny remedies (true facts) for health problems back in the early 1800s.

Consumption could be cured by eating the fried heart of a rattlesnake.

Lockjaw could be cured by grinding up cockroaches into boiling water and serving the concoction as tea.

Mouth odor could be cured by rinsing one's mouth every morning with one's own urine.

Birthmarks on babies could be made to disappear by rubbing against the marks with the hand of a corpse.

(I will never again complain about the fee I pay to visit my doctor.)

Then, feeling drowsy, I took a nap right there in the den, with my head thrown back against the wall so that my neck would be nice and stiff when I woke up.

I had no idea what the sound was that woke me. Not at first, anyway.

Just glass breaking late in the night.

I clipped off the reading light, set Tasha next to Crystal and Tess on the couch, then groped my way through the darkness to the kitchen.

I'd left my Ruger on the table, which was where I usually cleaned it.

The second noise identified itself exactly. Somebody was firing bullets through my front window.

I got on my hands and knees and crawled through the small dining room. In the living room I went to the far window and eased my head up an inch or so for a quick look at the gravel road fronting my house.

A lone street lamp outlined the dark car parked across the road. There was a man inside holding a long rifle with a long scope on it. He didn't seem to be in any particular hurry. He didn't seem to be especially afraid.

He squeezed off the third shot.

He must have seen me because he took the window where I crouched. Breaking glass made a sharp, dramatic sound and then began falling, in jagged bits and pieces, on the top of my head and my shoulders. A few pieces cut me.

Long silent seconds passed. My body was chilled from cold sweat. My breathing came in hot gasps. My hands were shaking. Some people may get used to being shot at, but I'm not one of them.

I was just starting to raise my head again when I heard him gun his motor. And then he was gone.

I stood up and watched him race out of the circle of light the street lamp provided, roaring into the rolling prairie darkness.

Now it wasn't just my hands, it was my whole body shaking.

I went into the den and turned on the light and sat down next to the cats. They didn't look scared at all.

I leaned forward and slid open one of the lower panels on the small bar.

The Jack Daniels black label I took from there filled half a glass just right. I knocked the stuff back and had another one. I wasn't much of a drinker – in fact, on a bad night, two drinks can make me sleepy – but tonight I needed a little help.

I thought about calling the police but didn't want them to look into my background as an investigator. Local police tend to get unfriendly about such folks.

Two hours later, I fell asleep in bed, the cats sprawled out all over the foot, my Robert Louis Stevenson novel now taken over by Tess.

I had troubled dreams, none of which I could remember when morning came and sang her siren song.

# 5

'You asleep?'

'Uh-huh,' he says.

'I talk to you a little bit?'

'Gee, Henry, is it about—' Then he stops himself. Henry's gonna talk anyway. Henry always talks anyway. And it's always the same old thing. That operation he's gonna have someday.

'You think I'm pretty?' Henry says from the bottom bunk.

While he's on the top bunk sweating his ass off. It's been 104 degrees this July day. Can't be much cooler tonight, even nearing midnight. Now he has to talk to Henry.

'Yeah, Henry, I think you're a great lookin' guy.'

'I don't mean handsome – I know I'm handsome. People have always told me I'm handsome, even when I was little. The nuns, they told me I was handsome. There was this one nun, when I was about fourteen, you know? I think she wanted to fuck me. I mean, she was this big old fat nun with onion breath and warts and all kinds of shit like that and a Bride of Christ and all, but I think she wanted to fuck me anyway. I really do.'

'Was she any good?'

'Very funny. I wouldn't've touched her with your dick. But you didn't answer my question.'

'I must've forgotten what it was. I'm kinda sleepy, I guess.'

'You can't sleep in weather like this. You know, I heard from my friend in Kentucky that they've got air-conditioned slammers down there.'

'In Kentucky, huh?'

'So you gonna answer my question?'

'About you bein' pretty?'

'Yeah.'

27

*'You're gorgeous, Henry. Is that what you want me to say?'*

*'How come you don't want to fuck me, then? Everybody else here does.'*

*'I'm not gay.'*

*'You sorta look gay sometimes.'*

*'You sorta look gay all the time, Henry.'*

*'I take that as a compliment.'*

*'Good.'*

*Henry, miraculously, shuts his effing mouth for three or four minutes.*

*He just lies there basking in the Henry-silence. Sure guys are farting/coughing/sneezing/shouting/laughing/belching/talking – but not Henry.*

*Henry-silence, these weeks of co-habiting with Henry, has come to be devoutly desired.*

*Then (oh no):*

*'You know what they do?'*

*'What who do, Henry?'*

*'The doctors.'*

*'Are we gonna talk about your sex-change operation again, Henry?'*

*'Yeah. Unless you wanna be macho and talk about sports or something.'*

*'I hate sports.'*

*'You sure you're not gay?'*

*'Yeah, I'm sure. But it would come in handy in a place like this.'*

*'They don't whack it off.'*

*'They don't?'*

*'No. Everybody thinks they do but they don't.'*

*'Well, that's good news for somebody.'*

*'They invert it.'*

*'They what?'*

*'Turn it inside out and stuff it back up there so it's like a woman's.'*

*'Well, that's better than whacking it off.'*

*'I'm going to get my eyes done.'*

*'Good.'*

*'I mean, I'm gonna get all the plumbing done first but then I'm*

*gonna concentrate on my face. You remember a movie star named Gayle Hunicutt?'*

*'Sorta.'*

*'Late sixties, around there, she was kinda big for a while. Anyway, her.'*

*'Her?'*

*'Her eyes. That's how I'm gonna have mine done. If I can find a picture of her, anyway. That'll probably be a bitch, won't it? Findin' a picture for the doctors to go by.'*

*'It's one thing after another, isn't it, Henry?'*

*'Then I'm gonna get a huge set of knockers.'*

*'Great. Henry. I really am gettin' kind of sleepy.'*

*'You're gettin' uptight is what you're gettin'. Straights like you always get uptight when people like me start talkin' about their operations.'*

*'Maybe that's it. Maybe I'm gettin' so uptight that the blood isn't gettin' to my brain and I'm starting to pass out.'*

*'You really are a prick sometimes.'*

*'Henry, I just want a little fucking sleep, that's all. I think you're beautiful and I hope you get those eyes you want – Gayle Harcourt or whatever her name is – and I hope you get a set of tits out to here. But right now, Henry, I really need to get some sleep. Honest to God I do.'*

*'I just wish you weren't so pretty.'*

*'Oh, God, Henry, just knock off the bullshit for one night, all right?'*

*'Why don't you come down here and make me?'*

*'You know what's happening, Henry?'*

*'What is?'*

*'I'm getting pissed. You know how when you get all hot and sweaty and begin to feel real crabby? Well, that's what's happening to me, Henry. I'm real hot and sweaty, but I'm goin' right by crabby and directly into enraged. Real enraged. So, see, Henry, I may come down there all right but if I do, I'm gonna kick your fuckin' beautiful face in. Are we communicating, Henry?'*

*And there fell upon the prison cell, for the rest of that hot and sweaty night, many hours of pure and blissful and extravagantly wonderful . . . Henry-silence.*

# 6

The day was so sunny and bright, so charged with spring, that I took my coffee out on the front porch and watched the baby blue fog disperse in the piney hills. Then I went around the outside of the house picking spent blossoms from the daffodils, which the rain had pounded. Meanwhile the cats sat in the window going crazy over every birdie who swooped down on the porch railing.

Finished with coffee, I ran my one mile up and one mile back along the gravel road. Everything looked so damned good and clean and beautiful, all of it somehow making me feel immortal. But I kept thinking about last night, the gunfire through the window, the sounds of glass breaking, a car roaring off into darkness. I supposed he might be up in a tree watching me now, but that was a bit paranoid even for a former spook like me.

After my shower, I drove the Jeep to my bank, and then to a hardware store on the edge of Iowa City. One thing about Iowa City, when they find a style they like they don't desert it. Lots of 1968 hippie holdovers wandering the aisles here. I expected to hear a Jefferson Airplane Up The Revolution! ditty come blaring out of the overhead speakers.

I like hardware stores. The sawn lumber in the back yard smells boyhood sweet, while the hammers and nails and glass and shingles and bolts and saws and screwdrivers and cement all attest to the purposefulness of human beings. When you think that we originally came from the sea, and then you look at the shelters we've built, not to mention the monuments in Paris and Rome and Cairo and Washington, D.C., you have to take at least a little bit of pride in our species, even if we do screw things up every once in a while.

I bought three pieces of window glass, some fresh putty and a

30

putty knife, and went back home and put in the windows. The cats helped, of course, sitting prim and pretty in a little conga line a few feet behind me, making sure that I knew what I was doing.

By this time, it was 10.17 a.m. It was safe to assume that Nora would be up by now.

The receptionist at the Collins Plaza in Cedar Rapids rang Nora's room six times and then said, 'I'm sorry, sir. Would you like to leave a message?'

I left my name and number.

Then I took another cup of coffee out to the front porch and settled in with my morning newspaper.

She called twenty minutes later.

# 7

'I have a question for you, Nora.'

'I expected you would.'

'What happens if I catch him?'

'I'm afraid I don't understand.'

'If I identify who he is, or at least who I think he is, and then I tell you, what do you do?'

There was a long pause. 'You mean do I turn him over to the police?'

'Exactly.'

'Is this really any of your business? I don't mean to be rude but it seems to me that your job ends once you find him.'

'I'm not much for vigilantes, Nora.'

'Meaning what exactly?' She was getting irritated. Nice rich girls, for all their niceness, aren't used to being interrogated by the hired help.

'Meaning, I don't want you or your friend with the mirror sunglasses to kill him.'

'You must have a nice image of me, Mr Payne.'

'The name's Robert and I don't have either a good image or a bad image of you. I'm just trying to anticipate all the eventualities.'

'Of course, you may never catch him.'

'True enough.'

'In which case you'll have earned yourself a great deal of money, anyway.'

'I'll do my very best, Nora. I need the money, as you pointed out last night, but now I have a personal stake in this. I want to see if you're right about Mike being murdered. And if he was, I want to see the killer brought in. I also don't like the idea of some scumbag roaming the countryside killing little girls.'

'That's what I've been waiting to hear. A little bit of anger. You're a very quiet person, Robert.'

'If you mean is macho my style, no. I don't like hanging around guys who look like they just stepped out of a beer commercial. I saw too many of them in the Army and too many of them in the Agency. Quiet usually gets the job done just as well as Ape Calls. Sometimes better. And that's why Mike Peary and I got along, by the way. He didn't have any peacock blood in him, either.'

She laughed. 'I agree with you. About Quiet getting the job done just as well.'

'I'm going to take this assignment and I'm going to do the best I can, and by the time I finish, I hope to have the man who killed your daughter and my friend in custody. How does that sound?'

'That sounds wonderful. I'm sorry if I was a little peevish just now.'

'Now there's a word I haven't heard in a while.'

'Peevish?'

'Uh-huh.'

'One of my mother's favorites. You could throw your bunk bed through your second-floor window, and Mother would explain to the maid that you were "peevish" that day. She was one of those soft, wilted flowers who never figured out a way to cope with the world, God rest her soul.'

'When did she die?'

'When I was twelve.'

'I'm sorry.'

'Oh, my father took up the slack. I couldn't have asked for a better parent until I turned sixteen.'

'What happened then?'

'I lost my virginity. One night in a cornfield, as a matter of fact. Some seniors were having the first spring kegger. My father hated my friends. He said they were beneath me and looking back, I have to say he was probably right. Anyway, that night, I had two firsts – my first boy and my first drink. I was a mess when I got home and so naturally my father was curious and angry and I told him. I shouldn't have, it really wasn't any of his business, but I was still pretty drunk so the words just came out. If my mother had been alive, she'd have taken me in her arms and held me and cried right along with me. But my father slapped me. He was almost insane. And it was all pride. He didn't ask me how I felt or if I'd been hurt in any way. He just wanted to know who the boy was and what his father did for a living. He just couldn't believe that his prim little daughter would have given herself to a member of the lower classes.' A wan laugh. 'I never did get around to telling him that this boy had served a year in Eldora, you know, the reformatory. God, he would have gone berserk if he'd known that.'

'So after that you and your father didn't get along?'

'Oh, we tried, both of us, we really did, gave it our best effort. But basically my father and I have never liked each other – there's always been some tension there. If I believed in Freud I'd say we probably wanted to get into each other's knickers. And so he'd give me very strict hours and I'd break them, and he'd buy me new cars and I'd smash them up, and he'd pack me off to boarding school and I'd run away. I'm sure you've heard of girls like me before.'

I thought of the quiet, anxious, pretty woman who sat on my couch last night. I would not have deduced from her looks, her manner or her language this wild background she was portraying.

'Then there were all the usual problems with drugs and alcohol,' she went on. 'I have to admit I really put him through hell. No doubt about that.'

'Why is he so against you hiring an investigator for your daughter's murder?'

'He thinks I'm the same unhappy, foolish girl who used to come in after curfew all the time and then throw fits when he confronted me. He's very sorry that Maryanne died but he thinks I'm just wasting my money and my time by not letting the police handle it. "Pathetic" was the word he used just the other day.'

'I'm going to do my best, as I said.'

'I appreciate that. And I apologize again for being so—'

'—peevish.'

She laughed again. It was a nice sweet sound. 'I'll give you a phone service where you can leave messages for me. I'll get back to you as soon as I can. And I'd appreciate hearing from you every few days.'

'You will. I promise.'

'Well, we'd better check out now. I have to go down the hall to

Vic's room and pound on his door till he wakes up. He could sleep through a bombing raid.'

'I'll talk to you soon.'

Crayfish, shrimp tails, chicken entrails, hog melts, worms, night-crawlers, live and dead chubs, coagulated blood, sour clams and frog pieces were all in my bait bucket when I went fishing that afternoon.

Figured this would be my last chance for a time so I took advantage of it, doing a little bit of what they call drift fishing, wading out to the middle of the stream and staying there a couple of hours.

I saw yellow birds and red ones and blue ones, I heard dogs and owls and splashing fish, I smelled the rich dark spring mud of the riverbank and the piney scent of the woods and the aroma of hot sunlight on the denim of my shirt. I was on a gentle leg of the river that was almost a cul-de-sac. A doe stood in a clearing and watched me for ten full minutes and a water snake at least two feet long slithered up from a muddy hole, looked around, and vanished back into the hole again immediately, apparently not liking my company. A cow with docile brown eyes and a swinging pink udder appeared in the same spot the doe had chosen and took up the watch, trying to figure out just what it was this two-legged creature was doing out there in the middle of the gentle blue river.

Easy to imagine the time when the Mesquakie Indians had laid claim to all this rich land. See the gray of their campfire smoke against the soft blue sky, hear the pounding messages of their drums echo off the limestone cliffs to the north. As a boy I'd combed these hills for buried arrowheads, almost obsessive in my search. In all those summer days I'd found only one. I still had it in my bureau at home. Kathy had always referred to it as 'the start of my Indian museum.'

I reached home at dusk, just when the invisible birds in the trees were making enough noise to awaken every Mesquakie laid to rest in the burial ground three miles to the west.

I got inside and turned the light on and said, 'Shit.'

We've seen it in the movies so many times that we should be

35

used to it, the way a house looks after thieves have gone through it, trashing everything in their search for hidden treasure. Your living quarters are a jumble of scattered papers, neckties, overturned chairs, emptied desk drawers and magazines that have been rifled through and then tossed on the floor like so many dead splayed birds.

I had a good notion of what my visitor had been looking for, and it wasn't treasure. Not of the monetary kind, anyway.

He'd wanted something germane to the investigation of Maryanne Conners's murder.

I worked my way through the house room by room. By nine I had everything pretty much fixed up, shoving a stack of paperbacks under the end of the couch where he'd broken the leg, putting all the classical CDs that had been Kathy's back in their proper slots, wondering in a bemused moment what he thought of all my underwear and socks that had been worn down to little more than holes with elastic banding at the top.

I felt raped, and for all the coolheadedness I'd bragged about earlier to Nora, I wanted to get my hands on the bastard.

Six hours later, deep into the night, the cats snoring at my feet, the phone rang.

I picked up.

'Leave it alone, Mr Payne. Just leave it the fuck alone.'

Perfectly androgynous voice. Perfectly.

'You understand, Mr Payne?'

And then he-she hung up.

I lay back down in my bed of shadows.

Knowing that I was now on my back. Tasha took the opportunity to walk up my body and snuggle down on my chest, which she had found a most inviting bed.

I hadn't had to ask what the caller wanted me to leave alone.

# 8

Cellmate the first year is a fifty-one-year-old farmer named Renzler. Frank Renzler.

Frank, who has told him this story so many, many times, was a farmer with a wife and two kids. Bank foreclosed on him after two bad droughts in a row, so Frank couldn't help it. One day he just picked up his hunting rifle and drove into town and blew away the banker. Took maybe one-eighth of his head off with two shots.

He cries, Frank does. No, check that. Not merely cries. Sobs. Lies on his bottom bunk and just goes effing nuts.

Talks about his wife. His kids. How much he loves them and misses them and how all he ever wanted was to be a fucking farmer like his old man and his grandpa and why did the bank have to fucking foreclose on him, anyway. Why did the bank have to foreclose, huh?

He's also the one with the bowel problems. Guy must have diarrhea three times a day. Just sits there on the crapper, no more than four, five feet away from the top bunk, and cuts away.

In the spring, Frank finds the puppy.

Nobody can explain how it got inside the prison unless it was a stowaway on one of the potato trucks that come in here twice a month.

But there one day in the machine shop where he works, just all balled up in a pile of rags, is this sweet little puppy.

And Frank (as Frank tells it) just starts bawling like a little kid. Proclaims his discovery a miracle. 'I know God put the little stinker there so I'd find her, so I'd have somebody to love till they let me out of here' (that's another thing, Frank is serving life without parole but is always pathetically alluding to 'the day they let me out of here').

37

*All of which is too good to pass up.*

*He lets Frank go six weeks always keening and blubbering on about what a sweet little puppy Angel is (that's what Frank calls her, Angel, her being an emissary from God and all) and then one day late, just as everybody is leaving the shop, he sneaks in there and does it.*

*Understand something.*

*He knows exactly what he's doing.*

*When he was a kid, he used to do stuff like this all the time.*

*Used to find neighborhood puppies and take them down in the storm sewer (the one place he was expressly forbidden to go) and then he'd experiment with puppies and kittens.*

*Cut off one leg and see if they could hobble around. Usually start with one of the front legs.*

*Then he'd take the opposite leg in the rear. See if they could limp around that way.*

*Of course all the screaming and thrashing about and all the blood—*

*Well, that was part of the fun, too, not just the crippling.*

*So in the machine shop, with the help of a knife his two-thousand-dollars-a-month bodyguard Servic got for him, he works over the puppy real good.*

*In the morning, Renzler finds Angel (he hears about all this later from other cons) and falls on the floor and goes into some kind of seizure.*

*They never seen nothing like it before, except one con who once saw a sixth-grade girl at Catholic school have an epileptic fit.*

*The guards come running and they see Renzler there on the floor and it takes four of them to hold him down.*

*Finally, finally, he stops screaming and throwing himself around.*

*Then he gets real quiet, tears streaming down his cheeks and he looks at one of the guards and says, 'You gotta loan me a knife so I can kill her.'*

*The guard looks over at Angel there on a pile of bloody rags. Some bastard has cut all her poor little legs off. Amazing that she's still alive.*

*The guard, this big thick German not known for sensitivity, has tears in his own eyes looking down at the obscenely maimed animal, and nods, and takes out this big-ass pocket knife, one of those gizmos that have a dozen different blades on them for opening cans and wine bottles and stuff like that, and he hands Renzler the knife. It's certainly up to the job. The blade is six inches long.*

*And Renzler gets down there with Angel and he kisses her sad scared little face and he says a couple of parts of a couple of different prayers and then he rolls her gently over for a better take on her heart and then he kills her.*

*And then he sits down right in the middle of the floor and he picks Angel up like she's his little baby or something and he starts rocking her back and forth in his arms and he's crying these really eerie quiet tears and kind of singing some lullaby he remembers his mama singing to him and the big German guard hasn't noticed as yet that Renzler hasn't given him the knife back and then—*

*And then it's too late.*

*Because Renzler picks up the knife, the blade still shiny with poor little Angel's blood, and he brings the knife up to his right eyeball and drives it deep into his eye socket, right on through to his brain.*

*He screams but not for long.*

*And then there's two of them dead, Renzler flat on his back now, his foot twitching crazily, little Angel hugged tenderly to his chest.*

*Eight days later, he gets a new cellmate.*

*Hard-core criminal, this one.*

*Killed a man in a 7-11 stick-up.*

*Brags so much about his sexual conquests, he quickly gets marked as a latent fag.*

*But what a relief to hear about stick-ups and dangerous guys his new cellmate has known and all the girls he's bopped—*

*Certainly preferable to slow sad Renzler with his family farm bullshit and his fantasies about getting out of here someday and how little Angel was sent to him directly by God.*

*Oh yeah, this new cellmate is a lot better.*

# Two

# 1

I reached New Hope next morning, just in time to see an Amish couple in a horse-drawn wagon irritate the hell out of a nice-looking young mother in a shiny new van. She had her kids with her and was obviously in a hurry. The wagon wasn't about to go any faster, there was too much oncoming traffic for her to pass, so all she could do was crawl along at 10 mph and glower a lot.

As I would soon find out, this little drama was a sort of metaphor for life here.

Yes, New Hope was one of those beautiful old Iowa towns that had sprung up along with the railroad back in the 1870s; it had a town square complete with bandstand and Civil War monument, with huge oaks and elms forming a natural canopy on the main drag, and striped awnings on all the proud little businesses that lined the four-block downtown – the men's haberdashery, the supermarket, the ice-cream store and the tobacco shop.

This was the bucolic New Hope, the New Hope that existed in the secret heart of everybody who had ever grown up, like me, in the small-town Midwest, all long lazy sunny afternoons fishing, and chilly football Friday nights out at the ramshackle old stadium, and Christmas carols on the loudspeaker as you jostled for gifts at the town's one and only department store, which was basically four big rooms with a lot of different stuff piled into it. And the Amish, of course, their horses clopping hollowly down the asphalt roads, the pretty women peering out from beneath their dark bonnets, the men with coarse gray beards and inscrutable eyes.

The old New Hope.

The new New Hope was McDonald's and Burger King and Motel 6 and the video stores with lurid sexy posters in their windows; Wal-Mart and a four-screen movie theater and what was formerly a furniture store converted into SOCIAL SERVICES.

Where the old New Hope belonged to the people who lived in town and worked at one of the three local factories, the new New Hope, its homes built in the hills surrounding the town itself, belonged to the married couples in their thirties and forties who drove their BMWs and Audis and vans to Cedar Rapids, where they worked, rubbed shoulders with as much modern culture as you could find there, and then escaped every night to live out their fantasies of Andy and Opie and Barney and Aunt Bea.

There were inevitable clashes, the nastiest, I'm told, occurring when two members of the school board pronounced themselves 'born again' and proceeded to list twenty-six novels, including *The Great Gatsby* and *Catch 22*, that had to be struck from the high school curriculum. If nothing else, this move got all the young professionals interested in the governance of the small community where they lived. They announced that in two years' time, they would be fielding their own school board candidates, and they sure as hell wouldn't be people who found Mark Twain 'sinful.'

Welcome to New Hope, located in the northeast corner of the state, *pop.* 14,683.

There was a motel right downtown, a good base to work from, pretty much equi-distant between the old New Hope and the new housing developments in the hills surrounding it.

The drive had been four hours so I needed food and coffee. I decided to try the downtown to get a human sense of the place. The downtown of somewhere, no matter its size, is where you can get your quickest sketch of a town's sociology.

I had two fried eggs, two pieces of wheat toast with raspberry jam, one glass of orange juice and three cups of coffee.

I ate these at the counter of a tiny place called Dickie's Diner where, nearing noon, most of the customers were male, roughly half of them dressed in the kind of suits and sports coats you get at Sears, the other half dressed in uniforms of denim, khaki, cotton, all bearing the caps and sew-on badges of gas companies and electric companies and bug-spraying companies. Mixed in with these folks were farmers, all weather-lined faces and big knuckly hands wrapped around chipped white coffee mugs. Not a single young professional in sight.

The talk, as I picked it up in snatches, was about a new state sales tax the legislature was proposing, and what a bunch of worthless fucks that legislature happened to be, and how bad most of the National League teams looked this year and – this from the businessmen – how the young professionals thought they were too good to shop in downtown New Hope. 'They do it all in Cedar Rapids. Not the one goddamned bit of support for us!'

Near the end, just as the third cup of coffee was starting to put a little twitch into my fingers, I heard a name that sounded familiar.

'Eve McNally find that husband of hers yet?'

A snort of laughter. 'Not unless she knows how to crawl through sewers.'

'How a man can do that to a woman like Eve sure beats me.'

'I really thought the last time he went down to Iowa City to dry out he'd be all right.'

'Lasted two months. Two damn months is all. Then he was back to the bottle.'

These were two of the suits sitting at the counter. McNally was one of the men mentioned in Mike Peary's letter as a possible suspect. They had me curious. He appeared to be missing, presumably on a drunk. From Mike's profile, a man who drank a lot – maybe to suppress the memories of what he'd done – would fit perfectly.

I paid my bill and went outside and stood on the corner for a few minutes, enjoying the spring air.

There was a phone booth across the street. I walked over and looked up the name *McNally, Richard.*

I got the address and drove out there. The town was laid out on an extensive grid broken only by the public square downtown. Railroad tracks cut north-south.

The houses were eclectic, everything from small Queen Annes to what they used to call 'corn belt' homes, square white clapboards of two stories with the inevitable squeaking swing on the inevitable front porch. The pastel pre-fabs that came in after WWII looked a lot older than the houses built eighty, one hundred years ago.

The McNally place was a small white clapboard, sitting in the middle of a green acre with a windbreak of shade trees and an aged but sprightly red barn in back. It was out on the north edge of town. The yard was carefully mown and well-tended, magnolia trees and apple blossoms charging the air headily.

I knocked. Inside a dog barked and then a soft voice shushed it and then she was there, framed in the glass of the storm door. She looked to be about my age, and probably not quite at her ideal weight, maybe five, six pounds over a very slight frame, with silken dark hair and silken dark eyes, the left one of which was spoiled by the fading remains of a black eye. She looked scared and miserable but even so, appealing in a kind of sad way, the sort of woman you try hard to make happy because you suspect they've never been happy before.

Of course, that was a tradition among pioneer women, out here, unhappiness. Despite all the macho cowboy movies, women pretty much kept things running on the frontier. Sure, the men had to plow and till the fields, and hunt the meat, but study up on pioneer women and you'll see why the suicide rate was so high among them – eighteen, twenty-hour days seven days a week during which they did everything from boiling up dyes for coloring cloth from barks and berries and roots; weaving cloth on a loom; cooking all meals; tanning hides and cutting patterns out for shoes; washing, ironing, mending; taking total responsibility for a brood of kids that probably ran to seven or eight; giving her man sex on demand; and being priest, doctor, teacher; and in her 'spare time' pitching in and helping with the planting and, later on, the harvest.

The woman in the doorway looked like a lineal descendent of those pioneer women.

'Hi,' I said.

'Hi.'

'That's a nice dog.' And it was, a golden retriever with a sweet-sad face that made you smile while it was breaking your heart. Beyond Eve, I got a glimpse of an inexpensively but very handsomely appointed home. The homey smell of baking came from the kitchen.

'Sara. She's the gentlest animal I've ever known.' She relaxed enough to lean down and pet the slender dog on the head. Sara's tongue licked her fingers pinkly with quick gooey love. 'Why

46

can't everybody be as sweet as you, honey?' the woman asked her
dog. She stood straight and looked at me. 'I've got some cookies
in the oven so I'm in kind of a hurry. Can I help you with
something?'

'I'm looking for Richard McNally.'

Fear became more pronounced in her eyes. 'Richard McNally
is my husband.'

'My name's Hokanson. I'm a freelance writer.'

'I don't know what you could want with my husband. He sells
gourmet honey.'

'But I understand he travels.'

'Yes,' she said. Suspicion joined fear now. She seemed to
stiffen her entire body inside her designer jeans and prim white
blouse. 'Of course he travels. How else would he make his sales?'

'Well, that's why I'm in town for the next few days. I'm doing a
piece on how small Iowa towns are becoming bedroom communities, with a lot of people commuting to their work.'

'Oh. I see.' That seemed to calm her some.

'Maybe I could find him at the office?'

She shook her head. 'No. He's – gone. Anyway, he doesn't
have an office. He just works out of the house here.'

'I see.'

'What's your name?'

'Hokanson. Jim Hokanson.'

'And you're with—?'

'I'm a freelancer. I'm writing this for Fenroe Publishing. I'm on
a kind of retainer set-up with them.'

I dug out a card and handed it over to her. Obviously, she
wasn't as yet completely satisfied with my little tale. She'd
probably dial that Chicago number and probably talk to somebody at good old Fenroe Publishing, Inc., but she'd probably
never figure out that it was nothing more than a small room in a
small office building in a bad section of Chicago used by the
Agency as a cover for many of its domestic people. Even though I
was officially separated, they still let me use it when I needed to.

She looked straight at me and said, 'I don't believe you.'

'About me being a freelancer?'

'Right.'

'Why not?'

47

She shrugged. 'I don't know.' She paused. Handed the card back. 'I want you to leave.'

'But ma'am, I—'

'You don't have any right to be here. And when I ask you to leave, that's what you should do.'

'But ma'am, I—'

She leaned down and took Sara by the collar and eased her back beyond the threshold. Then she slammed the door shut.

I stood there feeling like an Amway salesman on a very bad day.

A moment later, apparently thinking I'd left already or apparently unable to restrain herself, Eve McNally began sobbing.

It got to me. I wanted to go in there and hold her and just let her cry. She needed somebody to do that for her. I was like that after Kathy died.

On the sidewalk, I turned and started back toward town, watching a golden butterfly sit tentatively on a hedge already occupied by a quick bright cardinal. There were days when I wanted to be a boy again, when my biggest concern was where to find an even bigger steelie than the one I had, and when the next *Batman* comic would make its appearance down at Choate's Rexall pharmacy.

Before I got three steps, a gray car pulled up to the curb and a gray little man stepped out of it and walked quickly toward the McNally home. He too had a Sears suit on, a brown one. He wore a buff blue shirt and a yellow tie. It seemed to me that this kind of get-up should be illegal. I wasn't exactly a dandy but not even a blind guy could be excused for wearing this particular combo.

I stopped him. 'Are you going to see Mrs McNally?'

He seemed confused. 'Yes. Why?'

I shook my head. 'She's not in a visiting mood right now.'

'Is something wrong?'

'Just some family problems.'

'Oh,' he said. 'Oh. Then that makes sense.'

'What makes sense?'

'Are you a friend of the family?'

I nodded.

'I'm Don Murphy, assistant principal at Wilson Middle School. Where Melissa goes.'

'Oh, yes.'

'Well, she's hasn't been there for nearly a week and we've been very concerned. We've talked with Mrs McNally on the phone a few times and she assured us that Melissa would be back soon but – well, it seemed more appropriate to just drive out here today rather than waste any more time on the phone.' He grimaced. 'Family problems?'

I nodded.

'The husband, as usual, I suppose? No offense.'

'No offense.'

'She's such a decent woman,' he clucked. 'And Melissa's just about a perfect student.'

'Why don't I have Eve call you when she's feeling a little better?'

'I'd appreciate that. Today if possible.'

'I'm just going to get her a few things then I'll be back and tell her.'

'I appreciate that. I really do.'

He was gone, then, and I walked back downtown. The husband was missing, and the daughter hadn't been to school in nearly a week, and Eve McNally was given to sudden fits of sobbing.

I wondered what the hell was going on here.

# 2

Lunch, a couple of hours later, after a morning spent sitting in the tiny red-brick library looking through newspapers to acquaint myself with the town, was a Big Mac and fries eaten at a bright orange table in a bright orange seat next to a curiously sinister poster of Ronald McDonald. Ever since John Wayne Gacy, who murdered at least thirty-six young boys, often while wearing a clown costume, clowns sort of spook me.

The main drag told an interesting story. If I'd sat at this window a few years ago, I'd have seen brand-new cars and brand-new pick-up trucks parading down the street past the two- and three-story buildings.

But no longer.

In the 1980s the rural economy, like the urban economy, suffered a set-back from which it had never recovered. People talk about the urban underclass, those ragged bleak denizens of rattling rusted-out hulks that emit clouds of black smoke and that idle as if they're in death spasms – well, there's a rural equivalent and I saw a lot of them on the street today, coming into town for more food stamps or a visit to the free clinic, or to apply for a minimum-wage job at one of the fast-food places.

I was just finishing my Pepsi, just starting to want a cigarette the way I still do after each meal, when I looked up and saw a tall, red-haired woman with cat-green eyes and a cute dinky nose and enough freckles for three people standing there watching me.

'Are you Mr Hokanson?'

I was out of practice and so the question caught me off guard, but at least I was smart enough to respond 'Yes.'

'Mind if I join you?'

'Not at all.'

She had a kid-sister grin touched with a certain disingenuous eroticism. 'Even brought my own coffee. I'm a real cheap date.'

She sat down on the other side of the small orange table. It wasn't easy. Slim as she was, her big leather rig – holster and gun and night stick – took up room in quarters this cramped.

'I should introduce myself, I guess. I'm Jane Avery. I'm the Chief of Police.' The grin again. 'I know that sounds impressive but just keep in mind that it's a very small police department.'

'I'm impressed anyway.'

This time it was just a smile. She sipped her coffee, looked over and waved at somebody who waved back and called her name. At noon, the customers consisted of downtown workers, people who looked retired, and truckers. The back lot held maybe ten sixteen-wheelers.

'I forgot to tell you, Mr Hokanson, I'm also a celebrity.' She took another sip. 'Boy, that's hot.'

Her name was called again, this time by a guy who had to be a banker. He looked born to it.

She waved.

'They seem to like you,' I said.

She shook her head, her short red hair baby-gold and baby-soft. She wasn't exactly beautiful, she wasn't even exactly pretty, but she sure was fetching. 'Guilt.'

'Guilt? Over what?'

'The way they treated me when I first came here, three years ago.'

'They weren't nice?'

'Not nice is an understatement. The Mayor, a man named Glickson, he's dead now by the way, saw a piece about me in a Des Moines newspaper, about how I was a young cop who was getting her Masters in Criminology at night school. His Police Chief had just quit and so he offered me the job. It was good timing. My husband had just asked me for a divorce. He'd never been happy about me being a cop, he found it a very unfeminine job, and he couldn't help himself and gee whiz he was sorry but he'd fallen in love with a woman at the ad agency and gosh wouldn't I just give him a divorce so we could all be happy? So I took the job here.' She laughed softly. 'At least it distracted me from my broken heart, though God knows why I

51

was broken-hearted about Ron. Anyway, among many other misdemeanors, some of the old boy network in town here pinned a Kotex on the antenna of my police car, and called me at all hours of the night and day with all kinds of sexual suggestions, and tried three different times to have the Mayor fire me. I think he had a heart attack and died because of all the stress. Then the young professionals in town finally got sick of hearing about it and took my side and that put everything into a kind of stalemate. So here I am.' The grin again. 'Boring story, huh?'

'Hardly. I'm just amazed you're still here. With that kind of harassment, most people would have left.'

She shrugged the shoulders of her stiff police shirt. 'I was an orphan. This job had a lot to do with my identity and self-worth, if you'll excuse the jargon. It was very important for me not to run.'

'I can understand that.' I looked at her carefully. 'In fact, there's only one thing I don't understand.'

'And what's that?'

'Why you came over here and sat down.'

'Oh, that's simple enough. A citizen asked me to investigate you.'

'Would this citizen's name be Eve McNally?'

'Could be.' She leaned forward into an angle of sunlight. Her eyes were vivid green. 'Do you have some ID?'

'Are you serious?'

She nodded. 'Afraid I am.'

'My name's Jim Hokanson. I'm a freelance writer. Sometimes I do retainer work for Fenroe Publishing.'

I dug out my billfold, extracted a white business card, handed it to her.

She didn't look at it, just left it lying next to her elbow.

'Anybody can get a card printed. I really need to see some ID.'

To the casual eye, we might have been lovers having a quick lunch at McDonald's. She looked so sweet and relaxed sitting across from me.

I got out all the Hokanson stuff and handed it over, license, medical insurance card, Visa card.

She went through it carefully, turning everything over and over

in her slender fingers, even bending the Visa card a little.
She handed it back.

'So tell me,' she said, 'who are you?'

'You saw for yourself.'

'None of that's ever been used.'

'What?'

'All brand-new. Your Visa card, for instance, use that a few
times in one of those machines, it gets scratched a little. But it
isn't scratched at all. Same with your license. Not a mark on it. So
who are you?'

'You must've read an awful lot of Nancy Drew when you were
growing up.'

She smiled. 'I did, as a matter of fact. But you're not answering
my question.'

'Who am I, you mean? That's a pretty heavy philosophical
question for this time of day.' I looked across the small-town
street where people stood in twos and threes beneath the shadows
of awnings and discussed small-town news and gossip. There was
a pizza place on the corner named *Mike's*. 'Does Mike make good
pizza?'

'Who?'

'Mike. Across the street.'

'Oh. Yes, pretty good. So who are you, Mr Hokanson?'

I smiled. 'I'm on the same side you are, let's put it that way.'

'That's a very elusive answer.'

'That's because I'm a very elusive guy.'

Her beeper went off. She frowned. 'Excuse me.' She walked
back to a pay phone, deposited some coins and talked for a
minute or so. She came back but this time she didn't sit down.
'Bad car accident, I have to leave. I may see you later, whoever
you are.'

I waggled the Visa card at her. 'Says right there that I'm Mr
Hokanson.'

'Right,' she said. 'And I'm Katharine Hepburn.'

# 3

In the driveway sat two matching white Lincoln towncars. Brand-new. There was money in the God business. Far up the drive that curved behind a stand of pine trees, I could see a large white house, new and prosperous-looking against the backdrop of a pasture where cows loitered contentedly.

The church was small and modern in a repellent sense, all sharp angles and juts, like a piece of glass sculpture that had been dropped and smashed and then ineptly glued back together. The message seemed to be that God was a schizophrenic and a clumsy one at that.

But for all the trendiness of the design, the wailing song that poured forth from its open front doors was at least as old as the famous tent revival shows that played the Midwest and South back in Depression days – a bit of bayou blues and Jimmy Rodgers white boy hobo song combined with the stirring religious themes of working-class Baptists.

For all the fanciness of the exterior design, the interior was plain, thirty rows of oak pews and an oaken altar. And by the altar stood a thirty-ish man in a singles-bar Country & Western get-up of brilliant red shirt with blue piping, skin-tight jeans and a pair of Texas boots that were no doubt the real lizard they purported to be. He was good-looking in a chunky Irish kind of way – maybe Edmond O'Brien had been his grandfather – and he was gone gone gone on the song he was twanging out on his electric guitar, Elvis himself having never been more gone gone gone back when he was nineteen and known only in Memphis and signing his name on the top part of ladies' breasts.

He was singing all about how God understood him and why he did the things he did, and how God would cradle him someday

54

and purge him of sin and loneliness and want, and I couldn't help it, I actually enjoyed hearing him sing, his voice echoing off the vaulted ceiling and trailing out of the open side windows.

And then he paid it off, a big finale with him working hard on his guitar, eyes still closed, whole body surging with the grief and ecstatic eternal promise of the lyrics.

The church sounded obscenely quiet after he'd finished, as if its only purpose was to be filled with his song, and now it was spent and empty of reason to exist.

'You're really good,' I said.

For the first time, his eyes came open and I was almost startled by the clear green fury in them. Oh yes, this man knew whereof the demons he sang.

'Didn't know I had an audience,' he said in a young voice that made me slide his age down to twenty-five. 'Reverend Roberts says I should bring in an audience even when I'm practicing. I still get stage fright, you know, on our TV shows and all.'

He set his blue Fender down on the carpeted floor by the altar then walked down to meet me.

After shaking hands he said, 'I'm Kenny Deihl. If you ever saw the Reverend's show, I'm one half of the talent.'

'Haven't seen the show, I guess.'

Something subtle but serious changed in his startling green gaze. 'You're not from around here, are you?'

'No, I'm not.'

'You're not a follower of the Reverend's either, are you?'

'No. Afraid not.'

'Then just what the heck're you doing—'

'Kenny, I'll handle this. No need to get upset. We're all children of the Lord.' He stood in the back of the church but I had no trouble hearing his greased and mellifluous tones at all.

He looked just about the way you might imagine – $250 worth of moussed dark hair, a face that was youthfully handsome in an almost diabolical way, like a mask that didn't quite work, a blue conservatively cut suit that would give offense to no one, and one of those firm-handshake quick-grin manners that let you know you were in the company of a Psycho for Jesus. He smelled of hair spray, after-shave and chewing gum.

He came over and said, 'Kenny, why don't you run downtown

55

and pick up that case of Pepsi for tonight? You know how dry we get when we cut those radio shows.'

'I'll bet he's a reporter,' Kenny said. 'I'll bet he is.'

'Remember Thirteen Hebrews verse two, Kenny: "Do not neglect to show hospitality to strangers, for thereby some have entertained angels unaware." '

Kenny knew just what look to put on his face. He still hadn't forgiven me for coming here but he knew how to take his cue from the Reverend. 'Sorry, mister. Guess I just got carried away. After the state paper went a-spyin' on us—'

He looked at the Reverend, quit talking with a shrug then walked to the side door at the front of the church and disappeared.

'When I found him two years ago,' said the minister, 'he was singing in a motel lounge in Sioux City. He's changed a lot since then, become a truly saved soul, but he developed a distrust of strangers after the state newspaper did a very unflattering article about myself and two other Midwestern TV evangelists. Kenny takes criticism of me especially hard. When you save a man's soul, the way I saved Kenny's, well, he's naturally grateful to you and he gets very protective of you.' He shook his perfectly moussed head. He resembled an actor who might have been a leading man a quarter-century ago. 'The Devil has so many friends, and the Lord so few.'

'Well,' I said, 'that's actually what I am – Kenny guessed right – I'm a journalist. But I'm not doing an exposé. I'm writing a piece on how small towns are becoming bedroom communities for a lot of people.' I told him who I was profiling here.

'Well, Mr Hokanson, I'm sure you're telling me the truth, that you're not going to do an exposé and all, but I think you'll understand why I may not want to do an interview with you.'

'You'll see the copy before it gets printed.'

'That's what the other fellow said, too.'

'How about you think it over for a while and I'll call you back tonight?'

'Why don't you tell me where you're staying and I'll leave a message there. We're on thirty-eight radio stations in a three-state area and we have to cut half-hour radio shows once a week. I give a sermon and Kenny does two songs and then Mindy does two songs. Then, of course, I ask for help, financial help. Mr Hokanson, I'm not afraid to say those two words together – *financial help*. You can't do the work of the Lord without financial help, nobody can. It costs money to live in Satan's world, Mr Hokanson. That's what that reporter fellow couldn't understand, that virtually every dime donated to my church goes to helping other people.'

I tried hard not to think of the matching white Lincolns in the driveway.

The good Reverend suddenly made a bitter face. 'He even mocked me, that reporter. I was trusting enough to tell him about my wife, who has cervical cancer, and about our trips up to the Mayo clinic and about how I'd nearly lost my faith several times when I saw – through the test results – that my Betty wasn't getting any better. Wasn't that a legitimate question? To ask the Lord why He answered so many of my prayers for others who were sick, but wouldn't answer my prayers for my own wife?'

Tears stood in his eyes now, and spittle sprayed from his mouth, and he made deep animal sounds of mourning.

He started poking me in the chest as he made his point.

'I say to people "The Lord hasn't answered me because I've been a sinner" and they say, "Oh, no, Reverend Roberts. Nobody lives a more exemplary life than you. It can't be that." "Then why won't he help Betty get better?" I ask but they never know what to reply. So you see, it's got to be my sins. I am a sinful man.'

He wanted me to disagree but I wasn't about to. I still doubted that Jesus, back on earth today, would tool around in a new Lincoln.

'I hope your wife gets better.'

He looked at me hazily, as if he were coming out of a trance, as perhaps he was. Bible-thumpers often worked themselves into real frenzies.

'I thank you for your charitable thoughts, sir.'

'You'll get a hold of me tonight?'

'I most certainly will. I most certainly will.'

I nodded and walked out of the church, watching the play of shadow and light on the oak walls, and hearing him mutter prayers to himself up near the altar. This had to be for my benefit. Isn't there a psalm about the most sincere prayers being those whispered in the heart?

Outside, I saw a young blonde woman in white shorts and a blue halter hosing down one of the Lincolns. She had the somewhat overweight and overripe sexuality of a fifties *femme fatale*. She wore too much make-up and too much hair spray, but her particular persona worked anyway. She was appealing in a slightly tawdry, vaguely comic way.

I was five feet away from her when she turned and saw me and then, very slowly, she leaned over to take a sponge from the sudsy red plastic bucket by her bare feet. In bending over, she gave me a nice lingering look at her considerable cleavage.

'Hi,' I said. 'You've got a nice day for it.'

A knowing but tentative smile. She still hadn't figured out if I'd be worth any serious flirting.

'I could stand it ten degrees warmer,' she said. 'I'm from Houston and I just can't get used to what you all call a heat wave!' She gave me the benefit of enormous eyes made violet by contact lenses. 'Actually, I could stand it a whole lot hotter.'

Being a gentleman, and being somebody who hates corny lines, I decided to take what she said without any implication whatsoever.

'I was just in seeing the Reverend. Mr Roberts seems like a nice guy.'

She eyed me skeptically. 'Somehow you don't seem the type.'

'The type'

'You know, the church-going type. There's just something about you. I don't mean any insult, either.'

I told her who I was. 'You're the second good guesser I've seen in fifteen minutes.'

'Oh?'

'Yeah, Kenny Deihl guessed that I was a journalist. And I am.'

She had a good nasty grin. 'That isn't all that Kenny is good at guessing, either.'

And with that, and before I could inquire what her obscure remark had meant, she turned back to the car and sprayed water all over the roof and driver's door.

She shouted above the din of water on metal, 'He lets me drive this if I keep it clean. Part of my pay, I guess.'

'Are you Mindy?'

'Right.' She grinned her nasty grin again. 'I'm the girl singer for the Reverend.'

'He said he found Kenny in a Holiday Inn. Where did he find you?'

'A Motel 6.'

'In the bar?'

'Motel 6's don't have bars, if you get my drift.'

I went right on past that one. 'You three travel a lot?'

'Me and the Rev and Kenny?'

'Uh-huh.'

''Bout four months of the year, all told.'

'The Reverend do much travelling on his own?'

'That's kind of a strange question, seeing's how your article's supposed to be about a bedroom community and all.'

'Not really. I'm just curious about how he holds his flock together.'

She laughed. 'So that's what you call them – a flock. I've been wondering what name I'd use.'

She picked up the sudsy sponge and stood on tip-toes to wash the roof. She had a great bawdy body and knew it. Another five years, it would mudslide into fat if she wasn't very careful, but right now it was bedazzling.

She had given the roof a few swipes when I heard a beeping sound and saw for the first time the beeper clipped to the waist of her shorts.

'Oh, shit,' she said. 'Pardon my French.'

She stopped work, shaking her head miserably. 'That bitch.'

'Who's a bitch?'

'Betty Roberts.'

'The Reverend's wife?'

She heard the discomfort in my voice. 'He sold you on it, too, huh?'

'Sold me on what?'

'Her cancer.'

'She doesn't have it?'

'Hell, no, she doesn't have it. He just says that so the flock as you call them will feel sorry for him and give more money.'

'You sure you should be telling me all this?'

She plopped the sponge into the suds, wiped her hands on her hips and said, 'I'm splitting in a week. Don't matter to me any more who knows what.'

The beeper erupted again.

'She's up there at her bedroom window watching us with binoculars. That's all she does all day. The colored woman who works for her, it's her day off so Reverend Bob makes me be her go-fer.'

'This is quite a set-up here.'

'Yes,' she said, grinning that nasty grin. 'Isn't it, though?'

# 4

*What most people don't know about prison is that it's a bureaucracy and you have to treat it that way.*

*Early one spring, he decides he wants to start writing – just to give himself something to do other than listen to all the jailhouse lawyers talking about how they're going to get themselves out early, or some con whining on about how unlucky he's been all his life, or watching one of the guards drooling at the prospect of cracking a skull or two . . . But the assistant warden won't let him have a typewriter.*

*'Why not?' he asks.*

*'I wasn't aware I had to give you any reasons for my decisions,' the assistant warden says.*

*'According to Anderson you do.'*

*'Ah yes, Anderson. God, I get sick of jailhouse lawyers.'*

*'I could file a form, you know.'*

*The assistant warden doesn't say anything for a time, just stares out the window. Then: 'A BP-9.'*

*'What?'*

*'A BP-9. That's the form you need to file. Its official title is "An Administrative Remedy Appeal." File the form, maybe the warden'll give you that typewriter you want. Of course Anderson, being a good jailhouse lawyer, he can tell you about the BP-9 or the BP-10 or the BP-11.'*

*Then the assistant warden pauses a long time and says, 'You killed that little dog, didn't you? The one with its legs cut off.'*

*'Don't know what you're talking about.'*

*'You think I don't know about you? You think I buy all this altar-boy bullshit you spread around? You're the most dangerous man in this entire prison system.'*

61

*He says nothing. Just watches.*

*'Did it make you come, when you cut up that dog that way? Did it make you feel good about youself?'*

*The assistant warden shakes his head wearily.*

*'I can handle the thieves and the con artists and even some of the killers – but it's the monsters I can't deal with any more. The people like you.'*

*'Sounds like you need a vacation.'*

*'I want you to know something.'*

*'Yeah? What?'*

*'If I can ever figure out any way to do it, I'm going to kill you. Cut your throat the first chance I get. That's a promise.'*

*'Is there a complaint form for that?'*

*'For what?'*

*'For when somebody threatens to cut my throat?'*

*'You think this is funny?'*

*'I was just asking a question.'*

*'I couldn't sleep for a month, thinking about what you did to that little dog.'*

*'You think you can prove it?'*

*'I don't need to prove it. Not to my satisfaction, anyway, because I already know you're guilty.'*

*'I'm going to ask Anderson about that form. That BP-9.'*

*'You do that.'*

*'You want to put a little side bet on whether the warden lets me use that typewriter?'*

*'Just get out of here.'*

*'Yes, sir, Your Majesty.'*

*He leaves the office, smirking.*

*'Assistant warden says I need to file a BP-9,' he says to Anderson that afternoon on the yard.*

*'He still won't give you that typewriter?'*

*'Uh-huh.'*

*'What a prick. And damn right we'll file a BP-9. And we'll file it right up his ass, too.'*

*Time passes.*

*A) Obviously the assistant warden never cuts his throat.*

*B) Two months and three forms later (Praise the Lord for those BP-9s), he gets his typewriter.*

*C) Fourteen months later, the assistant warden is diagnosed with liver cancer. Thirty-eight years old. Wife and three kids. Good upstanding Methodist. And he gets liver cancer.*

*D) Six weeks after the diagnosis, the assistant warden is dead.*

*On the afternoon of the announcement, Anderson – they're on the yard again, a really ball-chilling April afternoon – comes over and says, 'You're a dangerous guy.'*

*'Yeah?' he grins.*

*'Yeah. I mean, I got my BP-9s 'n shit but you must have voodoo or something. I mean, that assistant warden gettin' liver cancer and all.'*

*The grin again. 'Yeah, maybe that's what I do have.'*

*'Voodoo?'*

*'Yeah,' he says. 'Voodoo.'*

# 5

A dozen people said hello to me on the way back to my motel. Half a dozen waved. I'd never seen any of them before but they reminded me that the twin of small-town suspicion was small-town openness. I saw dogs chase butterflies, bees seek honey, and cats loll in sunlight. Walt Disney would have had all of them singing merry little songs. He had the right idea. Even if the universe wasn't a merry little place, what was the harm in pretending it was every once in a while? Of course, my generation didn't believe much in Disney, except for *Fantasia* which had just been another giggly excuse to get stoned. No, my generation would have shown the dogs taking a shit on the lawn, the bees stinging innocent babies, and the cats eviscerating doves.

I was two blocks from my motel when I saw the Caddy. My first reaction was, No, you're imagining things. Must be a number of blue Caddys around. Anyway, what would Nora and Vic be doing here?

A block from my motel, I saw the blue Caddy sitting in an alley. The windows had been darkened so that I couldn't see in. But I had the clear impression that I was being watched carefully. I also had the clear impression that it was Nora and Vic in the car. Why were they following me around?

In my motel room, I called a friend of mine at the State Bureau of Investigation in Des Moines. I asked him to run a check on the good minister and on both Kenny Deihl and Mindy Lane. I was not exactly a trusting soul. He said to call him back in a few hours.

Before leaving, I looked around the room. It smelled of disinfectant and was dark enough, on this sunny afternoon, to give The House of Usher a few pointers on gloom. I opened the drapes, cracked the window a quarter-inch, spent a long minute watching a jay perched on the window ledge, and then raised my eyes and looked across the street to the parking lot adjacent to the steak house.

Big blue Caddy just sitting there.

I left the room, found the rear EXIT sign and took it.

If they had decided to follow me around, I'd make them work for it.

They were going to be sitting there for a long time waiting for me to walk out that front door.

Lochinvar Antiques was a refurbished Queen Anne-cum-Victorian building that had enough gingerbreading for at least three such houses. It sat on its own acre lot on the edge of a residential area. The grass was in need of a quick trim.

In the front yard, a slender woman with a blonde ponytail sat next to an aluminum tub where she was bathing a feisty young kitten. I couldn't see her face but something about her blue work shirt and jeans and the heavy Navajo turquoise earrings signaled me that she was going to be young, no more, say, than thirty.

I walked over and watched the kitten shake off water and soap suds. The woman laughed most pleasantly then looked up at me.

The eyes were young, brown and quick and intelligent, but the skin of her face was deeply lined and aged.

A momentary sadness shone in her eyes, as if she was used to people being surprised by how old her face looked when they finally saw it. The odd thing was that she was very pretty, even with the wrinkles and grooves in her face.

The kitten, who was calico and very young, four pounds of kitty at most, was covered with suds and water that made her fur stand straight up like spikes. She made a lot of mad little noises, her eyes chiding me for not taking her away from this murderous woman who imprisoned her.

'She hates it, Ayesha does,' she said, wrapping the wriggling kitten in a nubby white towel.

'Ayesha, that's a great name.'

'From H. Rider Haggard,' she smiled. 'I was one of those girls who always liked boys' books better than the ones for girls. Ayesha was the eternal goddess in *She*.'

'That's right, I forgot. I used to read Haggard, too.'

'Give me a minute, I'm going to run her inside.'

While she was gone, I walked to the edge of the small hill the house sat on and looked at the blue river in the yellow sunlight. There was a breeze, one scented up with apple blossoms, and as I watched the river I thought of how white pine had been rafted down these waters to the eager mills. For fifty years, just after the Civil War, the towns in this part of the state had boomed with furniture factories. But then in Burlington, which was the center of all this activity, a fire had destroyed a full five blocks of factories and the business never quite recovered, and the sight of white pine being ridden by lumberjacks down the blue blue waters was seen no more.

'She's still mad at me,' she said when she got back. She put out an elegant hand, its touch telling of hard honest physical work. 'I'm Joanna, by the way.'

I told her my name and gave her my pitch.

'I guess that's the trendy phrase for it now, huh? "Bedroom communities?" '

'I guess so,' I said. I nodded at the house. 'This is quite a place. Really well-kept.'

'Interesting history, too.'

'Oh?'

'I don't know if you know anything about this part of the state but back in the 1840s and 1850s, people around here hid runaway slaves. A lot of slave hunters – they were pretty much like bounty hunters – combed this area looking for runaways. They came up from the South; you know, hired by the plantation owners. That's why people had trap doors and sub-basements for slaves to hide in.'

Her enthusiasm made me smile. She was a girl again, eager to share a story. I liked her. 'One night a couple of slave hunters killed a little slave girl in cold blood. They were trying to impress all the slaves with how merciless they were. But they didn't count on the people of the town here. Six men from New Hope got together and spent all night tracking the slave hunters. They found the hunters in the morning and lynched them on the spot. Left them hanging for five days. The bodies probably looked pretty awful by then.'

'So much for the theory that nothing ever happens in nice little Iowa towns. Or used to, anyway.' I looked at her and smiled. 'But you were telling me about your husband and this being a bedroom community.'

'Well,' she smiled but it was a smile that bore more pain than pleasure, 'he certainly travels a lot.' She hesitated then said, 'As women throughout the Midwest can attest.'

I didn't know what to say so I immediately went to the inane. 'You've really got a great view from here.'

'I'm sorry to put all that on you.'

I looked at her. 'I don't mind. I just wasn't sure what to say.'

She shrugged. 'We used to be a matched set, my husband and I. Six years ago we were Zelda and Scott, the most beautiful, the most desirable, the most sought after. Then about five years ago, my face—Well, you see what happened. Tried everything. Nothing helped. The dermatologists call it solar elastosis. Did it to myself. Too much sunlight, too many cigarettes.'

She walked to the edge of the hill and looked down. A bright red canoe with two blonde girls paddled past.

I walked up next to her.

'He was always unfaithful – he really is quite handsome – but after my face started to go . . . Well, I don't suppose I blame him, really. We were both very vain people when we met. I was a real heartbreaker, very shallow and insincere, just as much as he was. The only difference is that with my face this way—'

She looked at me and smiled. 'Well, now I've been forced to look at life the way mere mortals do. You know, walk into a room and have men be courteous but not interested in me in the slightest bit. Or see the pity and the horror in the eyes of beautiful women who worry that this may happen to them some day.'

'He's gone now?'

She nodded, staring at the river again, down the brambly hill and past the sandy shore to the sunlight-painted water and the occasional splashing fish.

'He'll be back tonight. You can call him around eight if you want to catch him.'

'I'll set up a time for an interview tomorrow.'

She eased her arm through mine, led me back toward the beautiful period dwelling.

'Are you married, Jim?'

'Not any more.'

'Divorce?'

'She died.'

'Lord.'

When we reached the sidewalk, she slid her arm out from mine and said, 'Maybe I'll use you to make him jealous. You're a nice-looking man.'

'Thanks.'

'Would you mind?'

I leaned over and kissed her on the cheek. 'Not if it'll make you feel better.'

'For a little while it would.'

'Then go ahead and do it.'

'I'll tell him that you took me to lunch and that we spent the afternoon walking in the woods. God, it's been so long since he was jealous.' She laughed suddenly, heartily. It was good to hear. 'God, you probably think you stepped into a local production of *Sunset Boulevard*, some nutty old broad carrying on this way. Do you know *Sunset Boulevard*?'

'One of my wife's favorites.'

'I'll bet you were faithful.'

'I was.'

'And I'll bet she was faithful, too.'

'Far as I know.'

This time, she kissed me on the cheek.

'I think I'll go inside and lie down and have a fantasy about you, Jim.'

I smiled. 'That's when I'm at my best. In somebody else's fantasies.'

I gave her arm a squeeze and walked back to town.

# 6

He found out soon enough that cons like to brag about crimes they'd never been charged for.

Dumb goddamned cops this, dumb goddamned cops that.

You know. That sort of thing.

His second cellmate went by the name of Shay. Decent enough guy. Kept to himself. Didn't ask all sorts of questions. Kept his part of the cell clean. Was as discreet as he could be, given the circumstances, using the toilet. Was even known to read a book or two.

But sometimes he couldn't help himself, Shay couldn't. He'd give in to the con habit of bragging about himself and his criminal past.

'Eight frigging burglaries in the same three-block area in the same two-week period and they didn't catch me. Can you believe it?'

Or:

'Man, did I have to hightail it out of that town, believe me. That cute little waitress I said gave such great head? Guess how old she turned out to be? Fourteen fucking years old, man. Fourteen. Her old man told the cops and then came after me himself with a couple of these assholes from the bowling alley. Man, they would've torn me limb from limb. Fourteen years old!'

Or:

'I bet this other guy, see, bet him I could do it with the cops sittin' right across the street in a squad car. And I did it, too. I mean the place is all lit up and everything, and I just kind of stroll real casual-like onto the lot and I get in this red Plymouth convertible – I figure I may as well steal a car that's got some style – and I slide behind the wheel and I hot-wire the sonofabitch right across the *street from the cops, and then I pull off the lot. And they don't do anything – not a fucking thing – till it's way too late! I took that baby for a joyride and then ditched it. They never caught me!'*

*A guy can't keep hearing and hearing about how smart and cool and gifted his cellmate is without feeling a little bit competitive.*

*Isn't he also smart and cool and gifted?'*

*Hasn't he himself pulled off a couple of stunts that would make his cellmate's pale by comparison?*

*So, knowing that his cellmate will never believe his tale, putting it down to standard jailhouse fantasy, he decides to tell his cellmate about one night outside Miami, Florida.*

*The speedboat he's using overturns – he's probably had a little too much vino to manipulate such a craft in the stormy waters, a downpour having started an hour earlier – and damned if he doesn't wash up like a castaway in an old silent movie.*

*Now what?*

*Starts walking. All he's wearing is a pair of swimming trunks. Even left his Rolex behind.*

*Walks through the night and the rain for half an hour before he sees this little cabin set in a wash of white sand, meager little light showing.*

*Walks down there. Knocks.*

*Lady answers. Forty-fivish. Bit overweight. But dressed in a bikini and an open man's shirt, she has a voluptuous quality that is undeniably sexy.*

*Tells her his dilemma, she invites him in.*

*Which is when he meets the husband, chunky guy with balding gray dome and so much gray hair on his barrel chest that he looks like he's training to become a bear. Unfriendly as hell. Can tell right away that this is one very possessive guy. Doesn't appreciate your eyes on his wife's breasts. No sir.*

*They're drinking some kind of A&P generic beer and are actually pretty wasted on it. And listening to some Cuban station. Now that he gets a longer look at her, she has a Cuban air about her as a matter of fact. As for the guy, what he has on the wall is a bunch of Hemingway shit, this stuffed marlin that he probably didn't catch personally and this big color photo of himself in battle*

70

*gear in what looks to be Vietnam.*

*Far as he can see, the place has three rooms and a bath. She suggests that he can sleep on the floor with some blankets she'll give him then in the morning her husband can give him a ride into town. Husband doesn't look all that happy about it. Keeps glowering at him.*

*They drink until two and by then he knows what he's going to do.*

*Really crazy idea. Dangerous idea. Absurd idea.*

*But of course he's going to do it anyway.*

*He's working up so much hate for her swaggering abusive macho husband – the kind of guy he really loathes, kind of guy who was always picking on him when he was growing up – that he knows he'll go through with it.*

*He gets up and pretends he's going to the bathroom, carrying his beer bottle to set in a cardboard box along with the empties.*

*But when he gets level with the husband, he turns suddenly, hits the bastard on the head, grabs a length of clothes-line he's been eyeing for the past hour, and then ties the husband in his chair. Then he grabs the wife and slams her against the wall and asks where her old man keeps his guns. She tells him. He finds a .38, loaded.*

*All the wife can do is scream and scream and scream. She's shocked she can't get herself together enough to help her husband at all. Blood is running down the side of his head, in a stream down his cheek.*

*Then he goes for the wife.*

*Rips her shirt off and then her swim suit and then throws her down on the table and spreads her legs.*

*He doesn't rape her till he's sure the husband is conscious and watching.*

*The guy, by this time, is all screamed out. He's called him every possible name, made every possible threat. And now he's hoarse. Literally, hoarse.*

*The woman is long past crying.*

*She just kind of stares; he's reamed out every orifice; she just slides to the floor and stares over at her husband.*

*Which is when, for his final act tonight, he rattles around in one of the drawers by the sink and finds the butcher knife.*

71

*He goes over and cuts the husband free and then orders him, at gunpoint, to stand against the wall.*

*'What're you gonna do?' the husband says suspiciously.*

*But he just smiles slow-like and hands the wife the knife.*

*'Stab him,' he says.*

*'What?'*

*'Stab your husband.' Terror has turned her meaty face ugly.*

*'I – I couldn't do that. I love him.'*

*'If you don't do it, I'll kill you.'*

*She looks at her husband. At the knife in her hand. Back at her husband again.*

*He shoots her in the calf of her right leg. She cries out.*

*'I'm going to keep shooting you till you stab him.'*

*An animal frenzy takes her over – she looks wildly about the room for some kind of escape.*

*He shoots her in the left leg.*

*She cries out.*

*'Stab him!'*

*And she does, lunges forward and gets him in the hairy shoulder, burying the knife much deeper than she'd probably planned.*

*'Wow,' Shay says. 'Stabbin' her own husband. That was a great idea.'*

*He smiles. 'Yeah, I kinda liked it myself.'*

*'Man,' Shay says, lying back on his bunk, 'you sure come up with some good ones. You sure do.'*

# 7

Two blocks from my motel, I saw the Caddy again. Cruising slow. Keeping me in sight.

But why? She'd hired me to do a job. Didn't she trust me?

When I got to my motel room, I went immediately to the window and peered through a slit in the dark and dusty drapes.

They were just pulling into a parking place. I watched as they got out and walked down the street to a restaurant. They were both dressed in jeans and sweaters. She had a slightly wide but very friendly sort of ass. They come in all temperaments, asses do, tight little dour ones, big friendly happy ones, perfectly shaped ones that are nice only after you click your heels and salute, and weary suburban ones that just want to be rubbed a little with a mixture of fondness and eros.

I went over and laid on the bed and looked at the patterns the damp stains had made on ceiling and wall. What the hell were they doing in town, anyway?

The person in the next room decided to take a shower. The wall behind me roared and thrummed with water.

I turned on the news. Dan Rather looked as psychotic as ever, just about ready, at last it seemed, to pick up a gun and shoot everybody on the set of *Nightly News*. All the time smiling that Norman Bates grin of his.

When I woke up, it was dark. *M.A.S.H.* was on. I'd clickered the volume down to O so it was a silent movie.

I knew exactly what I wanted to do, given the fact that Nora and Vic were following me around.

I got up, washed my face with a wash cloth that smelled musty, went over to the phone and dialed Des Moines information.

73

I was surprised that Richard Tolliver had a listed number.

I called it. A maid answered. 'I'm sorry, Mr Tolliver has gone out for dinner.'

'I see. Would you ask him to call me later tonight?'

A suspicious hesitation. 'May I ask what this is about?'

'Family matter. His family.'

Another pause. 'Do you know Mr Tolliver?'

'No I don't, Ma'am.'

'I see. All right, give me your telephone number, then.'

I gave her the number. 'Room 115.'

'Room?'

'It's a motel.'

'Oh.' Prim disapproval. I'm sure she had a picture of me naked and rolling around on the bed with five or six equally naked ladies, all of us wearing tattoos and lamp shades.

'It's important,' I said.

'I'll see that he gets the message, sir. That's all I can do.'

'Thank you.'

'Yes, sir.'

Click.

I went in and had a wash and changed into a blue button-down shirt that the cleaners had starched to razor-sharpness, dark slacks, dark ribbed cotton socks – the ones with the gold toes just as in my college days – and a red windbreaker in honor of James Dean. Sometime this year he'd be having a birthday. It seemed the least I could do.

I went over and peeked out the window. The Caddy was gone. It probably wasn't much fun, killing time while the guy you were following caught a nap in his shabby little motel room.

I checked my watch.

Still an hour to go before dinner.

I decided to make myself useful.

# 8

I drove to within a block of the McNally house, took my little black bag from the back seat and then worked my way down an alley so that I could watch the place from a relatively safe position.

Lights shone. I figured I would have to come back later, or even possibly tomorrow.

But then the downstairs lights clicked off.

Eve McNally came out the back door, moving quickly down the narrow walk next to clothes-lines still hung with white sheets that smelled clean in the starry dusk.

I crouched behind the garbage cans and peeked through a dusty garage window.

She got into a new Ford sedan, worked the garage door gizmo, and then drove away.

I heard her tires crunch gravel as they headed west toward the mouth of the alley.

A few minutes later, I stood in her small but well-organized kitchen that smelled pleasantly of spices.

And stared into the sweet earnest face.of her dog Sara. A little growl rattled in her throat and twice she let out a bark but when I got down on my haunches and put my hand out, she trotted over and I started petting her head. I almost hated to take advantage of her good nature this way. For the rest of the time, Sara followed me around, tail wagging.

On the ground floor was a living room, large bathroom, sewing room and the kitchen. Upstairs were three good-sized bedrooms, a room with a worn couch and an old Philco black-and-white portable 17″ TV, and a bookcase that leaned dangerously left-ward. It was filled with battered paperbacks running to romance

75

novels, which I've always considered to be science fiction for women. My otherwise educated, beautiful and most sophisticated wife had read them. I found her taste just as baffling as she found mine for private detective novels. 'They're just as much make-believe as my romance novels are,' she'd always said. And she was probably right.

Nothing is what I found. Nothing at all useful, not in any way, nothing that told me why Eve McNally looked so depressed and anxious this afternoon, or burst into tears as soon as she'd closed the door behind me.

The woman had real problems, but what were they?

I decided to try the basement – a large, dark, dusty room that would have made Bela Lugosi feel right at home.

The washer and drier were almost comically white and new against the backdrop of cobwebs and cracked plaster and rat droppings and empty battered coal bin in this basement.

There were several cardboard boxes filled with cobwebby Mason jars of homemade preserves. I lifted each jar and looked under it. Nothing.

Thanks to all the dust in the air, my allergies kicked in. I spent a few minutes sneezing, blowing my nose and coughing hard enough to give myself a vague headache. I groped in my pocket for the anti-histamine tablets I always carry, my allergies being what they are and all, and after taking two, and giving my flashlight a little nudge so that its waning batteries temporarily fed more juice to the bulb, I went back to my search.

There were drawers to be looked into, boxes to be opened and inspected, and an old metal desk that probably dated back to the forties to be gone through.

It was in the desk, bottom right-hand drawer if you really care, that I found the small white box and in it, the finger.

At first, I thought it was a fake. I have a nephew who is at that age when whoopee cushions and joy buzzers bedazzle the young mind. He once showed me a finger like this. As now, I started when I saw it. The difference was, it took me only a half-second to realize that Jamie's was a fraud. This one, however, was real. Fake ones don't come with cuts and bruises and the long red nail fiercely broken. Before this finger had been chopped off just below the lower joint, the woman to whom it belonged had been putting up some kind of fierce struggle.

The finger felt obscene in my hand, cold and inhuman.

I shone my light into the box and found the note. I used the edge of my handkerchief to extract the note – there might well be fingerprints on it – and set it down on the desk.

Neatly typed in the center was:

*This is what happens to your daughter if I don't get those tapes back. And if you go to the police, I'll kill her.*

There was no signature.

I replaced note and finger in the box, put the box back in the desk, and was just turning toward the stairs when I heard a wooden step creak.

I shone my light up there.

Her eyes glowed like a cat's.

It was Eve McNally. And she held a carbine – pointed directly at me.

'What do you think you're doing?' she said.

'Trying to help you.'

'Right,' she said. 'Trying to help me.'

'I found the finger.'

'I don't know what the hell you're talking about, and I don't care. I just want you out of my house.'

She told me much more in that last sentence than she meant to.

Most homeowners finding a burglar in their place would immediately phone for the police.

But it was obvious that Eve McNally wanted no police in on this at all.

I felt sorry for her. She looked alone and scared even with that carbine in her hand. She needed a friend. She really did.

Then there was the matter of the finger.

'You just come up the steps very slowly.'

She waved the carbine at me.

I didn't move. 'Mrs McNally, you really don't know about the finger?'

Her fear was now replaced by confusion. 'Finger? What're you talking about?'

'Have you been down in the basement lately?'

77

'No.'

'Let me just walk over and get something from the desk. Then I'll bring it back to you.'

She sighed a ragged sigh. 'This is some kind of trick, I know it is.'

'No trick. There's just something I want you to see.'

I turned and started walking to the desk. She didn't shoot me in the back. That was definitely a good sign.

Lower drawer, right-hand, small white box. You couldn't miss it. The one with the human finger inside.

I retrieved it and carried it back to her like a well-trained family dog.

When I got three feet from the barrel of her carbine, she said, 'Hand it over slow.'

She wasn't expecting it so it really wasn't too difficult, grabbing the barrel of her gun two inches or so down from the muzzle, and giving it a jerk that snatched the carbine from her hands and brought her tumbling down the stairs.

I put the gun down, went over and helped her up.

She was crying, hard, bitter crying, and I felt sorry for her again, so I brought her close to me and held her and just let her cry for a time, and then when her tears seemed to subside I helped her upstairs and put on a fresh pot of Mr Coffee in the kitchen and then we sat down at the formica-covered table and I pushed the small white box over to her.

While she was looking at it, I went into the bathroom and got her three Bayer aspirin, and then in the kitchen again I got her a cool glass of water.

The finger lay on the table, out of its box, ugly and terrifying.

'I knew he was involved in something like this.'

'Who?' I said.

She looked up. 'You know who.'

'Your husband?'

'Yes.'

She'd been wearing blue eyeliner, smudged now from her crying, and her cheeks were puffy and pink.

'The finger doesn't look familiar?'

'No,' she said. 'Thank God. I was afraid—' Then she stopped herself.

'Where's your daughter?' I said. 'I know your husband's missing but where's your daughter?'

She changed the subject deftly, nodding her smooth, attractive face at the counter. 'Coffee's ready.'

I brought us two cups of coffee and sat down across the table from her.

'Your husband's in some kind of trouble with somebody and now somebody has your daughter, isn't that right?'

She stared at the finger some more. 'You read the note. You know what it says.'

'You didn't see the finger until I showed it to you?'

'No.'

'And you don't know who your husband might be in trouble with?'

'No.'

'Did he tell you he was in trouble?'

'No.'

'That note makes it sound as if he might be blackmailing somebody. Is that something your husband might do?'

She hesitated. 'I— He has a dark side, I guess you could say. He only ever really wanted one thing in life and that was to own his own business. He just had a thing about that. Being his own boss and all, I guess. But we lost it two years ago – it was just like losing one of his children for him – and he's never been quite right since.'

'Do you think he could blackmail somebody?'

'I'd have to say yes.'

'How many days has he been gone?'

'Why was the finger in the basement?'

'He was hiding it from you. He didn't want you to know he was in trouble. Now, how many days has he been gone?'

'Two.'

'How many days has your daughter been gone?'

The pause again. 'Who are you? You haven't told me yet.'

'A friend.'

She smiled sadly. 'That's what the Lone Ranger used to say when people asked *him* who he was.'

I smiled back. 'Well, unfortunately, I'm not the Lone Ranger.'

'If you go to the police—'

79

'I won't go to the police.'

'You promise?'

'I promise.'

Her mention of the police made me look up at the wall clock and I saw that I was already twenty minutes late for my dinner appointment with Jane Avery.

'She didn't come home from school the other day.'

'And you haven't heard from anybody about her?'

'No.'

I looked down at the finger.

'We'll have to assume that he's got her,' I said quietly.

'He?'

'The man your husband's been blackmailing.'

She lost it again, put her head down and started sobbing so hard I was afraid she was going to vomit.

I went over and got down on one knee and stroked her dark hair and rubbed her back gently and told her over and over that these things usually turned out fine and that if we just had a little patience and a little time . . . But that wasn't true, of course. At the very least we were dealing with a person who could chop another person's finger off. I had no doubt that we were also dealing with the same man whom Nora Conners had hired me to find, the same man whom Mike Peary had profiled in his letter to Nora. The same man who had murdered all those girls.

She sat up, dried her eyes with the back of her small white hands, and sniffled. 'I really appreciate you being here.'

I stood up. 'I've got to go but I'll check back with you tonight.'

She nodded.

I went over to the door, opened it and said, 'If the man should call you, write down everything he says. Every single word, all right?'

'Yes.'

'And if you should hear any noises in the background, anything at all, write down what those were, too.'

'I will.' She smiled tearfully. 'And – thanks.'

I nodded and left.

# 9

*The nights make him crazy sometimes. Nobody can really describe night-time in a lumbering old whore of a prison like this one. Puke & shit & vomit & sweat & piss & saliva & jism & every conceivable bodily fluid on the floor & in the crapper & in the mouth & up the bunghole.*

*It all makes him sick.*
*It all makes him feel like a puritan.*
*He does not want to be one of them.*
*He is not one of them.*
*Even when he kills it is with a kind of purity.*
*He sometimes has dreams of his own particular dark god. A very goaty old bastard to be sure.*
*Bring him bone & bring him flesh & bring him life hacked unto death with a knife or blown unto death with a gun or choked unto death with good strong quick hands.*
*The goaty old bastard likes it.*
*He has such crazy dreams.*
*Is sixteen years old again/sitting in a 1963 movie house watching Sandra Dee & Bobby Darin/but it is a movie unlike any he has ever seen*
*Sandra Dee is delivering a baby*
*& Bobby Darin is peering down between her legs*
*& what is emerging*
*What makes even the suddenly-appearing doctor stand back & cover his eyes in disgust and horror*
*is this*
*thing*
*No other word for it – thing*
*a crocodile head on the body of a small hunch-backed human*

*child with fingers that are long slashing razors*
    *slashing Sandra Dee's face into bloody shreds*
    *severing Bobby Darin's neck from his shoulders*
    *& then leaping for the doctor*
    *knife-fingers ripping the man's blue blue eyes from their sockets*
    *the doctor screaming*
    *& covering his eyes again*
    *blood streaming from beneath his fingers*
    *& then running, running*
    *sirens just behind him & shouts just behind him & gunfire just behind him*
    *& into deep woods now*
    *lost & wandering in circles & circles & circles*
    *& a storm all crashing thunder & silver lightning that burns when its silver touches you*
    *& he knows who he is now*
    *& he is both the 1963 boy watching the movie*
    *& also the sad hideous terrible thing that is lost in the dark woods*

*'Hey, man, knock it off.'*
    *The coon upstairs.*
    *That's how he thinks of him.*
    *Guy in the upper bunk.*
    *Says he's white.*
    *But everybody knows better.*
    *Except the warden, who always puts him in with the white guys.*
    *And he has to endure the coon for another six weeks or so until the new section is put on the prison.*
    *'Your hear me?' the coon says.*
    *'Yeah.'*
    *'That musta been some fuckin' nightmare,' the coon says.*
    *'Yeah.'*
    *'Woke me up,' the coon says.*
    *Politeness now calls for him to say sorry. But not in prison where politeness is considered an effeminate sign of weakness.*
    *'Fuck yourself. You don't have nightmares?'*
    *'Not like yours,' the coon says.*
    *'Just go back to sleep.'*

*'Just go fuck yourself.'*

*It is at times like these that the claustrophobia comes. There is no place for privacy. You eat/sleep/piss/shit/shower/exercise/work/ read/pick your nose/ scratch your balls with people watching you. 24 hours a day. 365 days a year. Watching you. There are even cons in this place who like watching gang rapes. They don't want to stick their own dicks in another guy but they sure don't mind watching other guys do it. Watching. Somebody is always always watching somebody. True, in some respects, it is a jungle but unlike a real jungle it offers no trees no ravines no caves for privacy. None.*

*It is also at moments like these when he understands the suicides. There was a guy in cell block D, for instance, who beat his head against the wall until he killed himself. There was a guy in the infirmary who got his hands on some rodent poison and killed himself. There was even the guy who was so desperate to get it over with that he went down to the garage one day, poured gasoline on himself and set himself afire, like those Buddhist monks back during the Vietnam war.*

*'Next time you tell me to go fuck myself, man,' the coon says, 'you're gonna be sorry you said it.'*

*'Yeah?' he says. 'Go fuck yourself.'*

*But the coon is a coward and everybody knows it.*

*The coon eventually goes back to sleep. And he eventually goes back to his nightmare.*

*Back to the movie theater again. And back to the beast on screen who is really – himself.*

*Razor talons click as he searches for new victims.*

# 10

''lo.'

'Chief Avery, please.'

'This is she.'

'I just wanted to tell you that you've won a free *Mike's* pizza.'

'This could only be the mysterious Mr Hokanson.'

'I believe we were talking about pizza. Don't change the subject.'

'How do I get this pizza?'

'You give your address to our delivery man and after he's run a few other errands, he'll bring it over to your place. Maybe an hour and a half.'

'And the delivery man is—'

'A guy I know named Hokanson.'

'Why not? I have a gun and plenty of ammunition and a whole drawerful of arrest warrants. I guess I can take care of myself.'

'All I need is the address.'

Which she gave me.

Jane Avery's apartment house sat in a little nook of cedars on the edge of a narrow creek that ran silver in the moonlight. No lights were on. No car was parked out front. Maybe she'd gotten tired of waiting.

It was a night of crickets and barn owls and a quarter-moon, a night of lonely distant dogs and far roaring trains and creek water tumbling across rocks just right for frogs to sit on. No doubt about it, I liked the country life.

I left my car running and walked up to the apartment-house. I knocked on the screen door. Then I watched something white flutter to the concrete steps. This was my night for notes.

Jim,
There's been an emergency. I'm at the old Brindle farm.
Guess we'll have to try again. Sorry but this is very serious
stuff.

I stuffed the note in my pocket, got in my car and drove back to
my motel. Maybe I'd just have myself a good night's sleep and
start this investigation all over again tomorrow.

I kept checking my rearview for any sign of Nora and Vic. None.

After parking my car, I decided to treat myself to a 7-Up and a
Hershey bar (with almonds, of course), so I went to the motel
office and got some change.

'Big night,' the elderly clerk said as he fanned four quarters out
on the counter.

'Oh?'

'Yeah. One person killed, another one wounded bad out at the
old Brindle place.'

Jane hadn't been exaggerating. Serious stuff indeed.

'Fred over to the DX?'

'Yeah?' I said, pretending I knew just who Fred was.

'Just was out there. Said they sure ruined a nice new Caddy.
Blood all over the interior. And that's not the kind of stuff that
washes off, either.'

A few moments ago I'd been checking my rearview for any sign
of Nora and Vic. Maybe they wouldn't ever be following me
again.

'Can you tell me how to get to the Brindle place?'

'Sure. If you want. But Fred said it's pretty damned grisly.'

There must have been thirty parked cars lining both sides of the
winding gravel road that ran past the Brindle farm, which was
basically an aged and deserted farmhouse with the windows
boarded up, and a faded barn that some local kids had spray-
painted dirty words all over. Down close to a creek was another
barn that, while smaller, was also a lot fancier, with a gabled roof
and a cross-gabled cupola. The sprawling land to the east looked
as if it hadn't been cultivated in some time. Overhead, a state

85

police chopper hovered, its searchlights crisscrossing the rolling countryside.

I had to walk a quarter-mile till I reached the driveway and the ambulance and the two squad cars and the blue Caddy.

I saw Jane. She was talking to a short man in a dark suit. He carried a small leather bag and was presumably the medical examiner. Jane looked harried.

Up close, the house had an eerie quality I couldn't explain to anybody who hadn't been around crime scenes much. While most detectives won't come right out and tell you that some houses, just like some wooded areas and indeed some human beings, aren't exactly cursed or haunted, there is a disturbing, baleful quality to them that makes you want to get away as soon as possible. While the activities of satanic cults are greatly exaggerated by the press, I'd once seen a house used for rituals where a four-month-old child had been sacrificed to the psychotic whims of the cultists. It would never be, at least as far as I was concerned, a fit place for human habitation ever again. The baby's screams would never quite be stilled.

'Sorry, keep back.'

He was maybe twenty-five with a beer gut and a macho mustache. This was probably his first murder as an auxiliary deputy and he meant to make the most of it. He had a gun, a badge and a khaki shirt with heavy sweat rings under the armpits. He even had a little cigarillo clamped between his teeth.

I was about to tell him something obscene when Jane looked over and saw me, excused herself from the doctor, and dropped by to cool the official ardor of her auxiliary cowboy.

'It's all right, Fred, he's a friend.'

'He shoulda said so, then,' Fred said, swaggering elsewhere to shine his badge in somebody else's eyes.

'Fred's the Mayor's son,' Jane said.

'Now there's a surprise.'

She looked back at the blue Caddy in the driveway. She had a yellow pad in her left hand and a pencil in her right. She sketched in some more of the crime scene, which she had started earlier by measuring various objects in relation to the bodies. This sketch would later be refined into a finished product complete with a scale on the order of $1/4'' = 1'$. This would ultimately be used by the district attorney or the county attorney in making his case.

Just as she was finishing, the left door of the blue Caddy was opened by a startlingly young-looking woman in white coveralls and the process of bringing the bodies out was begun.

'One dead?' I said as I watched.

Jane nodded. 'Yes. A woman. The man's already been taken to the hospital. He's alive but not for much longer, I'm afraid.'

I saw her then, in that moment before the sheet was pulled over her for the final time, Nora Conners. She had been wearing a white sweater and jeans. Her blonde hair was streaked and damp with blood; her white sweater was bathed in the stuff. I couldn't see a lot from this distance but it appeared that she had been both shot and stabbed.

The attendants eased the corpse into the rear of the big boxy ambulance, quietly closed the doors and then moved unhurriedly to the vehicle's cab. There was no reason to hurry.

'You look funny.'

I was aware of Jane's eyes on me.

'I always look funny.'

'No, you don't. You usually look handsome and you know it. But now you look funny. Ever since you saw the corpse.' She hesitated, studied me a little more. 'I don't believe your journalist story, by the way.'

'You don't?'

'No. I called your publishing office.'

'Then they told you that I do work for them?'

'I have a brother in the FBI.'

'Ah. I'll bet you're proud.'

She smirked. 'Wise ass, aren't you?'

'I'm just trying to forget what that corpse looked like.'

And that was certainly the truth. When murder victims get worked over the way Nora was, all I can think of are slaughter houses, what we humans do to the animals we raise to eat, how they look just as we're knocking them out with long clubs, and then chop off their heads, and then hang them from their feet and open up their bellies with long shining knives. I always wonder, when I'm on the highway and I see a truck of cows or pigs headed to the slaughter house, I always wonder if they know. Perhaps it's our fantasy that they don't know because we can't face the truth.

Maybe they do know and the startled bleating we hear on the highway is the sound of one species crying out to another for help. I wonder if Nora knew, as the killer approached her car tonight, if she knew what was coming, what the killer was bringing, and whether she cried out for help.

'Did you know her?'

'Who?'

'The dead woman.'

'No.'

'Would you take it personally if I called you a liar?'

'You're the law around here. You can call me anything you want.'

'I've got good instincts.'

'Meaning?'

'Meaning somehow you know something about this.'

She was about to say more when a fat bald detective in a suit came over shaking a small black camera as if he wanted to smash it against the wall. 'I told the city council, I told the Mayor in particular, that we need a new 35 mm for crime scenes and as usual he gave me the standard bullshit about the budget. I'm supposed to be taking pictures and the goddamned shutter won't work. You bring yours along, Chief?'

'In my glove compartment.'

He looked at me and shook the camera again and said, 'You ever just want to smash something to bits?'

'All the time,' I said.

He went over to her car.

'He's not taking his tranquilizers,' she said.

'How come?'

'Claims that yes, they do calm him down but no, he can't urinate properly when he takes them. So he doesn't take them and gets pretty squirrelly.'

She looked back at the crime scene.

Here we were in the rolling prairie night, all these red and white emergency lights whirling around in the gloom, all these farmers and small-town folks standing in the gravel road partly thrilled and partly horrified by what had happened here tonight. I wondered what the birds made of all this, or the wolves running in the hills, or the owl in the old barn down the hill. Just one more dumb ass human doing one more dumb ass human thing, the animals were probably thinking. These humans didn't even kill each other for the only reason that justified killing, survival, these humans killed each other for money and sex and jealousy. They didn't make any sense, these beings, and owl and wolf and bird would be glad when the lights and the noise and the sweaty intense fascination were all taken away and the land was given back to the moon and the clouds and the fast-running creeks, that sense of order and peace and oneness I had only experienced when I was up in my biplane.

'I'd better get back to it,' she said.

She looked like she wanted to say more, but then somebody shouted her name, tugging her away.

Just as I was leaving, people had to stand to either side of the driveway so the ambulance could get through, bearing Nora into the night.

# 11

He spends two of his prison years working in the print shop, running a big press. The prison does a lot of cut-rate printing for the state.

It is in the print shop that the snitch is dealt with.

Five days before it happens, two white cons trap a black con in the showers and castrate him. They also, after cutting him up that way, use the same knife to cut his throat.

Prison, always a dangerous place, is now even more dangerous.

At meals, the blacks huddle against one wall and glare at the whites who sit huddled along the other.

On the yard, he witnesses the most violent fistfight he's ever seen, between this jig and this big Polack.

In less than two minutes – the time it takes for the guards to come running and separate them – they break each other's noses, the black guy busts two or three knuckles, the white guy fractures his arm, and both of them suffer what later prove to be brain concussions because of the ferocity of their blows. They are both bloody and unconscious by the time the guards reach them.

He is scared.

Can't sleep sometimes, he's so scared.

Even finds himself on the verge of tears, he is so frightened. But most of the cons are. They all know how terrible this thing could get.

Comes a particular moment, he is alone in his cell. The warden is moving everybody around again – the cons have started referring to cellblock F as the Transit Authority – and he just happens to be between cellmates.

Another night when he can't sleep.

90

*This night, he puts a pillow over his head and keeps his eyes shut and tries to block out all the screaming and the taunts as black men shout: 'You gonna pay, pussy!' and white men shout back, 'I'm gonna kill you, nigger!'*

*Not until tonight does he realize what a real prison riot must be like. All the chaos. But most especially, all the rage. He can't get Attica out of his mind. So many had died so savagely. The cons had even broken pop bottles so they could use the jagged edges to rip the eyes out of cons who had snitched in the past.*

*Tear out their eyes like that.*

*He tries hard to sleep.*

*But can't.*

Next morning, he's running his press, checking ink levels and grabbing an occasional page to scan, when Marley, a true maniac, comes up and says, 'You didn't hear nothin'.'

'All right.'

'Haskins.'

'Yeah?'

'He was the snitch,' Marley says.

'No shit. He seems like such a nice guy. You sure?'

'What the fuck's that supposed to mean? I say Haskins's the snitch, then he's the fucking snitch. Dig?'

'Dig.'

Two days earlier, the two whites who had castrated the black man had been identified by a snitch and put in the hole. They would soon be formally charged.

Now Marley says they found the snitch. And now Marley says, 'So if you hear somethin', you didn't hear nothin'. Right?'

'Right.'

He goes back to his press work.

A few minutes later he notices that a very pale, very scared-looking con named Haskins is being dragged toward the big storage closet in the room adjacent to the press room.

*Haskins looks right at him. Puppy-dog eyes. Imploring.*

*Please. Please do something.*

*Please help me.*

*Please be human.*

*Please.*

91

*They drag Haskins into the storage closet and close the door.*
*He actually doesn't hear much.*
*An occasional cry.*
*An occasional scream.*
*The press makes a lot of noise.*
*They're in there a long time, or at least a lot longer than he expects.*
*He runs his press.*
*None of my effing business.*
*That's the only way you stay alive in prison.*
*None of my effing business.*
*When they come out, they're sweaty and sort of mussed up. They're walking fast.*
*Marley just sort of nods to him.*
*And then vanishes.*
*He just keeps working on his press.*
*None of my effing business.*
*But when it's time to grab a mid-morning Pepsi from the machine, he routes himself right past the storage closet door.*
*And sees the blood flooding out from beneath the door.*
*Man, they really must have given it to that poor bastard. Which is the really weird thing. Because while the blood he spills while cutting up his own victims (murders the police know nothing about, murders that have nothing to do with his tenure in prison) does not repel him, the sight of somebody else's violence sickens and scares him.*
*He avoids getting the blood on his shoes.*
*Doesn't want to be implicated in any way.*
*He goes and gets his Pepsi and returns to his press and minds his own effing business.*
*After a while, a guard is cutting through the press room on his way to lunch, when he sees the blood on the floor and goes over and opens the storage closet door.*
*He suddenly looks real sick.*
*Rushes to the phone and then suddenly there are a dozen guards all over the printing room and they all take turns peeking into the storage closet and they all suddenly look sick.*
*Seems that Marley and his buddy did the same thing to Haskins that the other white guys did to the jig in the shower.*

*Castrated him and then cut his throat.*

*Well, he supposes there's a kind of poetic justice to this, but he still can't sleep very well at night.*

# 12

On the way back to my motel, my mind stuck on the photograph it had taken of Nora Conners's throat as she was being carried on the stretcher, the fleshy red mess of it. I had a difficult time changing the photo in the slide tray.

'Bad?' asked the old clerk after he waved me into the front office.

'Terrible.' He wanted details. People in hell want ice water.

On TV, Larry King was talking to a movie star about her new autobiography.

The office looked the same, ancient and shabby, duct tape covering slices in the green vinyl couch and armchair, the diamond-patterned indoor-outdoor carpeting worn to a flat black dirty color. At one time, I think, it had been a kind of maroon.

'Somebody said she was buck-ass naked,' the old guy said, still wanting scandal and gore.

'Sorry. She had all her clothes on.'

'Oh.'

'I'm sure it'll be in the paper tomorrow morning.'

'Not here it won't. We only got the weekly.'

'In the state paper, then.'

'Yeah, but they never give you jack shit, not like the Chicago papers. You ever read the Chicago papers?'

'Sometimes.'

'They give you everything. If they're naked, they tell you they were naked.'

'That's what first-class journalism is all about.'

He caught my sarcasm and for a moment looked like what he was, an old man dying out his nights at the front desk of a tiny

94

motel in the middle of nowhere on a planet nobody but us lonely animals had as yet discovered. I was being a prig. He wanted a few juicy details, just a natural human curiosity. I'm the sort of hypocrite who earnestly scans all those tabloid covers while waiting in the supermarket line then talks about how silly they are at dinner later that night, and how I can't imagine people wasting their time on them.

'There was a lot of blood.'

'No shit?' he said, all frayed red bow-tie and frayed polyester white shirt and frayed ancient blue cardigan. 'A lot, huh?'

'Cut her throat.'

'Goddamn.'

'And she was a looker, too.'

'Young, huh?'

'Young enough.'

'Goddamn,' he said to my back after I'd nodded good night and was starting out the door. 'Sure wish the Chicago papers was going to cover this.'

The screen door slammed behind me.

The old fart said, 'Hey!'

I stopped, turned around.

'You got a phone call.'

'From whom?'

'Guy named Tolliver. Is that the rich Des Moines Tolliver?'

'He leave a number?'

'Said you had it.'

'Thanks.'

'Is that the rich Des Moines Tolliver?'

'I'm not sure.'

He looked disappointed.

In my room, I locked up for the night, opened a Pepsi, sat down on the edge of the bed, lifted the receiver, obtained a long distance operator and dialed Tolliver. My room was shadowy and chilly, a tomb of secrets, furtive adultery and lonely masturbation, broken dreams and bright, doomed hopes.

The maid answered. I had the impression she didn't care for me awfully much. Maybe she knew I was a hypocrite about tabloids.

'I'll see if he's taking calls,' she said frostily and set the phone down.

'Hello,' said a deep voice that sounded both intelligent and curiously humble. I guess I'd been expecting the stereotype robber baron to answer.

'Mr Tolliver?'

'Yes.'

'My name's Jim Hokanson.'

'Yes, Mr Hokanson, that's what Katie said. Katie, my maid.'

'Well, I called you earlier tonight before it happened.'

'Before what happened?'

'Before—' I stopped myself. 'Have you heard from the police tonight, Mr Tolliver?'

'The police?'

'Yes. There's been – some trouble.'

'What kind of trouble?'

God, now I'd have to tell him.

'Mr Tolliver, I wish I didn't have to tell you this but – your daughter Nora's been murdered.'

A long enigmatic silence. 'My daughter Nora?'

'Yes.'

'Has been murdered?'

'Yes.'

'And you are who, exactly?'

'Jim Hokanson.'

'Are you a police officer?'

'No.'

'Are you a private investigator, then?'

'Something like that.'

'I see.' A pause. 'Mr Hokanson?'

'Yes.'

'Mr Hokanson, this is going to come as a shock to you, but I don't have a daughter.'

'I met her.'

'You met someone who perhaps told you she was my daughter, but she wasn't.'

'I feel pretty goddamned foolish right now.'

'As well you should, Mr Hokanson. As well you should. Now give me your exact location. I have a plane of my own and I'm going to fly over there tomorrow.'

'I'm really sorry about this.'

'Quit babbling, Mr Hokanson, and tell me where you're calling from. I want to find out just what the hell is going on.'

# Three

# VICTIM INFORMATION

25. This is Victim __1__ of __2__ Victim(s) in This Incident.
    (number)   (total)

26. Status of This Victim:
    1. ☒ Deceased (as result of this incident)
    2. ☐ Survivor of Attack
    3. ☐ Missing

27. Name: __Saunders, Eleanor J.__
    (last, first, middle)

28. Alias(es) (including maiden name and prior married names):
    __Nora Conners, Nora McAuley,__

    __Nora Tolliver, Rosamund Tolliver__

29. Resident City: __Chicago__   30. State: __IL__   31. ZIP: __60649__

32. Social Security Number: __479__ _ __82__ _ __1954__   33. FBI Number: __A0093-079__

34. Sex:
    1 ☐ Male          2 ☒ Female          99. ☐ Unknown

35. Race:
    1  ☐ Black        3 ☐ Hispanic         5  ☐ Other
    2  ☒ Caucasian    4 ☐ Oriental/Asian   99 ☐ Unknown

36. Date of Birth: __04__/ __04__ /__55__
    (mo) / (da) / (yr)
    99 ☐ Unknown

37. Age (or best estimate) at Time of Incident: __38__
    99 ☐ Unknown                         (years)

38. Height (or best estimate): __5__ feet __9__ inches
    99 ☐ Unknown

39. Approximate Weight: __130__ lbs.
    99 ☐ Unknown

40. Build (check one only):
    1 ☒ Small (thin)              3 ☐ Large (stocky)
    2 ☐ Medium (average)          99 ☐ Unknown

41. Hair Length (check one only):
    1 ☐ Bald or Shaved                 4 ☒ Shoulder Length
    2 ☐ Shorter Than Collar Length     5 ☐ Longer Than Shoulder Length
    3 ☐ Collar Length                  99 ☐ Unknown

42. Hair Shade (check one only):
    1 ☒ Light                 3 ☐ Neither 1 or 2 Above
    2 ☐ Dark                  99 ☐ Unknown

43. Predominant Hair Color (check one only):
    1 ☐ Gray and/or White     5 ☐ Black
    2 ☒ Blond                 6 ☐ Other
    3 ☐ Red                   99 ☐ Unknown
    4 ☐ Brown

# 1

This is the page that Jane Avery – make that Chief of Police Jane Avery – pushed in front of me while I was eating breakfast in a sunny booth in Fitzwilly's Café the next morning. She wore a crisply laundered new blue police shirt and dark blue pants with knife-sharp creases. In the sunlight, her freckles were more vivid than ever, and her tiny nose and white white teeth more fetching than ever.

'Does any of this sound familiar?'

'I haven't swallowed my waffle yet.'

'I'm not kidding, Jim.'

'Neither am I. I've got a mouthful of food.'

'So swallow.'

I swallowed.

'First of all,' I said, 'this is a form that relates to sexual homicide.'

'After she was killed, she was raped.'

'Oh shit.' I tried not to think of the odd vulnerability that had always rested in Nora's eyes.

I looked over the form some more. 'Eleanor Saunders. Chicago. Age thirty-eight.'

'And her companion's name was Karl Givens.'

I just looked at her. Didn't say anything.

'Maybe you knew her under some other name.'

'Who said I knew her?'

'I watched you look at that blue Cadillac last night, when they were bringing the Saunders woman out. You knew her all right.'

A waitress came. Jane ordered coffee, black. It was nice in here, mote-tumbled sunlight streaming through the front window, an early 1960s Seeburg jukebox standing in the corner, with maybe even a few Fats Domino songs on it, and mostly quiet people in work clothes who knew and seemed to like each other. A place like this in the city, at 8.12 a.m., would have been a madhouse.

'You going to tell me about her, Jim?'

'Didn't know her.'

'Look at me and tell me you didn't know her.'

I raised my eyes from the last of my waffle. 'Didn't know her.'

'You're lying.'

'I didn't know that you called visitors liars.'

'You do if you're Chief of Police. And if your guest happens to be lying.'

The waitress came back with her coffee. 'Thanks, Myrna,' Jane said.

She sipped her coffee.

'You going to invite me over for dinner tonight?'

'I don't know yet, Jim. You really piss me off.'

I'd put our remarks down to normal man-woman banter until just now. She really was pissed but she was so quiet about it, I hadn't been able to tell until she'd told me.

'I'm sorry.'

'Then you're really not going to tell me how it is that you and the dead woman came to town on the same day, at the same time, and how she got herself murdered and how you claim not to have known her?'

'How do you know we arrived on the same day at the same time?'

'I checked. That's my job.'

'I wish you'd calm down.'

'I wish you'd tell me the truth.'

'How about the man with her?' I'd almost called him Vic.

'What about him?'

'Is he still alive?'

'Not for much longer. If he doesn't improve by noon, they're going to put him in a helicopter and take him to Iowa City. But even that probably won't do much good.'

'I really do wish you'd invite me over tonight.'

She stood up and clattered a quarter on the table. 'I really do wish you'd tell me the truth.'

She left.

# 2

In the car, I spent twenty minutes going through Peary's profile. Here we had three suspects:

Cal Roberts
Richard McNally
Samuel Lodge

According to Peary's profile, and he'd been just about the most skilled profiler I'd ever worked with, our man's personality characteristics made him:

Above average intelligence
Socially competent
Sexually competent
Demands submissive victims

At some point, I'd probably send the FBI Behavioral Science Unit all the material that Peary had gathered.

These days, the FBI is inundated with so many requests for help from local police departments that there's now a long waiting line. The budget doesn't allow for the FBI to take every case so the trickiest ones tend to get taken first.

This is where I can help small-town police departments. Because I'm a former employee, I know who to call and what kind of specific help to ask for. I can usually speed things up. Then, when the FBI returns its assessment of the material, I can show the local police how to implement it into their investigation.

Which is just what I was trying to do as I sat there, thinking of the three suspects in the light of Peary's eight-page profile.

104

The trouble was, the three men could all fit the profile – until I knew more about them and their patterns, anyway.

And that was going to take a lot more work.

# 3

The prison grapevine can get a story around in less than an hour. By then, virtually everybody in the place will know the same tale.

Well, this one day, there's a very special tale going around and its consequences can be seen in the cafeteria where this rabbity little guy with thick glasses sits eating his soup – alone.

Usually you see the little guy with his buddies but not today because he ain't got no buddies no more.

He learned less than two hours ago that he has the first confirmed case of HIV in the prison.

And nobody wants to be around him.

AIDS is just now starting to fill the TV screens and the front pages of newspapers and there's a lot of hysteria. Gays getting beaten up everywhere. An AIDS hospice being burned down in the middle of the night. Some little kid barred from school because a veritable lynch mob of parents come screaming to the school board.

Everybody in the prison industry knows that when AIDS starts to really hit this place, there is going to be hell to pay.

Anal intercourse being the most efficient method of transmitting the disease – well, in a prison full of horny men reluctantly willing to fuck each other even though they'd much rather fuck women . . .

Well, it's going to be terrible.

This is the background as he lies awake on the upper bunk one night and listens to the guy below him weep.

Tries to pretend he doesn't hear.

Tries to pretend he doesn't know what's really going on.

But he does know.

106

*This sorta pretty kid got passed around among all the important cons and now—*

*Well, you can bet there are a lot of important cons lying awake tonight, too, wondering if they're soon going to get the word from the infirmary that . . .*

'You awake?'

'Yeah.'

'Sorry for crying,' the kid says.

'It's all right.'

'It's just I'm scared.'

'I know.'

'You fuck anybody since you been in here?'

'Huh-uh. I don't like to fuck men. I like to fuck women.'

'You're probably all right, then.'

'Unless I pick it up some other way,' he says. He's a real hypochondriac. He wishes he had a different guy living on the bunk below.

'Don't you watch TV?'

'Yeah.'

'Well, they explain that. You can't get it from drinking out of the same glass or just touching somebody or anything like that.'

'That's what they say, anyway.'

'You don't believe them?'

'Huh-uh.'

'How come?'

'They're just trying to keep everybody calm. They don't want people rioting in the streets and shit like that.'

'You ever seen anybody with it in the later stages?'

'Yeah.'

'Pretty terrible.'

'Yeah.'

'I hope I die before I get that bad off,' the kid says. 'Except I'm scared to die.'

*Neither speaks for a long time.*

*Just listen to the prison night.*

'How about you?' the kid says.

'How about me what?'

'You afraid to die?'

'Sure. Especially from some faggot disease.'

107

*'I guess I don't like that.'*
*'Don't like what?'*
*'Being called a faggot.'*
*'Oh.'*
*'We're human beings, too, you know.'*
*'Just give it a rest, kid, all right?'*
*'I fucking resent it, man. I mean, if you really want to know. I don't call you names, why should you call me names?'*
*'You don't call me names because I'm not a faggot.'*
*'That's it, you fucking prick.'*
*And the kid jumps off his bed and puts his fists up like he's in some kind of bad-ass fight with an invisible opponent and then he starts coming closer and closer to the top bunk and—*
*He lashes his foot out and kicks the kid real hard in the mouth. The kid starts wailing and weeping right away.*
*All the cons who've been listening in are laughing their asses off.*
*Some fairy boy with AIDS, this is exactly what he's got coming.*
*The kid cries himself out, just the way little babies do, and then finally crawls back up on his bunk and goes to sleep.*
*Sixteen months later, the kid is down to eighty-one pounds and shits out any kind of nutrition they try to feed him in the infirmary.*
*He's shitting himself to death, literally.*
*The story is all over the prison.*
*God, eighty-one pounds.*
*Sure glad I never fucked him.*
*Benny fucked him. Benny won't admit it. But Benny fucked him.*

*During the time it takes the kid to die, eight more HIV-positive cases are reported in the prison.*
*His hypochondria is getting real bad.*
*Even though he's extremely careful never to touch anybody, he's terrified that he's going to get it anyway.*
*He's convinced that the government is lying.*
*He's convinced that he's never going to leave this prison alive.*
*No $2,000 per month retainer is going to help him now.*

*For the first time, he starts daydreaming about escaping from here.*

# 4

St Mark's Hospital was a four-story red-brick hospital with no flourishes or pretensions whatsoever. It had windows, doors, ledges and corners and that was it. Presumably it also had indoor plumbing.

I found the back door, then the back stairs and proceeded to go up. Earlier I'd talked to the hospital operator, pretending I was calling long distance about my brother Karl, and she told me he was in Room 408, intensive care.

I moved as quickly and quietly as possible up the echoing concrete stairwell. At the fourth floor, I opened the heavy green fire door and peeked down the hall, expecting to see the flash of white uniforms and hear the squeak of rubber soles.

The hall was empty.

I eased the door closed and started my search of the corridor. A hand-lettered sign taped to the wall said

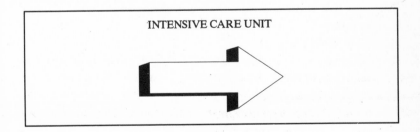

INTENSIVE CARE UNIT

I followed the arrow and ended up in another short hallway with four doors to it, two on either side.

The second left, a nurse with an ample bottom was backing out of the room. The first right, a young female doctor looking brisk and earnest was just saying a loud 'Good morning' to the patient inside.

The door I wanted was first left. I had to reach it before the nurse just leaving 410 saw me.

I took five giant steps, pushed the door open and lunged inside.

I was all cold sweat and ragged breathing for two long minutes.

Vic, or Karl, was in bed, unconscious, a pale corpse-like man who had so many tubes running out of his nostrils, his mouth and his arms, he looked like a creepy-crawly alien from a science fiction movie. His breath came in gasps. The room smelled oppressively of decay. There were no flowers or cute greeting cards or balloons in the shape of puppies.

I waited until my breathing was normal again and then I crossed over to the side of his bed and peered down.

He looked dead. There was no other way to say it. Waxen, still; some part of his soul had already crossed over.

He was all clean bandages, their heaviest concentration being across his throat. Across his middle were more bandages. Neither the slashed throat nor the two bullets to the stomach had killed him. Not yet.

I touched his shoulder.

His eyes flew open instantly.

He stared straight up at the ceiling, completely unaware of me.

'Who did this to you, Karl?'

Not even a flicker of recognition in his gaze.

'Who did this to you, Karl?'

A faint glimmer of awareness.

'Karl, I'm trying to help you.'

He seemed to hear me as if from a long way off, and then he turned his head no more than a quarter-inch and looked up at me.

He started crying. Suddenly, with no warning whatsoever, his entire body began to shake and tears were rolling down his cheeks.

He raised a trembling hand, a drowning man reaching up frantically for the final time, and I took it and held it.

'I'm sorry, Karl. But you're going to a better place.'

'Scared,' he said. And for the first time, some recognition of me shone in his eyes.

'I know, Karl. But you won't be scared for long. I promise.'

He fell to crying then, soft, almost silent crying, his lower lip twitching as he did so.

'Who did this to you?'

But he wasn't listening to my words, only to the sounds I made. 'Scared,' he said again. 'Scared.'

'I want to make this right for you, Karl. I want you to tell me who did this to you.'

'Conmarck,' he said messily, dribble and some blood glistening on the corner of his mouth.

'What?' I said.

He was looking at me but not seeing me. Just staring, the way a dead man would. He was going. Fast.

'Conmarck.'

I was about to ask him what that meant when the door opened behind me and a nurse said, 'This man is not allowed any visitors.'

Just as I started to turn away from Karl, he said it again, as if he had been programmed with only one word, 'Conmarck.'

I knew I had to do it quickly, and without giving her much of a look at me.

I put my head down, squared my shoulders, and plowed my way out of the room, the nurse chittering angry words at me as I did so.

I found the door, and the rear stairwell, and got out of the hospital.

Having no idea, of course, what 'Conmarck' meant.

I thought of Karl back there, his ragged frightened tears, crossing over now, crossing over.

I really did hope it would be better for him on the other side. Because then it might be better for me, too, when my time came.

111

# 5

The town had two sections, an older one where the blue-collar workers lived, and the newer one where the suburbanites nestled into their expensive homes. In the middle of the town was an aloof, impressive, French Second Empire courthouse and a wide main street that ran to small businesses that were likely here back when Frank Capra made all his wonderful movies about small-town America. On the south and east edges of town, you could see the official imposition of Progress, the strip malls and the franchise food places and the video stores with posters of half-naked ladies carrying Uzis. I stayed downtown. The older I get, the less I'm impressed with Progress.

For twenty minutes I forgot all about Nora and how she'd lied to me, and Vic whose real name was Karl and how he was nearby desperately clinging to life, and how disturbed Tolliver had sounded when I'd told him about the death of his 'daughter.'

I forgot it all. I bought myself a newspaper, just the way the businessmen did, and I strode around a little more, and then I bought myself a cup of coffee from the old-fashioned pharmacy with the big wooden fan in the ceiling and chipped and cracked but still honorable old soda fountain, and I sat down on a park bench where a pigeon perched, and I spent the next ten minutes engrossed in reading, while warm spring sunlight dappled the bandstand and the smell of apple blossoms floated on the breeze.

I probably wouldn't have noticed him except somebody honked at him. When I looked up, he was waving and about to get into a new station wagon.

There were some questions I wanted to ask him so I hurried across the street just as he was starting the engine.

'Morning, Kenny.'

He looked up, boyish in his black cowboy shirt with white piping. His gaze was anything but Christian or charitable. He rolled down the window. 'The Reverend told me not to talk to you.'

'Why's that, I wonder?'

'Said I'd just get us all in trouble.'

'Not if you don't have anything to hide.'

He shook his blond, Irish head. 'We argue enough as it is, the Reverend and me, no reason to make it any worse.'

He started to put the station wagon into gear.

'You want a cup of coffee?'

'No, thanks. I just need to get going.'

'Is Mindy having an affair with the Reverend?'

Kenny just looked at me. 'I gotta go.'

I reached in the window and put a hand on his shoulder. 'When you travel with the Reverend to different towns, does he ever go off on his own?'

'The Reverend was right.'

'Oh?'

'You're no magazine writer.'

'What's he afraid I'll find out?'

Kenny sighed. 'I haven't hit anybody in a long time, mister. I used to have this real bad temper and hit people pretty much when I felt like it. I don't want to have to hit you.'

'Does he go off by himself when you travel?'

Kenny sighed again. 'Yes. Now is that going to shut you up? Yes, the Reverend goes off by himself.'

'You have any idea where he goes or what he does?'

'I don't follow him, if that's what you mean. So how would I know what he does?'

'I guess that's fair enough.'

He watched my face carefully. 'Who are you?'

'A lot of people seem real curious about that.'

'Does your reporter bit usually work a little better than it has in New Hope?'

I smiled. 'Yes, a little better, anyway.'

'You don't want to get the Reverend pissed at you.'

'No?'

'He's got this mean pecker lawyer in Cedar Rapids. The guy

113

sues anybody the Reverend tells him to. And the Reverend tells him to sue a lot of people.'

I stood back from the station wagon and looked it over. Chrysler. This year's model. White walls. Leather seats. Big tape deck. I thought of the two matching white Lincolns. 'He sure must make a lot of money.'

'Our radio shows hit a lot of towns.'

'Enough to support everything the Reverend owns?' I looked at him directly. 'Where's the Reverend get all his money?'

'I told you. His radio shows.'

'Afraid you can't sell me on that. Lincolns don't come cheap. Especially not those models. And neither does a big boat like this one.'

'What're you saying?'

'I'm saying that the good Reverend must have some other source of income.'

'I'm going to tell him all this, you know. Everything you said.'

'I want you to.'

'You do?' he said.

'Sure. Because then he'll get nervous and when people get nervous, they make mistakes.'

'Why're you so interested in him?'

I laughed. 'Because I'm a reporter, remember? And reporters are always interested in people.'

Kenny Deihl stared out the windshield a moment, sighed. 'He isn't so bad, really.'

'He isn't, huh?'

'He's a hypocrite. I mean, if he believes all that religious stuff he says, you sure couldn't prove it by me. But he's been good to me. And good to Mindy. Neither one of us is exactly what you'd call a prize.'

'Oh?'

He shrugged. 'I was in a halfway house when he found me. I'm a drunk, an alcoholic, I guess you'd say. And as for Mindy—' He shrugged again.

'What about Mindy?'

'She'd gotten all beat up by this bar owner where she sang. The Reverend found her wandering around on the street. She's a coke head. At least with the Reverend, we have some kind of life.

We've each got rooms in the basement of the church, and he pays us enough to live on.'

'When you're traveling, you ever see anything strange happen?'

'Strange? Like what?'

'Nothing special. Just anything strange.'

'Not really.'

'He comes in real late, I suppose?'

'Sometimes.'

'You ever notice any kind of blood or anything on his clothes?'

'Blood? Hell no. What kind of a man do you think he is?'

'That's what I want you to tell me.'

'Well, like I say, he's a hypocrite and that's for sure, but hey, we're all hypocrites in some way. And you wouldn't believe the hope the Reverend gives to those in despair. You should see the mail he gets from people who're sick and dying. They love that man. They put him right next to Jesus Christ. They really do.'

This time he did put the car in gear.

'I've said enough.' He squinted up into the sunlight. 'I really am going to tell the Reverend everything I said. Otherwise I'd feel guilty.'

I nodded and stood back from the car so he could pull out of the parking place.

Just as he was ready to swing out into the street, he stopped the station wagon and said, 'You've got him wrong. You really do. He isn't perfect maybe but he's basically a decent guy. He really is.'

And with that, he pulled away from the curb, finding his place in the lazy morning traffic.

I stood there watching him fade down the street.

A little old lady in a little old Ford gently tapped her little old horn to remind me that I was blocking her space.

I gave her my best boyish grin and stepped out of her way.

115

# 6

There were five of them, women between the ages of forty and sixty I guessed, and they sat in a worshipful circle around him, laughing when his inflection said he was being witty, asking questions when his inflection said he was being profound. He ran to type, a sort you see in university towns, the handsome professor in his post-hippie phase, striped button-down shirts and $150 chinos out of GQ, graying hair caught up in a sweet little ponytail. It went well with his sweet little earring. You don't have to listen long to hear the sneer in the voice or see the arrogance in the gaze. Fifty years ago he would have been in Montmartre, seducing the frail daughters of European wealth while proclaiming himself a most serious artist. He was the sort of man Hemingway used to slap the shit out of when he was in his cups.

When he saw me, he looked as if he planned to have me arrested.

He had been standing in the middle of his front yard, right next to his easel and canvas, on the edge of which sat a huge monarch butterfly, demonstrating to the ladies the basic techniques of painting, when he heard me and looked around.

He frowned. 'You're Hokanson, aren't you?'

I nodded.

'I don't have anything to say to you. But I do want you off my property and right now.'

'Maybe I came to see your wife.'

'Off. And right now. Do you hear me? Off!'

The students, as one, turned to scowl at me.

Just then I saw Joanna coming down the stairs, looking thin and pretty in her designer denim shirt and designer denim jeans.

116

'I'll handle it, Sam. You go on with your class.'

'I forbid you to talk to him,' Sam said, sounding very silly.

She waved him away, swooped over by me and said, in little more than a whisper, 'The word's out about you.'

'The word?'

'Everybody knows you're not really a reporter. Even if you do have that business card saying otherwise.'

She slid her arm through mine, started steering me toward my car in the gravel drive, away from the house and the students, most of whom were still glaring at me.

'They don't like me.'

She giggled. 'Of course not. They all have crushes on him. He doesn't like you, therefore they don't like you.'

'What's he so angry about?'

'I wish I knew.'

'You really don't know?'

She shook her head. 'It's strange. For the first time, I think he's really hiding something from me. And I think it's a lot more serious than just one of his little affairs.'

'But you don't have any idea what?'

She shook her head again.

We stood by my car.

She was about to say something when Sam erupted again. 'Get away from that car, Joanna, and go back in the house! Get away from there right now!'

If he'd had a bullhorn, he would have sounded like a cop talking a killer out of a building.

'What an ass he can be,' she said, red daubing her cheeks suddenly. 'I'd better go back inside.' She dropped her gaze and then suddenly raised it again, looking right at me. 'Oh hell, I may as well tell you. I had a fantasy about you, just like I said.'

'I hope it was a good one.'

'It was a great one!'

'Joanna! You heard me! Get away from that car and go back inside!'

She glanced at me and smiled. 'I'm so proud to be married to him sometimes.'

Then, just as her daddy had demanded, she went back inside.

# 7

*That spring, one of the talk shows came to the prison – THREE
LIVE SHOWS FROM THE MOST DANGEROUS PRISON IN AMERICA!
as the announcer kept saying all week – and guess who one of the
inmate-guests was?*

*He certainly hadn't volunteered. Indeed, he hadn't even wanted
to do it . . . but when the TV lights came on in the big storage
room where an impromptu stage had been set up . . . there he was.*

*The show itself was pretty bland. They even gave the cons fake
names, to 'protect' them. The host mostly wanted to know if any of
his six inmate-guests had ever had sex with another inmate. The
guy looked pretty faggoty himself, truth to tell.*

*The only other topic the guy with the TV grin and the TV mousse
expressed any interest in was 'the hole.' What happened to a fella
when they put him in 'the hole.' The isolation. The fear.*

*So it went, the show that day, taped in interminable four- and
five-minute segments so dozens of commercials could be dropped
in later.*

*Only near the end did the host say anything interesting. He
raised the subject of how a number of beautiful women had
recently 'married' men in prison, even men on Death Row, despite
the fact that the women knew they'd never be able to consummate
their marriages.*

*The host then clicked through snapshots of these women with
their inmate-husbands. Some of them really were gorgeous. A few
of them even proved to be wealthy. Weren't they throwing their
lives away, wasting their prime years on men who could not
reciprocate real love?*

*'I mean,' said the host, 'look at what just happened in Los
Angeles. You have this woman on the jury who convicted this guy*

118

*of rape and murder . . . then she starts writing to the guy in prison . . . and ends up marrying him while he's still behind bars.'*
Then he looked at his guests and said, 'What is it you guys have got in the sex-appeal department, anyway?'

The inmates snickered and smirked and all the guys in the audience started cracking up.

'We'll look at this topic more closely tomorrow,' the host said. 'But for now we're out of time.'

They taped three shows in one day, a ball-busting schedule.

He was exhausted and irritable by the time the taping was done. The photos of the beautiful women had undone him. He lay on his dark bunk in his dark cell and clung to his cock like a drowning man at sea. He wanted one of those beautiful beautiful women for his very own. He would show them a kind of sex they'd never known before, a kind of sex that would rattle and alter their very existence, and then he would show them other things, so many other things too.

For the first time in all his prison years, he wept that night.

'Hey, man, you all right?' his cellmate said deep into midnight, the cell block all coughs and cries and furtive grunts of sex, the nightly cacophony of prison life.

'Yeah.'

'Seein' those chicks make you lonely?'

'Yeah.'

'Me too,' his cellmate sighed.

'I wonder what those women get out of it.'

'The chicks who marry guys in stir?' his cellmate said.

'Yeah.'

'You heard what the faggy host said,' his cellmate commented. ' "A pathological need to nurture." I ain't even sure what that means.'

'Which one did you like best?'

'The red-head in the green sweater. God.'

'She was somethin', all right.'

'How about you?'

'Dark-haired one, I guess. Just somethin' about her.'

'Great legs.'

'Yeah. But not just that. Something—' And then he remembered. She reminded him of a high-school girl he'd followed home from

119

*an ice-cream store one night. She made the mistake of walking by these woods. He just couldn't help himself. Raped and then killed her with his hands and then raped her one more time.*

*His cellmate yawned. 'I'm wasted, man. Gotta get some sleep.'*

*Two minutes later, his cellmate was snoring.*

*But not him. Oh no, not him.*

*He stayed awake all night, dreaming, dreaming.*

# 8

It's crazy what you can get sentimental about sometimes. For me, on this particular day, it was field glasses. I hadn't used this pair of Swarovskis since leaving the FBI.

I sat six car lengths down from the McNally house. Through the field glasses, I watched a man pacing back and forth in the side window, approximately where their dining room was, as I recalled. He was big and looked like he might have been tough once, before the beer caught up with him.

I assumed this was McNally. I also assumed, because of his frantic movements, that the McNallys had not gotten their daughter back. I tried not to think of what that finger in the box had looked like.

He slapped her.

She'd suddenly appeared inside the window frame with him, shouting at him, face raw with tears and fear and rage, and then he'd slapped her the way one man slaps another, enough to move her back at least a foot. Then he slapped her again, backhanded this time, and she disappeared from the window frame.

In the small town where I grew up there'd been a young married couple famous for their battles. In the early years, he'd given her a few cut lips and a black eye or two. A little later, he started giving her broken arms and legs, once a broken nose. You know the rest, how one night, the sixth year of their marriage it was, he slammed her head many times into an old-fashioned radiator and killed her before the ambulance arrived. She was twenty-four years old when she died. She was also my cousin. I still had the occasional dream of looking the sonofabitch up when he got out, and slamming his head into a radiator thirty or forty times. See how he liked it.

121

He came fast out of his house, McNally did, going around the far side to his garage. A minute later, he backed out of the driveway in a new gray Dodge. If he noticed me parked there at the curb, he gave no hint.

He headed west. I waited a minute and a half, then I headed west, too.

Following people in a small town is difficult. Following them in the country is nearly impossible.

Fortunately, after only three or four miles, I sensed where he was going. He was headed in the right direction for it, anyway, and I had this feeling – I'll spare you the lecture on 'hunches' that law enforcement officials always like to give civilians – I had this feeling that he knew something about Nora's murder last night.

I dropped back, giving him a two-mile advantage.

I drove slowly past farms, remembering what it was like to attach milker units to cows' teats at a frosty 5.30 a.m.; and what it was like on a sweet warm Indian summer afternoon to rake the corn you'd just chopped up onto a conveyer belt leading to the silo; and what it was like to lie on the sunny side of a summer hill and have five tiny kittens and two tiny rabbits crawling all over you and making you giddy with the pleasure of it. We'd been going to have kids someday and live on a working farm, Kathy and I, but of course it had never happened, not in reality anyway, though sometimes I could fancy it so vividly I'd swear it had actually taken place.

I pulled up on top of the hill overlooking the deserted farm where the blue Caddy had sat last night. The river, sparkling blue, ran behind the farm.

In sunlight, the once-white farmhouse was scabrous, and the ancient red barn almost comical in the way it leaned, and over all was a Poe-like pall, an unnatural silence where human life had been taken with obscene enjoyment. No animals, no flowers prospered here.

I left the car on the shoulder, grabbed my trusty binoculars, and walked down the dusty gravel for a better angle.

McNally had pulled his car down into the barn so it couldn't be seen from the road. He had yet to emerge from the cool shadows inside.

Far down the road ahead of me, I saw a car hidden inside a

great rolling wraith of gravel dust traveling fast toward the farm. Of course, it might well go right on past the farm and then right on past me. But, as I'd expected, it started slowing down when it got within a quarter-mile of the farm, slowing down and using its blinker to signal a left turn.

This car was a blue Toyota four-door, the family model.

The driver did the same thing McNally had, pulled straight into the barn, failed to reappear. I hadn't had any look at all at his face. I was damned curious.

I went back and sat behind the wheel of my car and turned on the radio to a news station.

No sense in making myself any more obvious than necessary. Sitting in your car was obvious enough. Standing out on the road with binoculars was pointing a bright red arrow at yourself.

They went fifteen more minutes and still there was no sign of them. They could be doing all sorts of things in that barn but I guessed it would have something to do with McNally's daughter. He might be a drunk and a wife-beater but even scum care about their children in their own scummy way.

In the interim, a big gravel truck roared by, rocking my ancient Jeep; a long vented truck filled with squealing pigs rumbled past; then a motorcycle with a young helmetless kid raced by; and finally two big bays ridden by two young girls clopped onward, leaving road apples of a curious iridescent green.

I mention all this so you'll know why I was numbed into indifference when I heard the next car come up behind me. Figured it was just another local pilgrim hastening on to farm or co-op or babbling brook.

Only when I heard the door *chunk* shut behind me did I realize that the car had stopped and pulled over to the side of the road.

Only when I heard the gravel crunch and pop did I realize that somebody was walking through it directly toward me.

By the time I got the window rolled down, she was there. She put her nice arms on my door and leaned in and spoke to me. She wore a sweet innocent perfume.

'You doing a little bird-watching?' she said.

'I didn't think you were speaking to me.'

'I shouldn't be, actually. I should be arresting you.'

'For what?'

'For what? C'mon, whatever-your-name-is, for withholding evidence.'

'What evidence?'

She sighed. She looked sexy in her blue uniform and dark dark shades. 'So are you going to tell me?'

'Tell you what?'

'What you're doing at the scene of the crime?'

'This isn't the scene of the crime.'

'It's very close.'

I was tempted to just tell her. For one thing, I liked her. For another, she would eventually find out anyway. But I had given the McNally woman my word that I'd keep her secret a secret. Given the stakes, her daughter being kidnapped and all, it was a promise I certainly meant to keep.

'How about if I buy you dinner tonight?'

'Are you trying to bribe an officer of the law?'

'You bet I am.'

'I don't know why I like you.'

'I'm just glad you do.'

'Maybe I'll seduce you tonight and get the information that way.'

'I think you're serious.'

She shrugged. 'Maybe I am. Or maybe I want to do both – get to know you and find out everything you know.'

'You wouldn't hear me object.'

She sighed again. 'Actually, I hate coy stuff like that. I shouldn't have said it.'

I smiled. 'I thought it was kind of sweet.'

'I grew up in a very strict household,' she said, 'so I guess I've still got some hangups about sex.'

'Most of us do.'

'You?'

'A little, I suppose. But I don't let it get in my way.' I looked at her a long moment. 'I'd tell you what I know but somebody may die if I do that. So right now I have to keep silent. I don't expect you to understand what the hell I'm talking about but I am telling you the truth.'

She took her own long look at me. 'You know what? I believe you. But I'm still kind of pissed.'

'I know. And I don't blame you.'

She looked down the hill at the ancient shabby outbuildings and the ancient shabby house, and shook her head. 'It's always different in the daylight, crime scenes, I mean. You always wonder how people can be such animals. But they seem to be different at night; they change, somehow.' She looked back at me. 'You could help me, you know.'

I was tempted again but said nothing.

'What kind of meat do you like?' she asked suddenly.

'How about if I bring a cheese pizza over?'

'Are you serious?'

'Sure. Why should you have to cook? You work a full-time job.'

'You wouldn't mind a cheese pizza?'

'Huh-uh.'

'I could make us some kind of dessert.'

'You don't have to make us anything. I'll bring a pizza and a six-pack of a good imported beer and we'll just enjoy ourselves.'

She smiled. 'Now if you'd just tell me why you're sitting out here.'

'Maybe tonight.'

'Now you're the one who's being coy.'

'Yeah, I guess I am.'

She was still leaning in and looking at me and didn't see them, McNally first, his friend second, backing out of the barn, reversing down the driveway and then heading off quickly in the opposite direction, lost in a gravel dust storm of their making.

'Maybe I'll follow you back to town.'

'I'm not headed that way,' she said. 'I'm going back to the farm.'

'Why?'

'See if we missed something last night.'

'You're thorough.'

She smiled. 'No, egotistical. I want to make sure that I do a very good job so that all the cynics in this town will know that a woman can be a very good police officer.'

'Is it all right to tell you that I like you?'

'Only if that thought is accompanied by your real name.' She stood up, stretched and grinned. 'I'll see you about eight tonight, then. With your cheese pizza.'

125

She gave me a little salute, walked back to her patrol car, got inside and drove down the hill, giving me a blast on her horn and a wave as she reached the farm driveway.

But by this time, I was preoccupied with wondering who McNally's friend was and what they had been doing in the barn together. I turned the car around and drove back two hills where, with my field glasses, I could watch Jane walk around the farm. She stayed twenty minutes.

When she was done, she left, and then I drove over for my own look.

I spent the next fifteen minutes peeking through shattered windows into empty farmhouse rooms littered with gray and white pigeon droppings, and with empty Bud cans and Pepsi cans, and old red Trojan wrappers that looked like lurid autumn leaves.

I had just stepped inside the barn when I heard the tires of a heavy automobile crunch through gravel.

I stood in the barn watching as Jane walked up to me.

'I thought you were going back to town,' she said.

I smiled. 'Thought you were, too.'

'Now'd be a good time to tell me who you really are.' If she was kidding, she wasn't kidding much.

I looked back into the barn. I wanted to scout around but not when Jane was here.

I checked my watch. 'Well, guess I'd better head for home.'

'Not going to finish checking the barn out?'

'And give you all my trade secrets?' I tried to laugh.

She walked me back to my car. She was going to make sure that this time, I left.

'Maybe I'll see you later,' she said.

Just then she looked tired and melancholy and I wanted to give her a hug but I knew better. You didn't hug women when they were wearing badges and holster rigs.

'I hope so,' I said, and drove off. This time I really did go back to town.

# 9

By the time I got back to my motel, I was ready for some lunch, after which I planned to go visit Mrs McNally.

A woman in a pink polyester uniform was sweeping the walk in front of my room, the sparkling dust motes getting to my sinuses immediately. When she saw me, she said, 'Your friend's in there waiting for you.'

'My friend?'

She shrugged. 'That's what he says. Your friend.'

She went back to her sweeping.

The scratched-up metal door and the rusted window screen and the dusty curtain behind it took on a sinister aspect now. My heart started hammering. This was like the old days in Cairo and Barcelona and Cannes. I loved it and hated it at the same time.

I went over, grabbed the doorknob and pushed the door inward hard enough to bang it against the inside wall.

The room was in shadow. He sat in the armchair with the dark blue slipcovers meant to hide cigarette burns and wine stains. A narrow beam of sunlight exposed him.

He looked like the world's youngest successful banker, with his snow-white hair and quick gritty blue eyes and a dark blue suit that must have cost a few thousand dollars. The face was the only thing that didn't go with the clothes. He had to be sixty but didn't look much older than forty-five or so.

'You're Hokanson?'

I nodded. 'And you're Tolliver.'

'Yes.'

He got up and walked over and we shook hands. He shook mine firmly but without any theatrics. 'Could you use a sandwich and a cup of coffee, Mr Hokanson?'

127

'I sure could.'

In the sunlight, what with his crow's feet and the sorrow lines at either side of his mouth, he looked a little older but not much, still giving the impression that he was an imposter of some kind, kid face appended to adult body.

We'd been here twenty minutes now and thus far he had told me the following, which I'd dutifully written down in my little black book:

1.  He had no daughter.
2.  He had had a son, but he'd died at age 25.
3.  Ten years ago a woman who subsequently pretended to be his wife, broke into his home and stole several credit cards; she ran up bills of more than $50,000 before the cards could be canceled.
4.  He had plans to possibly enter the Republican primary next spring and was afraid that 'Nora Conners' had been hired to discredit him in some way. Politics had become a very rough game. Thus far he had heard whispers that a) his main corporation was facing bankruptcy b) that he frequented houses where girls as young as twelve could be had and c) that he had once bought his way out of a drunken hit-and-run accident.
5.  He wanted to retain me to find out who she was and why she'd claimed to be his daughter. And what had led to her murder.

The place was small and made even smaller by the lunch-time crowd that had at least a dozen people standing and waiting for booths. It was one of those blissful oases of ignorance that had not yet heard that smoking causes lung cancer. Everybody, it seemed, had a cigarette going, even as he or she chewed his or her food. There were a couple of three-and-four-year-olds in the booth across from us. I was waiting for them to light up, too.

'Wouldn't it be quicker and cheaper just to take this matter to the police?'

He shook his white head. 'No, not as fast. And not as cheap, either. The press will be able to learn whatever the police learn but if you could find out who she really was and what she was up to – well, I could practice a little political damage control before it all becomes public.'

'Won't you look like a victim to people? Why would they blame you for a woman who pretended she was your daughter?'

He smiled. He was a trim man, neatly shaved, manicured, crisply dressed, all of which left just the faintest hint of priggishness. Maybe it was his thin mouth, and its constant implication of displeasure.

Before he could answer, our waitress came around again, filling our coffee, taking away the plates from the chips and tuna sandwich I'd had, and the Egg Beaters and toast he'd had.

'People don't remember things clearly,' he said. 'By the time this story filters through the public consciousness, it'll be generally believed that I'd had an affair with this Nora, and maybe even that I'd been a suspect in her death.' He paused and raised his head a little. His neck was the only thing about him that showed his real age. 'This morning I took the liberty of depositing ten thousand dollars in your bank account.'

This was my week for strange people wanting to give me a great deal of money. First Nora, now him.

'I'm not sure I buy your story.'

'Oh?' he said, his blue eyes hard.

'No. I think you're interested in Nora and Vic for some other reason.'

'What other reason?'

'I'm not sure yet.'

He laughed. 'Maybe you should investigate me first and then if you're satisfied with what you find, start on Nora and Vic.'

'You say you had a son?'

'Yes. He died a long time ago, just as I told you.'

'What about your wife?'

'She's dead, too. Nearly ten years ago.'

'Do you have a lady friend now?'

'No one special. I'm not sure I see the relevance of that.'

'Maybe Nora was angling for some kind of blackmail set-up. Sometimes that works best with somebody close to the person being blackmailed. A girlfriend who decides to cash in on her rich boyfriend tells an accomplice the boyfriend's darkest secret. And the blackmailer takes it from there, after agreeing to split fifty fifty with the girlfriend.'

'They sound like nice people, your girlfriend and blackmailer.'

'So nobody's blackmailing you?'

'Not that I know of.'

'And you don't have anything they can blackmail you for?'

He smiled. 'Do you know the Balzac quote that behind every great fortune is a scandal?'

I nodded.

'Well, I didn't make our fortune, my father did. The trucking business made him a millionaire many, many times over. All I did was inherit the fortune. My father had to cheat and swindle a lot of people to make his money. All I had to do was be the dutiful son – get at least a B average at Yale, and not do anything publicly excessive that would embarrass him – and I became a very wealthy man on the day he died twelve years ago. If there are any family enemies, they belong to my father and he took them with him to his grave.'

'And you want to run for office?'

'As I said, I'm considering it. I think I'm what the state and the country need.'

'What's that?'

'A conservative without an ideology. It's frustrating being a conservative these days; you always have to sit next to some lunatic who wants Creationism taught in our schools or something like that.'

'Think you have a chance?'

'I have the money, anyway. That's a big part of the battle. I won't have to depend on PACs.'

I looked at his ridiculously young face and his brilliant white hair and the quirky but stone-hard blue eyes. I didn't trust him, didn't believe anything he was telling me, but I didn't know why. He just seemed dishonest.

'You're going back to Des Moines?'

'Not right away. Thought I might stay here a few days and see what you find out.'

'Assuming I take the job.'

'Assuming you take the job,' he said. 'Of course.'

'I guess I'll do it.'

'I'm very pleased.'

'But when I do find out anything concrete, I turn it over to the local police chief.'

'After you tell me – that's all I ask. Tell me first. I'll contact my press aide and she can start to prepare our response.'

I stood up, dropped a dollar on the table for a tip, picked up the ticket.

He took it from my hand, then picked up the dollar and handed it back to me. 'I invited you, Mr Hokanson. I'm the one who should pay.'

Out on the street, in the fresh air and sunshine, he said, 'A friend of mine has a summer cottage here. You can reach me there.' He gave me the address. 'When your father was the biggest trucker in the state, you have friends everywhere.'

He put forth his firm but civil hand and we shook again.

I went east, he went west.

# 10

*'You screwed your own daughter. You hear that, guys? He screwed his own daughter.'*

*'That's enough, Spence,' the counselor says. 'This isn't funny.'*

*'He put the pork to his own frigging daughter.'*

*This is group therapy. Meets twice a week in a big echoing room near the prison library. Pistol-hot in summer, blue-balls cold in winter.*

*Standard number is the counselor and six cons, one of whom is this rather prim fellow named Dodsworth.*

*Past couple of weeks the cons have been kind of ganging up on Dodsworth. Few sessions back he told – they were playing this nasty game called True Life, where you tell the group the worst thing you ever did – he told the group that one night when he was really bombed, his fourteen-year-old daughter gave him this big sloppy kiss and he got this killer erection and then walked around for the next six weeks impotent because he was so ashamed of what he'd felt for his daughter.*

*You could tell when he raised his eyes and started looking around at everybody that he'd fucked up real bad.*

*Should never have admitted something like that.*

*Because everybody knows it's the truth.*

*See, the way to play the game is, you make stuff up. Like, 'Well, I guess the worst thing I ever did was after I robbed this guy, you know. I found this dynamite out in the back and I blew up his entire house. Boards'n bricks'n shit flyin' everywhere. It was great, man.'*

*And everybody laughs.*

*Because it's bullshit and you know they know it's bullshit and that's half the fun.*

132

*Other thing is, tell only stories that reflect well on you.*

*For instance, to a con, blowing up somebody's house can be a pretty cool thing.*

*That reflects well on you.*

*But plugging your own daughter?'*

*Or even having the thought?*

*Fucker's worse than a child molester.*

*'I don't want to be in here no more,' Dodsworth says to the counselor. 'Spence knows damn good and well I never fucked Bonnie. I wouldn't do nothin' like that.'*

*'That ain't what you said couple weeks ago,' Spence says. And winks. And everybody laughs again. 'Maybe since Bonnie ain't around you'd like to put the pork to one of us. Lesee now – who'd ole Dodsworth like to put the pork to—'*

*Another wink.*

*'Why, Mr Haines!'*

*Haines is the counselor.*

*'I bet that's who Dodsworth has the hots for. Mr Haines!'*

*Lots of laughter now. Mr Haines and Dodsworth both blushing.*

*Spence is a mean but very clever guy. You might not think so, him being such a grungy fat-ass with enough faded tattoos to start an art gallery. But he's got great cunning, Spence does, no brains, no power – but cunning. And that's what it takes to be important in here.*

*He tunes out.*

*Sits there seeing it all but not seeing anything, hearing it all but not hearing.*

*And has the thought for the second time: I need to escape. I've been here too long.*

*Couple days later, on the yard, he gets his protector Servic alone and says, 'You ever think about just walking out of here some time?'*

*'You gettin' a little crazy.'*

*'Yeah, I guess so, anyway.'*

*'It comes and goes, kid. You just gotta ride it, is all.'*

*'So you never thought about it?'*

*'Sure I thought about it. Who the fuck ain't thought about it. But see those guys?'*

133

*He points to the towers located at either end of the yard. The guards in them are armed with rifles and legend has it that they're damned good shots.*

*'You figure out a way to get past them guards, kid, you let me know.'*

*'Maybe there's another way.'*

*'Maybe. But if there is, I ain't never heard of it.' He pauses, looks at him. 'Somethin' happen?'*

*'Just all the bullshit. I got this group therapy session every week with Spence and—'*

*'Spence. Fuck Spence. Don't let him get you down, kid. He's just pissed 'cause his old lady's sleepin' with some coon back in Milwaukee.'*

*'No shit?'*

*'No shit.'*

*'No wonder, then.'*

*'Bein' mean's the only thing he's got left.'*

*Servic, who's been a lot nicer of late, looks up at the guard towers again. 'You ever figure out how to get past them towers, kid, you let me know.'*

*He laughs. 'I will. I promise.'*

*They walk back to the rest of the cons.*

# 11

There was a muffled cry and a scrape of furniture legs across a hardwood floor following my knock. Then there was just silence.

I stood on the McNallys' front porch watching a cardinal perched on a bird-feeder in a nearby oak tree. He bobbed and pecked relentlessly, red and vivid and sleek in this afternoon of graceful white butterflies and cute quick squirrels bouncing across the side lawn. It was springtime and I wanted to be up on the Iowa River, standing in my waders and casting my line.

I knocked again.

Half a minute later, Eve McNally came to the door. Her forehead and left cheek showed red from where something had slammed hard against her, a fist most likely. She wore a Grateful Dead T-shirt and a pair of red shorts. Her legs were nicely shaped but she was already having problems with varicose veins.

'I didn't invite you here,' she said. 'Go away.'

'I want to talk to your husband.'

'He's not here.'

'He's inside, Eve, and I know it.'

'He don't want to talk to you.'

'You haven't got your daughter back yet, have you?'

She glanced over her shoulder. If I hadn't known for sure that her husband was home, I knew now.

He appeared in the doorway, a big beefy man with hair so black it looked dyed, a blue panther tattoo running down the meaty biceps of his right arm. He wore a white sleeveless T-shirt and a pair of dungarees that hung precariously on the slope of his considerable belly. The panther looked angry, on the prowl. Presumably that's how his master looked most of the time, too.

'What the fuck you want?'

'I want to help you get your daughter back.'

'You get your ass off my property,' he said. I thought of angry Sam throwing me off his property a little earlier today. This wasn't my day for making friends.

'Tell him I'm trying to help you,' I said to Eve.

'He don't listen to me.'

'Out,' he said. And suddenly he was out the door and pushing me backwards off his porch.

'Don't hurt him,' Eve pleaded. 'He's tryin' to help us.'

I grabbed the railing to keep from falling down the four steps. I had just managed to get a grip on it when he hit me with a hard roundhouse right.

I suppose tough guys don't mind much getting hit but personally I've never cared for it a whole lot. For one thing, it almost invariably hurts. For another, it oftentimes inhibits your vision. And for a final thing, it makes you feel like a helpless child.

Unless, of course, you hit back.

He was still pissed, meaning he wanted to hit me some more despite his wife's screams.

I stumbled down the final three stairs, losing my grip on the railing. But by then I knew just what I wanted to do.

And I did it.

When he was on the bottom step, I kicked him directly in the crotch. He made a lot of frightening noise but then he did what I'd hoped he would do – sort of crumpled into himself, holding his crotch as he did so.

I hit him three times in the side of the head, hard. I wanted to hit him a fourth time but my knuckles were starting to hurt.

I grabbed him by his nice black hair and half-dragged him back up the stairs and inside. He took a swing at me once but missed. I returned the favor by slamming home an especially vicious kidney shot. I didn't miss.

In the living room, I pushed him on to the couch and stood over him. I had my Ruger out and was pointing it in his face.

'Oh God, mister, don't shoot him.'

'I just want to talk to him without him trying to hit me.'

'You fucker, I won't just hit you, I'll kill you.'

'You were out at the Brindle farm this afternoon. Why?'

He looked surprised, fear and curiosity blooming in his beady little gaze. He composed himself before speaking, sitting up straighter on the couch, tugging his T-shirt down over his little middle-aged male titties.

A grandfather clock tocked peacefully, measuring out the centuries in the sudden peaceful silence, and in the kitchen the refrigerator motor thrummed on. It was a nice modest home, this, a home where husband and wife should live happily ever after and children should be raised in safety and love and not get kidnapped, no never get kidnapped at all. Nor should two grown men, both with blood on their mouths, be in the living room sweaty and enraged and wanting to kill each other.

'You dumb bastard, even if you don't believe me or your wife, I am trying to help you find your daughter.'

But he was scared. His eyes kept blinking and he kept licking his lips. He daubed blood from his lower lip with the back of his hand. 'What's my daughter to you?'

'Well, for one thing, believe it or not, I really don't like to see little kids get kidnapped. And for another thing, I think she figures into a case I'm working on. By helping you, I'm probably going to help myself.'

'I don't know who took her.'

'I think you do. And I think you know why. And I think that's why you went to the Brindle farm this afternoon.'

He sat up even straighter, daubed at his split lip some more.

'Tell me about the farm, McNally. Who did you meet there?'

His gaze shifted subtly to the right. I instinctively understood the significance of that – he was watching somebody, namely his wife, do something behind my back – but by then there wasn't much I could do. I guess because she'd sort of taken my part with her husband, I'd figured she wouldn't help him hurt me in anyway. But you never know about husbands and wives. You just never know.

I started to turn to the right and that's when she hit me on the crown of the head.

I had no idea what her weapon of choice happened to be but whatever it was, it was damned effective.

I felt my head start to split open, a dark cold rush up my

nostrils and start to spread through my respiratory system, and then my knees went. And that was it; then I didn't feel anything at all.

# 12

'Let me help you up.'

'I'd appreciate that.'

'Maybe I hit you a little too hard.'

'I think you did.'

'Here. Just sit down here right on the couch. I'll get you a couple of aspirin. I mean, I'll bet your head hurts.'

'I suppose your husband's gone?'

'He's afraid – I've never seen him like this. Somebody's trying to kill him, I think.'

'Who?'

She just shook her head.

'I want you to tell me who was out at the Brindle farm with your husband this afternoon.'

'I don't know.'

She put her hand out as if to touch me, then stopped herself. 'I'll get you those aspirin.'

The dog lapped my face all the time Eve McNally was gone, big slurpy dog kisses and hard killer dog breath. When Eve returned, she handed me a glass of water, dropped two aspirin tablets into my palm and then shooed Sara away.

'I'm sorry, mister,' she said. 'I really don't know who he met at the Brindle farm this afternoon and I really am sorry I hit you so hard.'

And just what the hell was I supposed to say to that?

# 13

I took another break and looked over more of Peary's notes for the second or third time.

'*Killings abruptly stopped,*' he noted in pencil. '*I doubt this was because the killer lost his passion for the hunt. More likely, he found a better way of disposing of bodies.*'

I found a pay phone and called one of my friends at Quantico, asking him to run a search through the FBI computers. I wanted to know if there was a precedence for a case where a killer abruptly changed the way he was disposing of his victims. The computer would search through tens of thousands of cases, checking patterns to see if this abrupt change had been noted before.

I told him that this was real urgent. He told me to call back in a couple of hours.

# 14

Dearest Reece,

When your letter arrived last Tuesday, I canceled a tennis date at the country club I was telling you about. I didn't want anything to interfere with the pleasure of reading your letter. As I told you when I first wrote you, since I saw you on that talk show, I've been able to think of no one else but you. No one else even remotely interests me.

I can't tell you how many different feelings your letter evoked in me – joy at knowing that you want our relationship to continue; sorrow at knowing that, for the next few years anyway, we won't be able to be together physically; and pride that somebody like you would find worth and value in somebody like me. I really am, as I've told you, the classic poor little rich girl . . . raised on a great deal of money but no love at all thanks to my mother dying at so early an age and a father who was too busy with his girlfriends and businesses to give me any real love.

I was afraid that you'd lose interest in me if I told you the truth about my marriage record – three strikes and you're out? Isn't that the baseball rule? Well, I've been married three times and none of them lasted longer than six months. I know this is supposed to be a reflection on me but I hope you interpret this the way I do . . . that I simply hadn't met the right man until you came along.

I've gone on a diet. Even though you can't see me – though I do plan to visit you soon – when I saw you on TV I said to myself, 'There's a man who appreciates a good female body.' You're so handsome, Reece, and yet there's such kindness and tenderness in your eyes. I want everything to

141

be perfect for you. So I'm planning to lose eight pounds in the next two months. So that when we meet—

I have nightmares of you in prison. A few years ago I read a '*Good Housekeeping*' article written by a woman whose husband was behind bars. Until then, I'd had no idea how terrifying a place prison can be. Nor did I have any idea of how many prisoners are killed inside.

You don't belong there, Reece. I know that you've made some mistakes in your life – but who hassn't? As I told you, thanks to the inheritance my father left me, I've already contacted a very high-powered New York criminal attorney and he believes we have a very good chance of getting you a new trial. And, if the state supreme court orders one, thère's at least a fifty/fifty possibility, he says, that the district attorney will decline to try you again, given how much time has passed since your conviction.

Then we can be together, darling. Forever.

Remember how I told you that your letter evoked so many different feelings in me? Well, last night, when I got in bed, I lay there naked for a long time in the darkness, your letter upon my breasts. And I had a sexual experience like none other in my life, Reece. With my three husbands, I had a very difficult time reaching satisfaction but last night—Well, last night, with your letter on my breasts and my TV image of your face in my mind, I had no trouble at all. I was a complete woman at last. Just imagine what it will be like when we're actually together . . .

I'm enclosing a Tibetan prayer I learned when I studied with a very legendary Maharishi in Connécticut a few years ago. I've found that in moments of conflict and crisis, this prayer helps me find my true inner self and become calmed. I hope it helps you as much as it's helped me.

A few days ago, I called the warden's office and asked his rather snotty secretary if I could send you some things. She disallowed about half of what I was going to box up and send to you. I was so angry by the time I hung up, I called Senator Paxton's office and demanded to speak directly to him. My father was a major contributor to the Senator's various campaigns so he not only took my call but also agreed to help me with the warden.

Dusk is falling outside my bedroom window now; the sky gray-blue except for the horizon which is a kind of pearly pink. Even though it's a little chilly, I keep two of the French windows open slightly so I can smell the clean new spring. You'll love this manor house when you come to live in it, darling. I suppose you'll be a little intimidated by it as some of my friends have been, but the staff here always do their best to keep people at ease. After showing you the house, the first place I'll take you is to the stables. My father had two horses that nearly won the Kentucky Derby and one horse that actually won the Preakness in 1971. I'm sure you'll love the horses as much as I do. I'm sure you will.

Well, that's all for now, darling. You're in my mind and soul every waking moment.

In a few minutes, I'll be turning off the light and slipping into bed again. Your letter will soon be touching my naked breasts.

Eternal love, darling,
Rosamund.

*What he did with the letter, first night he had it, was wait until his pal in the other bunk was snoring, and then he took the letter and wrapped it around his cock and masturbated with it, his jism running into her delicate handwriting, becoming one.*

# 15

After leaving the McNally place, I went to a drugstore where I bought some headache powder and drank a milk shake and looked through a science fiction magazine. Then I went back to my little temporary hutch.

A motel room at mid-afternoon is an especially lonely place. With all their earnest drunken noise, the night people at least lend the place a festive air. But afternoon is wives on the run from rickety marriages, the kids in tow with dirty faces and sad frantic eyes, missing their daddy and yet hating him at the same time for how he treated Mommy; and traveling salesmen wearing too much Old Spice and knowing far too many dirty jokes; and afternoon lovers from insurance agencies and advertising firms and department stores, giving each other quick hot sex of the sort their marriage partners gave up on years ago.

I saw samples of all these types passing by my window as I sat in the armchair, talking on the telephone, yellow pad on my knees, telling a friend of mine all about Mr Tolliver.

'You want to know everything about him?' Sheila said.

'Everything.'

'It'll take me a little while.'

'I know.'

'He's prominent enough that I think you could probably pick a lot of it up at the library. I really hate to charge you these rates but it's how I make my living.'

Sheila Kelly costs half as much as other computer search services I've used, yet she apologizes constantly for her prices.

'You'll find out things I'll never find in the library.'

Sheila is one of that new breed of human beings who spend half their life using a computer as an extension of their mind.

144

Mike Peary had used her on several investigations and told me the information she'd turned up had helped him resolve the cases in a day or so. I'd had similar luck. Sheila performs hacking services that are not, strictly speaking, legal. But they sure are useful.

'Why don't you give me your number?'

I gave her my number.

'Is that a motel?'

'Right.'

'Is it a nice place?'

'Well, the toilet flushes anyway.'

She laughed. 'My husband and I stayed in a place like that in South Dakota once. It was like motel Hell. We could only get one station on the TV and that was a local show that had pro wrestlers performing between Country and Western singing acts.'

'Well, this isn't quite so bad.'

'You probably won't hear from me till tomorrow.'

'Whenever.'

Ten minutes later, after stripping down to my boxer shorts, I laid down on the bed and opened up my Robert Louis Stevenson.

I read until I got drowsy and then I napped for a while.

When I woke up, the sunlight was waning behind the curtains. A car door opened and chunked shut. Hearty laughter, man and woman. The night people were arriving.

I went into the bathroom and washed my face and combed my hair and when I came back out I picked out a shirt and trousers for my visit to Jane Avery's tonight.

Then I looked down and realized that my bare feet had stepped in something that I was tracking across the rug.

I turned on the lamp and looked down at the stains I'd made. I raised my foot and turned it so I could see my sole, which I daubed at. Something sticky.

My eyes moved back up the trail I'd left. It stretched from where I stood to the closet door.

I went over to the closet and looked down. So much for the sharp eye of the detective. I'd walked past the small puddle beneath the door without noticing it until I'd accidentally stepped in it. No doubt about it. The Detective League of America, or

145

whatever organization it was that detectives belonged to, was going to kick me out.

The closet door was louvered and dusty. I opened it carefully, on dry hinges that creaked, and looked inside at my clothing hanging from the rod that had been positioned at eye level. A string attached to a light socket above hung in front of my face. I gave it a tug. The naked bulb was burned out.

From here, below the line of shirts and trousers, I could see only a pair of legs from the knees on down. The shoes were tasseled and expensive cordovan loafers. The trousers appeared to be dark blue and hand-tailored. But I wasn't going to learn much this way. I pushed all my attire to the right side of the small dusty closet for a better look.

Even though I'd only seen him once, and then from a distance, I recognized the handsome and imperious face of Sam Lodge. He was still handsome, still the sneering art instructor and antique shop owner, but his charm was gone. The large butcher knife that had been shoved deep into his chest, almost to the hilt, lent him a violence that no amount of charm could have disguised anyway. The killer had shoved him up against the back of the closet so that his neck appeared broken, head resting at an awkward angle on his left shoulder. His blue eyes stared without interest at some point in the room behind me.

I closed the door and stood for a long moment trying to figure out what he'd been doing in my room in the first place. We hadn't exactly been the best of friends. But even so, the enormity of death, of extinction, took me down for a few moments. After my wife died, I'd felt the same way, knowing that never again would she ever exist, not on this world nor on the billions of worlds filling the universe, never exist again no matter how remarkable were the discoveries of future science, never touch others with that special loveliness and grace and quiet self-effacing wisdom that had been so precious to me. And somebody was going to be feeling these same things about Sam Lodge, probably his wife and certainly his parents, when they learned that he was now broken and forgotten in a closet in a shabby little motel in the middle of a nowhere planet in a nowhere backwash of the dark and rolling cosmos.

I did the only thing I could. I went to the phone and called Chief of Police Jane Avery.

# CONDITION OF VICTIM WHEN FOUND

136. There Is Reason to Believe the Offender Moved the Body from the Area of the Death Site to the Area of the Body Recovery Site:
    1 ☐ Yes        2 ☒ No            3 ☐ Unable to Determine

137. Evidence Suggests the Offender Disposed of the Body in the Following Manner:
    1 ☐ Openly Displayed or Otherwise      3 ☒ With an Apparent Lack of
        Placed to Insure Discovery                Concern as to Whether or Not the
    2 ☐ Concealed, Hidden, or Otherwise        Body Was Discovered
        Placed in Order to Prevent Discovery    99 ☐ Unable to Determine

138. It Appears the Body of the Victim Was *Intentionally* Placed in an Unnatural or Unusual Position *after Death* Had Occurred (e.g., staged or posed):
    1 ☐ Yes        2 ☒ No            3 ☐ Unable to Determine

139. Body Was Discovered...
    1 ☐ Buried                           5 ☐ In a Container (e.g. dumpster, box
    2 ☐ Covered                           refrigerator)
    3 ☐ In a Body of Water (stream, lake, river,    6 ☐ In a Vehicle
        etc.)                               7 ☐ Scattered (body parts)
    4 ☒ In a Building                    8 ☐ None of the Above

140. If the Body Was Discovered in Water, Was It Weighted?
    1 ☐ Yes — — With What? _____    2 ☐ No

141. Was the Victim Bound?
    1 ☐ Yes                            2 ☒ No (go to Item 146)

142. Article(s) Used to Bind or Restrain the Victim or the Body:
    1 ☐ An Article of Clothing          4 ☐ Chain
    2 ☐ Tape                          5 ☐ Handcuffs or Thumbcuffs
    3 ☐ Cordage (e.g., rope, string, twine, wire,    88 ☐ Other (specify): _____
        leather thong, etc.)                    _____

143. The Evidence Suggests That the Restraining Device(s) Was (check one only):
    1 ☐ Brought to the Scene by the Offender    3 ☐ Both 1 and 2 Above
    2 ☐ An Article Found at the Scene by      99 ☐ Unknown
        the Offender

144. Parts of Body Bound (check as many as apply):
    1 ☐ Hands or Arms                5 ☐ Hands and Ankles Bound Together
    2 ☐ Feet, Ankle(s), or Legs          88 ☐ Other (specify): _____
    3 ☐ Neck                         _____
    4 ☐ Arms Bound to Torso

145. The Bindings on the Victim Were Excessive (much more than necessary to control victim's movements):
    1 ☐ Yes        2 ☐ No            3 ☐ Unable to Determine

146. The Body Was Tied to Another Object:
    1 ☐ Yes                            2 ☒ No

147. Was a Gag Placed in or on the Victim's Mouth?
    1 ☐ Yes (describe): _____     2 ☒ No
        _____                    99 ☐ Unknown

148. Was a Blindfold Placed on or over the Victim's Eyes?
    1 ☐ Yes (describe): _____     2 ☒ No
        _____                    99 ☐ Unknown

149. Was the Victim's Entire Face Covered?
    1 ☐ Yes — — With What? _____    2 ☒ No
                                          99 ☐ Unknown

# Four

# 1

*Six days ago, he had to change cells again. Five times in a year and a half.*

*Another one of the warden's grand plans. Probably got the idea from one of his effing sociology tests.*

*He did what he always did, put his toothbrush and toothpaste and shampoo and hairbrush and deodorant and shaving cream and razor into his gym bag and shambled in line behind a guard who led him to a new cell block.*

*Guy in the cell is this big dumb shaggy hick with warts or something all over his face.*

*Guard locks him in.*

*First thing he does, he starts sniffing the air.*

*What in hell is that* smell? *So dirty, so overwhelming, he feels like he's choking.*

*'Name's Lumir.'*

*He nods to Lumir.*

*'Not as loud over here in this cell block. Not as many jigs.'*

*But he's still sniffing, trying to figure it out.*

*'You don't mind, I like the top bunk.'*

*'You cut your stools with water, Lumir?'*

*'Huh?'*

*'After you go to the bathroom, do you throw a glass of water into the toilet?'*

*'Huh-uh.'*

*'You should.'*

*'How come?'*

*'Kinda smells in here, Lumir.'*

*'I don't smell nothin'.'*

*'Yeah, well, I do.'*

151

*That was six days ago and by now he knows what the trouble is. Or, troubles (plural) are:*

1) *Lumir doesn't cut his stools with water, something some of the more thoughtful cons learn to do for each other.*

2) *Lumir does not partake of the morning shower any more than two mornings a week.*

3) *Lumir does not use deodorant because he claims it 'makes me break out, like a rash on a baby's butt donchaknow, and then I'm just ascratchin' and ascratchin' my armpits.'*

4) *Lumir is constantly picking his nose and eating the boogers.*

5) *Lumir is constantly snuffing up phlegm and spitting it haphazardly at the toilet.*

6) *Lumir changes socks no oftener than once a week.*

7) *Lumir can scratch his balls in a really noisy way; and Lumir scratches his balls eighteen hours a day. Some day Lumir will no doubt become the first man ever able to scratch his balls while he's asleep.*

*Now, all these things are the stuff of great high hilarity when you're sitting in a bar ten years later recounting them.*

*But he has to spend day-in, day-out with Lumir and there's nothing funny about that at all.*

*Nights . . . he just lies there. He never gets used to the smells . . . the really foul stomach-turning odors of Lumir's stools . . . or the rancid stink of his socks . . . or the sweet-sour stench of his unbathed body.*

*For the third time, he finds himself thinking seriously about escaping.*

# 2

An hour later, I stood in the motel parking lot, leaning against my car, listening to Jane become more and more irritated with my dishonesty. Night was coming now, and with it the immortal teenagers in their immortal hot cars cruising up and down the main street, the joy of their radios obscene against the grim business in my room.

'You didn't know him, right, Jim?'

'Right.'

'But somebody killed him in your room.'

'Guess so.'

'Just by coincidence.'

'That's the only thing I can figure out,' I said.

'You think you'll tell me what's going on before anybody else gets killed?'

'I would if I could.'

'What's that mean, "if you could." '

I was thinking of Melissa McNally. Kidnapped.

'If I could. Just what I said.'

Jane sighed. In the gathering dusk, the downtown lights had come on, a little outpost of civilization in a land where, only 300 years ago, Indians had roamed, killed rattlesnakes and worn them around their necks for good luck. Every once in a while you could feel those old winds blowing down the timelines, carrying the exuberance of the Mesquakie when this land belonged to them, and the peace of the vast prairie when it was nothing but wild corn and vivid flowers and freely ranging animals.

'You're wandering off,' Jane said.

'I'm thinking.'

She shook her head, leaned close. Some of the fifty or so

153

citizens filling the driveway had heard our sparring and moved closer for a more definitive version. We walked to the other side of the boxy white ambulance where we could argue without being heard.

'Why the hell don't you just tell me the truth?'

'Jane, listen, as soon as I can—'

The attendants were just now bringing the body out in a black bag on a stretcher. Inside, two of Jane's officers, who regularly went to Des Moines for crime scene training, were just now going through the room for fingerprints. Jane was irritated that the medical examiner, a man shared by several small communities, had yet to put in an appearance.

Jane was about to start talking again when one of her auxiliary deputies, the Burt Reynolds macho man, swaggered up and whispered something in her ear.

'Where?' she said.

'Down the block. Right at the end.'

'You're sure?'

'Heck, Jane, I used to help the guy move stuff. I should ought to know his car when I see it.'

Car. I'd been wondering about that, too. How had Lodge gotten here? While waiting for Jane to show up, I'd gone up and down the parking lot checking registrations. I hadn't found a car with Lodge's name on it.

I turned back for a look at the crowd. By now, what with all the lights provided by Cedar Rapids TV stations, the parking lot was starting to resemble a movie set, the crowd looking appropriately curious, the cops looking appropriately harried, the motel itself looking appropriately seedy. This would inevitably be a drama about a carousing husband who had met his fate in the very same motel room where he'd bopped innumerable married ladies and yummy teenage nymphets, most of whom were cheerleaders.

I saw him only because I felt his intense gaze at my back. I turned to the right and there he was, tall enough to tower over everybody in front of him. Despite the cool breezes, he wore only a T-shirt. But McNally didn't need a jacket. He had his rage and his fear to keep him warm.

I was still wondering whom he'd seen this afternoon out at the

154

Brindle farm. And why he'd seen them. And why somebody had kidnapped his daughter.

Just as I turned away, I saw a few more familiar faces. There, several yards from McNally, at the very back of the crowd and standing on a small rise of grass, were the good Reverend Roberts, Kenny Deihl and Mindy Lane. If they were here to save Sam Lodge's soul, they were a mite late.

'There's Doc Winick,' the auxiliary deputy said, referring to the rumpled little medical examiner making his way toward us.

'God,' Jane said, the stress of the moment clearly starting to tell on her mood. 'I sure hope he's sober.'

She started to walk away. I grabbed her elbow. 'Are we still on for tonight?'

She glared at me. 'You don't know how much I dislike you right now.'

'I'll pay for the pizza.'

She leaned in. 'You asshole.' But she was smiling. 'Double cheese.'

'I used to think that was my name until my mom told me different.'

'Very funny.'

'I'll even bring some ice cream.'

She frowned. 'We shouldn't be talking about food.' She nodded to the ambulance that was just starting to pull away. 'Not with Lodge dead like that.'

'I'll go get myself another room for tonight.' I pointed to the CRIME SCENE signs her two detectives were affixing to door and window.

'I meant what I said,' she said.

'You mean about the double cheese or me being an asshole?'

'Both,' she said, and was gone.

155

# 3

I decided to walk two blocks to the pharmacy where the town's only news-stand could be found.

As I reached the end of the motel driveway, I turned left and saw the auxiliary deputy who liked me so much.

He was leaning against a car, a cigarette dangling tough-guy-style from his chubby mouth. He looked pretty comic, so comic in fact that I felt a little sorry for him. This guy was obviously suffering from a terminal lack of self-esteem.

'You never seen a car before?' he said.

'A blue Toyota sedan.'

'Somethin' wrong with that?'

The mercury vapor lights gave his face a chilly aqua gleam.

'Just passing a remark.'

'You know somethin' about this car?'

'Nope.'

'You think there's somethin' weird about this car?'

'Nope.'

'You know who it belonged to?'

If I hadn't, his use of the past tense would have given me a big hint. I glanced across the street, in the front window of a diner. It was one of those strange May winds you get in Iowa sometimes, May but smelling of autumn somehow. The people in the diner looked very contented and very snug.

'Guess I don't.'

'Him.'

'Him?'

He shook his head as if I were the biggest pea-brain who had ever lived. 'Him. The dead guy. You know, Lodge. The guy in your closet.'

156

'Oh.'

'That's all you're gonna say? "Oh?" '

'What else do you want me to say?'

He shrugged. 'You sure don't act very shook up. Most folks would be goin' crazy, findin' a dead guy in their closet.' He looked at me sly, from the corners of his beady eyes. 'Less of course, they happened to have killed the guy themselves.'

I wanted to give him a little grammar lesson, about the parts of speech and how singular has to agree with singular and so on, but I hate people who do stuff like that so I kept quiet.

He was just about to say something else when another auxiliary cop suddenly appeared on the edge of the motel driveway and called, 'Chief wants you. Better get up here.'

'Shit,' he said.

'Don't blame you for hating crime scenes,' I said, figuring I should be friendly, given what I was about to do as soon as he dragged himself away from here.

'Ain't that. It's the smokin'.'

'Smoking?'

'Yeah, she won't let me smoke around her.'

'I see.'

'A man, he'd let you smoke.'

'He would, huh?'

'That's the trouble with havin' a woman Chief of Police. I mean, she's smart enough and all but she sure has a lot of rules.'

He pushed away from the car, dropped his cigarette on the sidewalk, and then crushed it to tatters with the toe of his cordovan Texas boot.

'You be around in case she's got some questions for you?'

'I'll be around.'

'I'll tell her.'

Before he left, he added an accouterment I hadn't seen before, one of those Western-style hats I call a junior Stetson. I believe Matt Dillon wore one like this in the old *Gunsmoke*. Unfortunately for my friend here, the hat dwarfed his small head and only added to the roundness of his cheeks. He looked like the meanest ten-year-old on Maple Street.

He gave me the sort of hard, measuring glance that men about

157

to have a gunfight give each other, and then strolled off, ready to slap leather.

I pulled out the pair of rubber surgical gloves at about the time he reached the motel drive. I carry the gloves for just such opportunities as this one. Plus you can put them on your fingers and make funny animal shapes. If you know how, that is. Not everybody does.

When he was gone from sight, I tried the back door of the Toyota. It was locked. I tried the front door, passenger side. Locked. I tried the front door, driver's side. Locked. I tried the rear door, driver. Unlocked.

I worked quickly, constantly watching front and back windows for sight of any casual strollers. They would certainly remember, later, seeing me going through the dead man's car.

Nothing, nothing, nothing was what I found until I came to the glove compartment, in which rested several envelopes held together with a wide rubber band.

Being the sort of inquisitive guy I am, and fully planning to give back every single thing I took – having years ago taken the Boy Scout pledge, I mean, and having lived my life accordingly ever since – I then, given my suspicious nature, started groping beneath the front seats. People often hide things there, apparently figuring that most crooks are so stupid they'll never think to look there. Your standard crook, of course, having graduated from a certified crook school knows enough to look under the seats right away.

I found nothing.

Soon as I could, I walked around to the rear of the car, glanced up and down, right and left, found the sidewalks momentarily empty, and went to work, picking the lock of the trunk as quickly as I could.

I was in and out in less than a minute, finding absolutely *nada* – unless you count a spare tire and a pair of jump leads.

I closed up the trunk and started walking slowly back to my motel, enjoying the clean clear cold. May in Iowa usually encompasses several seasons, including winter at least three or four of the thirty days. Sweater weather, the locals call it, evoking images of a blazing fireplace, a very hot hot toddy and a beautiful girl whose eyes dance with the reflection of the fire. I hoped my night with the High Sheriff of New Hope would offer at least a few of those pleasures.

So Samuel Lodge was the man who'd met McNally at the Brindle farm this afternoon. Presumably, anyway, since it was definitely his blue Toyota I had seen entering and leaving the barn.

And now Samuel Lodge was the man who'd been murdered in my room and stuffed into my closet.

These two thoughts kept me occupied as I walked back to my room.

I was engrossed enough in them that my mind didn't register the scene in the steak-house window until I was several feet past it. Then I did a sort of double-take, a subtle one, of course, nothing that Laurel and Hardy fans would like, and turned around.

I walked back down the street and looked in the window, which had a skin of moisture on it from the cold, and there they were.

The good Reverend and two of his flock, namely Kenny Deihl and Mindy Lane.

None of them looked especially happy to see me.

I went inside, told the cashier I was only popping in to say hello to a few good and true friends, and then wended my way through tables of older people sawing steaks and inserting pieces of them into their mouths, all that time gabbing, smiling and turning A-1 bottles upside down.

'Mind if I have a cup of coffee?' I said to the Reverend.

'Would Jesus deny you a cup of coffee?' he responded.

I wanted to point out that, strictly speaking, I hadn't been addressing Jesus, I had been addressing the Reverend, but I sat down and ordered my cup of coffee anyway.

Mindy looked exceptionally pretty in a white low-cut blouse with an oversized lace collar and her hair pulled up dramatically from her face. This, I assumed, was the Religious Mindy, the fleshy sexuality only hinted at in the somewhat sullen mouth and the dozy but shrewd green eyes.

Kenny Deihl offered everybody at the table a nervous smile, as if hoping to effect some sort of truce between us all. In his Western shirt, and with his empty handsome face, he was the perennial B actor whose purpose in the movie was to learn some tough lessons in life from a sardonic John Wayne.

159

Then there was the Reverend himself, funereal in blue suit and blue shirt and muted red tie. There was too much gold in his watch and cuff links for him to ever be a true friend of the Lord's, but he tried to make up for it in the almost oppressive piety of his gaze and the somnolent truths uttered by his TV voice.

The waitress took my order for coffee, but she wasn't going to give up on me as a customer. 'We've got some good meat loaf tonight,' she said, and God how good it sounded but I didn't figure that the High Sheriff of New Hope would appreciate me chowing down right before our date.

'Sorry,' I said.

I looked around the restaurant briefly at all the husbands and wives of so many years, some of them brides and grooms for sixty years, I imagined, and I sensed such peace and belonging in them that I felt cast out, to suffer in the darkness with these three who seemed, each in his way, profoundly troubled.

'I understand that the body was found in your room,' the good Reverend said.

'Yes, unfortunately.'

'Did you know him?' Mindy asked.

I shook my head. 'No, not at all.'

She smiled. 'He had a mighty sweet tongue on him, that one.'

The Reverend shot her a look of instant displeasure.

'What I remember about him,' Kenny Deihl said, 'was that letter he wrote the *Clarion* about us not getting a tax exemption.'

'It's no time to be speaking ill of the man, Kenny,' the Reverend reminded him, straightening his left French cuff. 'He was possessed of the Devil when he wrote those words. Maybe he got right with God before he passed on. You need to consider that, Kenny.'

'He didn't get right with God,' Kenny said. 'Not that cynic. No way.'

I already wanted to get up and run screaming from this odd trio. Maybe they were laying out all this bad dialogue for my sake – but it was even worse to think that they actually talked in this skin-crawling way when they were alone.

Mindy said, not bothering to hide her amusement, 'Sam didn't think that religions should be given tax exemptions. He said the state had too many bills as it was and needed to raise all the taxes it could.'

'He especially disliked religions such as ours,' the Reverend intoned. 'Where we take our ministry to the people rather than praying to false gods in crystal cathedrals or towers of the papacy.'

Towers of the papacy. I'd have to remember that one.

'If Jesus was with us today, in the flesh that is,' the Reverend said, 'He would own His own radio station.'

'Not TV station?' I asked innocently.

'You're like Sam Lodge,' the Reverend said heavily. 'You mock without understanding.'

Mindy looked at me and smiled. 'You don't want to end up like Sam Lodge, do you?'

'That's right,' the Reverend said. 'That's right indeed.'

I was still confounded by the youthfulness of his face. He was well into his thirties but he still resembled a student council president from a prestigious eastern university, all well-concealed ambition and blow-dry politics.

I looked at each of them. 'So you all knew him?'

'Indeed, we all knew him,' the Reverend said.

'Not out of choice,' Kenny said.

'Speak for yourself,' Mindy smiled.

If we didn't know by now that she had slept with the recently departed Sam Lodge, we were never going to get the hint.

'Did any of you kill him?'

'Is that supposed to be a joke, Mr Hokanson?' Kenny said fiercely. 'Because if it is, it isn't funny.'

'It's no joke,' the Reverend said in his best patriarchal manner. 'He's being serious.'

'Well, I don't think it's funny, either,' Mindy said. She looked right at me. 'Up until you asked that question, Mr Hokanson, I sort of liked you. Maybe Kenny here isn't the smartest person on the planet, and maybe I'm not always the good girl I should be, and maybe the Reverend here spends a little more of the church money than he should – but we're all basically good people. Good Christian people. And we certainly wouldn't go around killing people.'

She was serious. I kept looking at her for the sardonic smile or

161

the sarcastic phrase, something to indicate that she and I were still conspirators, that we knew the real truth about dopey Kenny and the relentless Reverend, but now I saw, and saw with great vast disbelief, that she was actually one of them, too – one of the Christian pod people.

I sighed a serious sigh, set down my coffee cup and stood up. 'Well, just thought I'd stop in and say hello.'

'You really piss me off, you know that?' Mindy said, tears choking her voice and filling her eyes.

'Mindy!' the Reverend snapped, seeing that other diners were watching us now.

She put her head down. 'I'm sorry I used that word. Forgive me, O Lord.'

I stared at her a long moment. Here I'd had her all neatly filed away under Good Time Girl but she wasn't that at all. She was something dark and mercurial and perhaps even dangerous.

'Excuse her vulgarity, Mr Hokanson,' the Reverend said.

I nodded.

'You better go,' Kenny said.

And go I did, glad for the street and the gathering night and the balming cleansing cold air.

# 4

*Later that year, in Cell Block D, a lifer serving time for cutting up two fourteen-year-old girls and then dumping their bodies down a grain elevator, got hisself hitched to a 348 pound babe from Astoria, Kansas. Not, you understand, that the lifer was any prize hisself.*

*Warden, being warden, wouldn't give them permission to set up an impromptu wedding chapel inside the prison, so they had to make do with a wedding in the yard, with the woman's blind mama and deaf papa. Also in attendance were several of the lifer's fellow convicts, including two killers, three bank robbers and six just kind of generally bad people. They all wore Aqua Velva, they all sang the Barry Manilow song* Mandy *(that being the bride's name and the lyrics having been typed out for them) and they all kissed the bride, three of them in the French manner. The bride's mama sang along, but not her deaf papa.*

*This would not be the way they got married, with such public scorn or ridiculous setting.*

*Oh, no.*

Dear Reece,

I've spent the last few weeks looking through bridal magazines. I dream of the day when I, attired in white, and you, attired in a good blue suit, approach the altar and quietly take our vows.

I read the newspaper clipping you sent about the in-prison wedding and, honestly, I was appalled. Don't these people have any self-respect? Don't they understand that they're being mocked? They're the type of people who go on *Oprah* and *Geraldo* without seeming to understand that they're

163

being used as buffoons. Yesterday, Geraldo's topic was 'Women Who Sleep With Their Daughters' Girlfriends' and here we had three women blithely talking about having affairs with teenage girls. I just couldn't believe it. I know you think it's silly that I read romance novels but that's exactly why I do – to block out all the filth and despair and lunacy I see every single day in this sorry old world.

I'm enclosing a novel I hope you like. Chapters six and nine were especially entertaining. I thought so, at any rate. Not my usual cup of tea, I admit, but I also admit to being engrossed.

Oh darling, I know our day will soon come and I'm so happy that you agree that I shouldn't come and visit you in prison. I don't want our first meeting to be behind bars. That would set a tone for the rest of our lives. I'm glad you believe that Roger is a good enough lawyer to get you a new trial. He's working at it diligently and believes we'll soon see some results.

In the meantime, darling, read the novel I've enclosed. I hope you agree with me that it's a most instructive book.

Wild Wanton Love My Darling,
Rosamund.

*The novel was a shiny new paperback that showed a kind of studly young cop holding a punk up against a brick wall. Cop had a big Magnum pushed right against the punk's head. The title was:* Battleground, Miami – Blood Bath. *He hated these dim-wit kind of books. All these fucking hero cops. Not a dishonest, sadistic, stupid or incompetent one among them. All pretty-pretty boys with their sweet summer sweat, and every fucking one of them a hero.*

*Why would Rosamund (by now, she'd told him her real name but he, like her, preferred Rosamund) who loved gentle and delicate and beautiful things, enjoy a book like this?*

*He tried reading it straight through. He was no literary critic, to be sure, but as far as he could see this Robert David Chase guy was the hackiest of hacks.*

'Giff turned and fired his Magnum, chuffing death into the startled face of the drug dealer. But it was more than just bullets that were destroying this lizard's life. It was freedom and the American Way and summer nights on Indiana porches and snowball fights on Christmas Day that were really killing this shit-eating scab-sucking criminal. This scum-bag coke merchant was like a vampire, see, he couldn't stand the light of decency and honor, and now he was going down down down, way way fucking down, into the darkness, into the pit, into the eternal fucking abyss, man, way way way way down, man. Way down.'

*He couldn't be sure, having always fallen asleep in his English classes, but this Robert David Chase seemed like a really awful writer. Really, really awful.*

*Those were his feelings, anyway, till he came to Chapters Six and Nine, both of which were told from the viewpoint of one Haskins P. Washington, a self-described 'entrepreneur of the flesh' i.e. a pimp.*

*Haskins, it seems, this all told in flashback, had been incarcerated for life before finally escaping six years into his sentence.*

*Here's how it went. When prisoners worked farm detail, they worked outside the prison walls, usually in fields not far from highways or arterial roads on which there was heavy truck traffic.*

*Haskins decided to take advantage of this by 1) getting himself on farm detail, which took fourteen months and by 2) then having a friend of his rent a truck and drive by a certain field on a certain day at a certain time, at which point the friend stopped the truck at a certain place and two other friends with Uzis jumped from the back of the truck, firing hundreds of rounds to protect Haskins P. Washington who came barrel-assing across the road from the field, and who then hopped in the back of the truck which then sped away.*

*This was Chapter Six.*

*Chapter Nine contained another escape plan – this time involving abducting a prison official and putting a chopper down in the middle of the yard – but this was pure Hollywood and sounded crazy as hell and completely bogus as a serious escape plan.*

*But Chapter Six, now that was another matter.*

*Chapter Six, he practically memorized as he began making plans of his own . . .*

# 5

After buying *USA Today*, *The Wall Street Journal* and *The Chicago Tribune*, and after eating a small piece of pie mostly because I wanted to sit at the old-fashioned Coca-Cola fountain and pretend it was 1958 and that I was a popular quarterback and all-around nice guy, it having been a far, far better world back in those days, I tucked the newspapers under my arm and strolled back to the motel.

It was misting now, a chill shimmering prairie spray, and it gave me the animal desire to be in some place snug and warm, the way I'd felt passing the restaurant window earlier.

The crowd had pretty much gone. Once the body had been removed, what was the point in hanging around? The police, in and out, in and out, carrying small plastic evidence bags, sure proved to be disappointing as spectator sports. So drift home or drift to the tavern and speculate on who killed Sam Lodge, and why, and if you got a chance to embellish on the basic tale ('I heard they decapitated him. I mean, I'm not sure of that but I think that's what somebody told me'), so much the better. A couple of brewskis and some bone-chilling bullshit horror story. What could be better?

If it had resembled a lively movie set before, the parking lot now looked its old shabby self again, even shabbier in the mist.

I went to the front office and asked the old-timer where I'd be sleeping tonight.

'Room 167,' he said.

He got me the key and said, 'Some folks're sayin' you know his wife.'

'Whose wife?'

166

'Whose wife? Who the hell do you think's wife? Sam Lodge's wife.'

I shook my head. 'You mean they're saying I had an affair with her?'

'Something like that, I guess.'.

'Well, I hate to disappoint them, but I've only laid eyes on her twice. And that's all I laid, too. Eyes.' I held up my hands surgeon-style. 'These puppies have never known her fleshy pleasures. So tell all your friends that for me.'

'No reason to get pissed.'

'Yeah, I should enjoy being called a murderer.'

'Hell, you won't find no wet eyes in this town. Sam Lodge was a grade-A asshole.'

I'd had enough of this conversation. 'How about the key to 167?'

'Soon as you give me the other key back.'

It was like an exchange of prisoners.

We swapped small golden keys, and I started to leave.

'There was a call for you,' he said.

'You know who?'

'She didn't say. Just said she'd call back.'

'Thanks.'

'Sorry if I pissed you off.'

'I'm just kind of tired. I probably overreacted. Don't worry about it.'

A different set of ghosts greeted me in 167, each room being the sum of what has transpired within its walls down the years. The Agency, back in the days when they spent a lot of money on such things as telepathy and ESP, concluded that certain rooms could bring on subtle stress because they had not been warmed by sunlight for long periods of time. The humans who briefly occupied the rooms seemed to know this somehow and responded in various neurotic ways. Allegedly, the Agency people could duplicate this experiment perfectly every time out, but when it was finally written up in article form several Agency scientists argued with how the test had been set up in the first place. Personally, I think the test results were probably correct. We do seem to respond in unconscious ways to rooms we're in. That's why I believe in ghosts of some sort, though not necessarily of the chain-clanking variety.

The motel folks had been nice enough to stash all my clothes in the closet, this one being the economy model, coming without a corpse included.

I called Jane Avery's house but all I got was her machine. I assumed she'd have a lot to do tonight, what with Lodge's death and all. Our pizza would likely be later than either of us wanted.

I stripped down to my underwear and did a hard fifteen minutes of exercises, five running in place, five doing push-ups, five doing sit-ups. I had been starting to slide into a vexation of some sort – dead bodies having that effect on me sometimes – and usually my only out is exercising. Breaking a sweat seems to have a kind of healing effect on me.

I was in the bathroom, toweling off, when the phone rang.

I was hoping for Jane. I got, instead, Eve McNally.

'Is it true?' she said.

'True about what?'

'You know. About Sam Lodge being murdered.'

'Yes. Yes, it is.'

'My Lord. It's all getting out of control.'

'What's getting out of control, Eve?'

There was a long pause. 'Have you seen my husband tonight?'

'No. Was he planning to look me up?'

'No – I just meant . . .'

That pause again.

'Any word about your daughter?'

'No.'

'Are you worried about your husband?'

'A little, I guess.'

'When was the last time you saw him?'

'He stopped back around suppertime. I – I sort of lost control. I started screaming at him and hitting him because of Melissa. I'm worried she might already be – you know.'

She couldn't say the word and I didn't blame her.

'He started crying. I never saw him cry before. It was hard to watch. It was like he didn't know how to cry or something. His whole chest just kind of heaved and there were tears rolling down his cheeks and – I felt sorry for him. I'm real mad at him, for getting Melissa involved in all this, but I felt sorry for him, too. You know?'

'I know.'

'I told him to go see you.'

'You did?'

'Uh-huh. I said maybe you could help him without going to the police. You know, have two minds working on it.'

'Working on what, Eve?'

The long silence again.

'If he wants to tell you, he'll tell you. Otherwise I just have to keep my mouth shut. I'll get her killed for sure.'

For the first time in this conversation, she started crying again. Soft, almost silent tears.

'I just keep saying Hail Marys over and over again but sometimes I wonder if there's any God at all. I know I shouldn't say that but that's how I feel. I mean, I hear my voice talking out loud in the silence and I think – why am I doing this? Nobody's listening. Nobody's out there.'

'We all have those doubts sometimes, Eve. It's a part of our faith, dealing with doubt.'

Another long silence. 'If he calls you, will you let me know?'

'Sure.'

'Tell him – tell him I'm sorry I got so mad.'

'Eve, you had a right to be mad. Something he did got your daughter kidnapped. I'd be pretty mad about that.'

'He says he can get her back. Soon as he—'

'Soon as he what, Eve?'

'Soon as he—'

But then, of course, silence. Utter silence.

'Eve?'

'Yes.'

'You can trust me.'

Silence.

'You really can.'

'I want to but—'

'But the only way I can help you is if you're honest with me.'

'I know.' She sounded like a contrite child. 'Will you have him call me?'

'Yes I will.'

'I'll talk to you later.'
'All right, Eve. Good night.'

Twenty minutes later, all shirted and jacketed and trousered up, I tried Jane's place again, only to get the machine once more.

I was antsy, the way I'd been in my college days before a date, pacing and eager for the night to begin.

Then I decided to call Herb Carson, a wealthy cattle rancher who'd given it all up to devote himself to a small airplane museum about twenty minutes from here.

Herb was in and happy to hear from me.

'You haven't been here since we got our parasol monoplane.'

I laughed. 'Still after the most exotic birds, aren't you, Herb?'

'Damn right. I want to make this the most unique museum in the country.'

'Sounds like you're doing it. I'm an airplane buff, Herb, but even I don't know what the hell a parasol monoplane is.'

He chuckled. 'I was waiting for you to ask.'

So he told me.

Back in 1929, when aviation was still the most romantic of callings, an eighteen-year-old garage mechanic with a sixth-grade education came into a very small inheritance with which he bought a Heath Airplane kit. Talk about a hardy breed. In those days, some Americans built their own airplanes. Which is what the kid did. He welded all the parts by himself, shaped all the wooden pieces by himself, stretched the oiled silk over the plane by himself, and, as the final touch, installed a Henderson motorcycle engine by himself. Most folks bet that the plane would never 'fly' in any real sense. Back then, you saw a lot of would-be planes that would reach thirty or forty feet and then crash. Folks were scared for the kid. But on a warm October day in 1929, the kid took the plane up and it flew beautifully. The name Bobby Solbrig may not mean much to you, but to old-time aviators it was legendary, Solbrig probably being the greatest stunt pilot who ever lived after getting his start in an Iowa cornfield just about the time President Hoover, another Iowa boy himself, was telling us that the economy was in great shape if we just left it alone, and that those people who worried about a Depression were nothing but nervous nellies. Bobby Solbrig had a little more success than poor President Hoover.

'And guess what I bought last week?' Herb said after finishing his story.

'What?'

'A biplane just about like yours.'

'You're kidding. Where d'you find it?'

'Louisiana, of all places. Bayou country, actually. It's in beautiful shape.'

'I'll have to see it.'

'You bet you will. Why don't you stop by tomorrow and I'll let you take it up.'

'I'm not sure what time I can come out.'

'Just call the house before you set off. Make sure I'm here.'

'Thanks. It'll be good to see you.'

The laugh again. 'Yeah, and it'll be even nicer to see my biplane.'

After we hung up, I tried Jane's place.

'Hello?'

'You're home,' I said.

'I sure wish you'd tell me what's going on in this town of mine,' she said, sounding tired. 'Two murders yesterday and now another one tonight.'

'You probably won't believe me, but I'm not sure myself. Not yet.'

'Will you give me a little time to take a shower?'

'Sure.'

'Let's make it an hour then.'

'That's perfect. That's about how long it takes for Domino's to prepare a gourmet pizza.'

'Double cheese.'

'Double cheese it is.'

# 6

'It's kind of a pit, actually,' Jane Avery said after I got the pizza box open and handed out bottles and white paper napkins and grease-stained coupons entitling us to $1.00 off our very next Domino's pizzas.

I had complimented her in the usual casual way one always compliments a person on her apartment. The trouble was, she was right – about it being a pit, I mean.

What you had here was the standard modern middle-class apartment. You had your four rooms and a bath, you had your wall-to-wall carpeting, you had your stove and refrigerator and garbage disposal, and you had large sliding windows that over-looked just about the two cutest little dumpsters I'd ever seen.

And then, imposed on the sterile right-angled order of the apartment itself, you had Jane's delirious messiness.

I'd used the bathroom right after getting here and had found one high heel black shoe in the sink. I'd gone out to the kitchen to get glasses and ice for us while she visited the bathroom, and hanging off the knob of the door leading to the back yard, I found a pair of panties, bright yellow and quite clean. But hanging from the doorknob? In the living room, an array of magazines ranging from *People* to *Police Science Quarterly* squatted everywhere in short stacks, like kittens waiting to be patted upon the head. A glass half-filled with what appeared to be milk sat atop the TV set; I imagined it tasted just dandy. A red skirt – which I knew she would look nice in, her shortie white bathrobe having just given me my first peek at her legs – was draped over the back of an armchair while next to the small dark fireplace was an ancient Hoover upright, either waiting to be employed, or having been sitting there ever since it had been employed.

172

'I don't know why you say your apartment is a pit,' I said.

'Gee, I don't either,' she said, giving me a sarcastic smile as she was about to push her third piece of pizza in her mouth. After swallowing, she said, 'That really used to get him.'

'Get who?'

'My husband.'

'Oh.'

'He's one of those guys who believes that God genetically programmed women to *like* doing housework. And I'm serious. He once said that maybe I should see a counselor because I never liked to do any of the housework.'

'I think you should see a counselor, too, but not for that reason.'

'Funny.'

'I think you should see a counselor because you hang your underwear off doorknobs.'

'You saw that, huh?'

'Is that a religious practice or something?'

She shrugged, looking cute as hell with her short red hair still wet from the shower, and her freckles evoking sunny afternoons on the fish-filled creeks of my youth. 'I always drop stuff when I bring the laundry up from downstairs. Yesterday I dropped a pair of panties. That's how they got there.'

'Ah.'

'This is really good pizza,' she said.

'You look great.'

'I thought we were talking about pizza.'

'You were talking about pizza. I was talking about how great you look in that white terrycloth robe with your hair all wet.'

There was one piece of pizza left.

'God, we sure pigged out,' I said. 'That was an extra-large pizza.'

'I'll arm-wrestle you for the last piece.'

'Hey, are you serious?'

'Sure I'm serious. I had three older brothers and they made me arm-wrestle them for everything. I don't blame you, though – I'd hate to be beaten by a girl, too.'

We were sitting on the floor, using the coffee table for pizza and beers.

To arm-wrestle, all we had to do was angle our bodies closer to the coffee table and set our elbows down.

'You know something funny?'

'What?' she said.

'I really want to beat you. I really do. I mean, I feel competitive about this.'

'Good. You should. Because I feel competitive, too.'

'But I don't want to hurt you.'

'What a he-man!'

'No, I'm serious. If I start getting carried away, you just tell me.'

'Sure.'

She gripped my hand. 'Ready?'

'Remember now, if I get carried away, you let me know.'

'Right.'

She put my arm down flat against the table.

'I mustn't have been ready.'

'Oh right, that must've been it. You weren't ready.'

'You really think you could've just flattened my arm like that if I'd been ready?'

'I told you I had three brothers.'

'Well, I had three sisters, so what does that prove?'

'Did you really have three sisters?'

'No. But that wasn't any dumber than saying that you had three brothers.'

This time I was ready and right away you could see the difference. She didn't put my arm down flat in ten seconds this time. Nope, on this second outing it took her at least twenty seconds.

I stared down at my arm as if it had betrayed me.

'Tell you what,' she said.

'What?'

'We'll cut the piece of pizza in half.'

'No, no way. You won fair and square.'

'Aw, God, don't be noble. My husband was like that, noble noble noble, and he was a real pain in the ass.'

'I seem to remind you of your husband an awful lot.'

'You couldn't possibly be as big a dip-shit as he was. Nobody could.'

'Boy, there's a glowing endorsement.'

'Now, c'mon, we'll split the piece of pizza. And afterward you can try me again.' She leaned over and gave me a chaste little kiss on the cheek. 'Maybe I just got lucky.'

'You have a cute big toe,' she said, twenty minutes later.

'You only say I have a cute big toe because you want to spare me the embarrassment of pointing out the hole in my sock.'

She smiled. 'I noticed you looking around.'

'Nice place.'

'God, Payne, will you stop saying that. It's a pit.'

Gentlemanly behavior dictated that I once again tell the saving lie and compliment her apartment.

But unfortunately my mind was fixed on the fact that she'd called me Payne. She should have called me Hokanson. That was the name I was using in New Hope.

She'd picked up on it, too. 'I think I'm in trouble.'

'I think you are, too.'

'Calling you Payne?'

'Uh-huh. How'd you find out?'

'The day we had coffee, I waited down the street till you left then I rushed back there and lifted your cup. One of the deputies is real good with fingerprints. I checked you out. Your prints are on several national files. You were in the FBI.'

'I see.'

'So what're you doing in town, Payne?'

'I can't tell you.'

'In a couple of minutes, Payne, I'm really going to get pissed off. My sworn duty is to find out who killed these three people. I believe that you have information that could help me. Ergo, I need you to be honest with me.'

'Ergo?'

'It means consequently.'

'I know what it means. I've just never heard a cop use it before.'

'So what're you doing in New Hope?'

'I can't tell you.'

'How about if I give you a back rub?'

'Are you serious?'

She was serious.

Dark wind blew silver rain in through the screen and sprinkled drops across my neck and arms. Sweet spring night was on the wind, intoxicating.

I was spread out on her floor in the position that Indians always put John Wayne in whenever they wanted to cover him with hundreds of hungry red ants.

She was straddled across my lower back, her hands expertly working the muscles in my neck, shoulder and back. She was deliciously good at it.

'I read up on you, Payne.'

'Oh? Then you know about me winning the Nobel Peace Prize?'

She was charitable enough to laugh. 'No, but I know that you did some pretty interesting stuff when you were in the FBI. And I also know your wife died.'

I didn't say anything.

'I'll bet she was nice.'

'She was wonderful,' I said.

She redoubled her efforts at massage. I closed my eyes and drifted on the dark cool winds and the dappling drops of chilly rain on my shoulders. This all reminded me of college dates, when you'd end up at a girl's apartment feeling intimate enough to relax but not intimate enough to know what to do next. Especially since I wasn't sure what *I* wanted to do next.

'You give great back rubs,' I said. I was going to say more, maybe something craftily romantic, when the phone rang.

'Oh, darn it,' she said.

And grabbed the phone from the end table.

'Chief Avery.' Beat. 'When?' Beat. 'Does Eve know who did it?' Beat. 'I'll be right there.' She hung up.

'I have to go,' she said.

'What happened?'

She was up already, pulling on her clothes.

'You think we'll do this again?' she said.

'I certainly hope so,' I said. 'So what happened?'

'Eve McNally.'

'Right. I know who she is.'

'Somebody beat her up pretty badly tonight. She won't say who and she won't let Milner take her to the hospital.'

'Milner?'

'A patrolman.'

'Oh.'

'So I'm going over there. Talk to her myself. She's the classic battered woman – she'll never say a word against her husband even though he's the one who always beats her up.'

'So this has happened before with Eve McNally?'

'Too many times.'

The final thing she did was snag her badge on her turtleneck and wrap her gun and holster around her narrow hips.

I got up off the floor and picked up my jacket and then followed her out the front door, which she paused to lock behind her.

'Sorry if I humiliated you at arm-wrestling, Payne,' she said. And grinned.

'Yeah,' I said. 'You sound real sorry, too.'

Then she was gone, moving at a trot now to the official black Ford sedan tucked into the corner of the lot.

I moved slowly to my car, my mind fixed on the question of why Eve McNally might have been beaten up.

# 7

*Rosamund never did visit him in prison.*

*When the time came, when the last appeal was turned down and the plan was set in motion, she dispatched a man to visit him, a man whose name she gave as Givens.*

*Well, two days before Givens's arrival, there had been some trouble three cells down, a guard getting hit pretty hard on the back of the head, so the warden, being the mean stupid vituperative sonofabitch everybody knew all wardens to be, decided to punish everybody in the block.*

*One of the things he did, the sweet bastard, was suspend the usual visiting privileges.*

*Usually, the prisoners were led into a long, narrow visiting room where they sat at a long, narrow table, on the other side of which sat the visitor, usually a loved one or lawyer.*

*But the warden decided to make the men of Cell Block D use the booth in which inmates were forced to use the telephone to speak to visitors who were on the other side of the Plexiglas window.*

*Mr Givens showed up in an expensive suit and a look of distaste on his handsome face. He looked very anxious to get out of here.*

*Chit-chat was how you'd characterize most of their fifteen-minute conversation.*

*Wasn't Rosamund a fine lady? She sure was, he said. Wasn't it nice of Rosamund to wait for him this way? It was indeed. Wouldn't it be nice when they were married and leading a normal life? Absolutely.*

*Only toward the end, only when the fat-ass uniformed guard with his nightstick and his Magnum, started to look antsy, the way he always looked when he was about to shoo visitors out . . . only then did Mr Givens come to the point.*

'Damn,' he said.

'What?'

He tapped his gold Rolex. 'My watch seems to have stopped.'

'Huh?'

'At 10:25 a.m. On May 26.'

'Gee, a Rolex stopping like that. Who would've thought that—'

Only then, being a very slow learner apparently, only then did he realize what Givens was doing.

May 26 was four days away. How could his watch have stopped at a future date when—

Aw, shit.

He really was a dumb bastard.

Here Givens had done everything except write it down and hold it up for him and he still hadn't caught on.

10:25 a.m. on May 26.

Of course.

'I noticed the soybeans over on the north side. They look great,' Givens said.

10:25 a.m., May 26, soybean field on the north side.

There it was.

His way out of this fucking place.

Thanks to Rosamund.

Then the guard came by.

'Time's up,' he said.

And tapped his nightstick against the Plexiglas. Just so Givens would know who was really in charge here, just so Givens would know that this was one tight-ass prison and that the guards planned to keep it that way.

'I'll tell Rosamund you send your love,' Givens said.

'I'd appreciate that.'

'You're the only thing she talks about any more.'

Guard tapped his nightstick again. 'You hear me, mister? Time's up.'

'I thought,' said Givens, 'we still had five minutes left. According to what they told me—'

'You want to take the time and go up and ask them again, fella? If you do, I'll dock your friend here five minutes on his next visitation. You want me to do that?'

Givens sighed, shook his head.

179

*'Take care of yourself,' Givens said, standing up.*

*He watched Givens walk out of the visiting room.*

*Guard looked at him and grinned. 'You assholes over in D. You think you're going to get away with hittin' Bernie the way you did, don't you?'*

*'I didn't hit him.'*

*'Yeah, but it was your friend who hit him.'*

*'He isn't my friend. I don't even know him.'*

*'You assholes are all the same, don't matter whether you know each other or not. You stick together.' He knocked his nightstick against the Plexiglas. 'Well, us guards, we stick together, too.'*

*That night, an inmate got his nose and three ribs busted up, same guy, by a big coincidence, who was the cellmate of the guy who'd hit Bernie the guard.*

*This was the talk of D for the next three days, how the guards had deliberately busted up the guy, and how D was going to pay the guards back.*

*But who gave a rat's ass?*

*He was, at long last, going to get out of here.*

*10:25 a.m., May 26, soybean field to the north.*

*Yes, ma'am. Oh yes, yes, ma'am.*

*He let the other cons lie on their bunks and stew and sulk about that nasty guard and that poor defenseless con.*

*All he thought about was the soybean field.*

*The soybean field . . .*

# 8

One day, I got authorization to go up to the Office of Technical Services, which is where the Agency keeps all of its James Bond devices, and a very friendly old chap spent an hour with me bringing me up to speed on devices for tapping phones and photographing documents and new ways to plant bugs. Most people don't realize this, but the Agency employs a good number of cabinetmakers, leatherworkers, woodworkers and general carpenters who do nothing but devise better ways to conceal electronic bugging devices. When the old man had finished telling me about his department, he said, 'There's only one thing we haven't come up with yet.'

'And what's that?'

'Some way for you agents to occupy your time while you're on a stake-out.'

How true.

I gave Jane Avery a ten-minute head start and then I drove over to the McNally block and parked at the far end, between two cars, so I'd be less conspicuous.

Her police car sat right out in front of the McNallys'. As I drove by, I'd seen both of them in the lighted window, behind the gauzy cover of sheer white curtains.

Jane had been in there more than an hour.

As for me, I now had time to brush up on my three favorite sports, thumb-twiddling, sighing and keeping the cheeks of my backside from going to sleep.

Oh yes, and one other sport: playing guess the Sears house.

Around the turn of the century, a lot of Iowa people bought house kits from Sears. These weren't little shacks, either, the homes from these kits. In fact, the most popular in-town model

181

was the Dutch Colonial, a two-story job with a gambrel roof and authentic reproductions of 'Colonial sidelights' flanking the front door.

There were probably three or four hundred Sears houses still standing in Iowa, which said something about the quality of craftsmanship in those days.

Unfortunately, I didn't see any Sears houses on Eve McNally's block, no matter how hard I looked, no matter how many times I lifted my binoculars and checked them out.

Maybe the owners had done what the Mesquakie Indians used to do, before the white man came. They made houses from reed mats that lasted about seven years, which was also the time it took to exhaust the firewood in a given area. So the Mesquakies never, as it were, sought a home improvement loan; they just moved on to a new area where they built new houses and started life afresh, members of a truly mobile society.

Jane Avery came out just as I was starting to rub my backside, prickly numbness having started to overtake it.

I slid down in the seat, figuring her lights would sweep across my door when she pulled out. As they did.

After a flash of headlamps, there was just darkness again. I pulled myself up, opened the door and walked across the street.

It was misting now, a chill spray that reminded me of lying with Jane on her bed. I smiled.

At the door, Eve McNally peered out through the dark glass before turning on the porch light. An aged yellow lamp above my head came on. It had probably chaperoned teenagers back in the days of Benny Goodman and swooning over Sinatra.

After recognizing me, she shook her head, waved me away.

From inside my jacket, I took a number 10 white envelope that was folded inside my shirt pocket. The envelope contained nothing more exciting than some notes I'd scribbled down about my biplane. But Eve McNally didn't know that.

I held the envelope up and pointed at it importantly.

She was nice enough to fall for it.

It was an awful trick to play on a woman whose daughter had

182

been kidnapped – she was likely hoping against hope that the envelope contained word of Melissa – but I didn't have much choice.

She said, 'What's in the envelope?' Her words were muffled by the glass and the dusty door curtains.

'You need to let me in first.'

She shook her head again.

'I've got news,' I said.

A kind of frenzy overtook her. News? Of Melissa?

She looked confused a moment – should she let me in or not – and then she made her mind up.

The inside door was jerked open.

All that separated us now was a screen door. I tried the handle. She had the door latched.

'What news?'

'I lied. I shouldn't have gotten your hopes up that way.'

'You lied? You lied?' She sounded hysterical. 'About having news? You are really a dirty sonofabitch, you know that?'

'I am. Yes, I am. I'm really sorry.'

'I thought—'

'I know what you thought. And I apologize again. I know you don't believe this but I'm trying to help you.'

'Oh, sure you are.'

'Just let me in a moment. Please.'

'You didn't need to lie to me,' she said, then surprised me by quietly lifting the latch and stepping back.

She went in and sat down on the edge of the couch and stared forlornly at the floor.

She was close to the end table lamp so I could see her face now, the bruises, the cuts above her right eye, most likely the result of a ring scraping her as she was being punched.

I went over and sat next to her on the couch. At first I didn't know what to do or say. I still felt bad about having raised her hopes.

She was staring at the floor as if she were in a coma. Most of the room was in darkness; we were in a little ring of light.

I slid my arm over her shoulder and said, 'You need a friend.'

'I just want my daughter back.'

'I know. And I really do want to help.'
'You don't know how bad I wanted to tell her everything.'
'Jane Avery?'
'Uh-huh.'
'So you didn't tell her anything?'
She shook her head. 'I couldn't. Just like I can't tell you anything.'
'Including who beat you up tonight.'
'Melissa'd be dead for sure, if I told you that.' Then she turned and looked at me and said, 'But there's one thing.'
I didn't say anything, just let her come to it in her own time. She wore a faded KISS T-shirt that made her sad little breasts seem very vulnerable. The shoulder of the T-shirt had splotches of dried blood on it.
'I found something tonight, going through his stuff.'
'Your husband's?'
'Right. You want to see it?'
'Of course.'
'I would've told her but she's the law. And you're not, right?'
'Right. I'm not the law.'
'I'll be right back.'
She vanished into the darkness. I heard her opening a drawer in a room off the hall that divided the small house in two.
She returned carrying a single sheet of paper.
She handed it to me then took her place again on the couch.
'Any idea what it is?'
'Not yet.'

201 Lawlor Avenue, S.E.
Mar 1 $475.00
Apr 1 $475.00
May 1 $475.00
Jun 1 $475.00

325 River Street, S.E.
Jul 1 $635.00
Aug 1 $635.00
Sep 1 $635.00

```
No.    3706                                    April 01      19  93

Received from      Heartland Rental Properties

        Six Hundred thirty-five and                no
                                                          100  Dollars
For Rent of         325 River Street SE

from          April 01              to     April 30              19    93

$  635.00                          Donald Hargeson
```

The numbers and the rent receipt had been Xeroxed on one side of a sheet of plain white paper.

'Does any of that mean anything to you?' About mid-point in her question, she winced and touched a delicate fingertip to her puffy lower lip. She'd been hit pretty hard.

'Well, Lawlor Avenue and River Street are Cedar Rapids addresses.'

'That would make sense, I guess.'

'Make sense how?'

'My husband goes to Cedar Rapids a lot. Whenever he wants to hit a lot of taverns.'

'You have a Cedar Rapids phone book here?'

The towns around Cedar Rapids were now treated by the phone company folks as satellites if not suburbs of Iowa's second largest city.

She walked over to a small desk, rattled around in the middle drawer, and brought forth a phone book which she carried over and handed to me.

I turned to Taverns and went down the list. Though there were roughly seventy-five taverns in and around Cedar Rapids, none of those listed was on either Lawlor Avenue or River Street.

'No luck,' I said.

I set the phone book on the coffee table and then turned back to her.

'Every time I lie down and close my eyes and try to sleep, all I

185

can see is Melissa. I just keep imagining all the things that might be happening to her. All the things I've read about in the papers over the years—'

I took her hand. 'She's going to be all right, Eve. You've got to keep saying that to yourself. Over and over and over. You've got to believe that.'

She smiled her sad smile. 'You should've been a doctor. You've got a nice manner.'

'I don't suppose you've changed your mind about telling me who beat you up tonight?'

'No. I'm sorry.'

'Just the way you talk about it, I know it wasn't your husband.'

She said nothing, obviously not wanting to answer my question either way.

I stood up to leave and told her she could call me any time, night or day.

'Do you think those addresses have anything to do with Melissa?'

'There's no way of knowing without checking them out.'

'Would you even consider doing that?'

I nodded. 'Tomorrow morning, I'm going to take a plane up for a short ride. Then maybe I'll drive into Cedar Rapids and see what I can find out.'

'You really are a nice guy.'

'Thanks. You're going to get Melissa back and she's going to be fine,' I said, reaching the door and turning around again.

In one of his books, Graham Greene noted that despair is a serious sin and the older I get, the more I understand what he meant. All we have, when all else has deserted us, is faith and hope. It was enough to bring our species from the sea millions of years ago, and it's enough now to take us to the stars.

'You don't want this?' she said, holding up the paper with the figures on it.

'No. Don't need it, thanks. And I'll say a few prayers for Melissa tonight.'

'I'd appreciate that.'

I nodded and left.

# 9

*After more years than he cares to believe, he gets his first chance to go before the Parole Board.*
*Cons are filled with advice on how he should handle himself. One con even hands him a list.*

## Always

1) *Always look humble.*

2) *Always wear your hair in a part.*

3) *Always wear some kind of religious symbol they can see, like a St Christopher medal.*

4) *Always tear up a little when you mention your parents/wives/children and how you've let them down (they may suspect you're faking but they'll be moved anyway).*

5) *Always speak softly.*

## Never

1) *Never say 'ain't'.*

2) *Never sigh – they'll think you're irritated or angry.*

3) *Never look at the women very long.*

4) *Never yawn.*

187

*5) Never squirm; shoulders straight, back straight.*

Comes the day.

They arrive and take you (and thirty other cons) over to a different building and then you wait in the hall as one con at a time goes into the room where the Adult Authority conducts its interviews.

In his case, being near the back of the line, the wait takes all morning and most of the afternoon.

When the cons come out, they all grin and give you the finger secret-like and shake their heads disdainfully.

Cons never want other cons to think that they've become broken by the institution. So they're always performing these little defenses of their honor and individuality, none of which the Adult Authority is likely to approve of.

'Well, now, good afternoon,' says the fat banker heartily.

Bulbous body; boozy nose; three-piece suit.

The banker's smile is joined by the priest's smile and the country club lady's smile. The banker and the country club lady, in fact, remotely resemble brother and sister. Same kind of middle-aged bodies; same kind of middle-aged do-gooder smiles. The priest is just plain worn out and keeps glancing at the wall clock. Probably time for him to get in his Godmobile and go out and save a few souls.

'Well, now,' the banker says, opening the manilla folder particular to the case at hand.

'Yes,' says the country club lady, looking at her own manilla folder. 'Well, now.'

Banker: *Looks like you've been a good skate.*
Him: *Good skate?*
Banker: *Oh. Sorry* (smiles). *Guess that expression's a little out of date. Looks like you've been a good prisoner, I mean.* (But there is irritation in his eyes. He obviously doesn't like to be challenged, even on this minor a thing.)
Lady: *What's that?*
Him: *This?*

188

| | |
|---|---|
| Lady: | *Yes.* |
| Him: | *St Christopher medal.* |
| Lady: | *You're Catholic, then?* |
| Him: | *Yes, ma'am.* |
| Priest: | *Do you feel that a belief in God gives you the power to change your life?* |
| Him: | *Absolutely. Absolutely.* |
| Lady: | *I don't find any prior skills listed here. You're in the print shop now, correct?* |
| Him: | *Yes, ma'am. And I really like it. My dad and mom, they really wanted me to make something of myself, and now maybe I am.* (Just a hint of nice wet tears on his eyes.) |
| Banker: | *Is there any place you'd like to settle if you're given a parole?* |
| Him: | *A small town would be nice. Where people, you know, still believe things.* |
| Lady: | *Things?* |
| Him: | *Well, you know, where they still have the old values.* |
| Priest: | *Jesus's values.* |
| Him: | *Yes, Father. Jesus's values.* |

'So how'd it go?' *Lumir of the acrid feet asks that night.*

'Real good. Real good.'

'You do all the shit you were supposed to?'

'I sat up straight. I didn't say "ain't." I didn't flirt with the woman. I got tears in my eyes when I mentioned my mom and dad. And they bought it.'

'No shit?'

'Absolutely. You shoulda seen them. They were impressed. Take my word for it.'

*His parole is turned down.*

# 10

In the earliest days of Iowa, back in the 1830s, most of the taverns doubled as stagecoach stops. In case you don't think that traveling by stage, or stopping at such taverns, was dangerous, consider this tip from a brochure handed out to stagecoach passengers:

> *Don't point out where murders have been committed, especially if there are any women passengers.*

*Merle's Rack 'n Snack* probably wasn't as dangerous as one of those early stage stops but with half a dozen Harleys out front and the old-fashioned kind of Country music blasting from the windows, I assumed that *Merle's* probably had its share of nightly violence – you know, the standard romp 'n stomp that makes bikers such delightful companions.

Which made the presence of the shiny new Lincoln in the parking lot all the more curious. A white Lincoln. Just like the pair the good Reverend Roberts had been sporting in his church driveway that day, and which the very pretty and very deeply disturbed Mindy had been washing and waxing that afternoon.

I went inside and soon enough learned what the *Rack 'n Snack* stood for.

'Rack', which I should have figured out for myself, referred to three bumper pool tables near the back, while 'snack' referred to two (count 'em, two!) small and rather battered microwaves behind the bar. According to the handwritten menu leaning up against several boxes of shotgun shells, and two feet over from car air-fresheners with nude women on them – you know, the sort you hang down from your rearview mirror and which your teenagers would be proud to see you buy . . . according to the menu you could choose between a:

BEER 'N BRAT
BEER 'N BURGER
BEER 'N BUFFALO

I hadn't ever had a buffalo burger and somehow I wasn't inclined to try one here.

As I walked over to the bar, the twenty or so customers, mostly drunken men, got their first good look at me and I got my first good look at them and it was pretty obvious that they wouldn't be inviting me to their birthday parties and I wouldn't be inviting them to mine. The air was ripe with cigarette smoke and beer, just as the john would be ripe with piss and puke. Maybe they had one of those naked-lady deodorizing dealies hanging from the ceiling in there.

In the jukebox darkness, I nodded to the bartender, a guy with a rather theatrical eyepatch and a kind of swarthy, feral face. He wore a T-shirt with a Confederate flag on it and a sneer that was all the more impressive for the white regularity of his store-boughts. He looked pretty much like his friends, whom I saw in the lurid light of the jukebox, all long dirty hair and shirts with the sleeves torn off and even a few headbands and peace signs on the backs of leather vests. I've always found it odd that the lower-class men of my generation ended up appropriating all the things they once so despised about all the hippies. But these weren't hippie faces, all spoiled middle-class piety and sancti-mony over the so-called decadent establishment – no, these were sad hardscrabble faces, faces you got growing up as one of a dozen kids who had to scratch for love and food and self-esteem the way you see chickens scratching for sustenance in barnyards. All those years of deprivation had made them dangerous, and you never knew when their sorrow was just going to overwhelm them and they'd take it out on you.

'Beer, please,' I said.

'We got lotsa beer, pal. What kind?'

'Budweiser,' I said, 'pal.'

While he opened one of the cooling drawers below the counter,

I looked around but there was no sign of Reverend Roberts.

He set my beer down, no glass. I had my dollar bill waiting on the sticky counter.

'The white Lincoln,' I said.

'What white Lincoln?'

'The one in your parking lot.'

We had to shout above Tanya Tucker.

'What about it?'

'Thought maybe I knew who owned it.'

'Who?'

'Reverend Roberts.'

He shook his head, grinned. 'That fucker would never come in here. Too good for this kind of place. But his old lady—' He leered with those perfect teeth again. 'Booth way in back, by that EXIT sign over there. That's where she always sits.'

I walked over, all eyes on me, and looked into the booth where a plump woman in a very tight red sweater designed to display her wares prominently sat sipping a drink. She had the sort of cute cheerleader face that not even years and weight could quite decimate, especially given the erotic quality of her full mouth. Her blonde hair was worn short, which was a mistake, and her eyes were heavy with too much eyeliner.

'Mrs Roberts?'

'Yes.'

'I wondered if I could talk to you.'

'Are you trying to pick me up?'

I smiled. 'That would be my pleasure but actually I want to talk business.'

She visibly winced. 'That means my husband the Reverend.'

I nodded.

'Are you police?'

'No, but I'm an investigator.'

She smiled. She had a killer smile. 'Why not? Maybe it could be fun.'

I sat down. 'Like a fresh drink?'

'No, thanks. I went through two different de-tox programs in the last year so I'm sticking to my own little kind of drinky-poos.' She hoisted her glass. 'Wine coolers.'

So much for the two de-tox programs.

192

'Did he get somebody pregnant again?'

'Your husband? Not that I know of.'

'Good, because the last time he did, it was really a mess. The mother dragged her daughter – who was all of fifteen – into the church and made a scene during a Sunday service. It was something out of a bad movie. A very bad one.'

'Didn't he get in trouble with the church members?'

'Oh, he did a Jimmy Swaggart. You know, one of those big, teary, dramatic spectacles on the altar. They loved it and they forgave him.'

'Did you forgive him?'

She smiled. 'Don't start looking at me like a victim. If I counted up all the men I've screwed on the side, I could probably fill a small stadium. I'm no prize, believe me.' The smile again, only sadder. 'Oh, back in high school I was a prize. I was a real doll, I really was. And these were the stuff of myth.' She delicately indicated her breasts with a long, graceful hand. 'The Reverend could never keep his hands off them. After we were married, he used to feel me up even when I was asleep. He just couldn't get enough of them. But then we went through some very bad years, eight or nine of them in fact. He got run out of two different churches – the other thing he couldn't keep his hands off was teenage girls – and we never had any money and my drinking started to be a serious problem. I wanted him to get a real job. I mean, in his heart he's no Reverend, not the way he violates the Ten Commandments – nobody could be that much of a hypocrite. But he enjoys *pretending* he's a Reverend. He likes all the corny stuff, the weddings and the christenings and the funerals. He gets so caught up in them, he always cries. It's pretty fucking amazing, when you think about it. I mean, I've seen him bury people that he despised, but there they were, these huge silver tears, streaming down his cheeks. He really is something else.'

I hadn't known until about halfway through her little speech how drunk she was. It took an awful lot of wine coolers to reach her present state of intoxication. I assumed she must have had something a little stronger earlier in the evening.

'You ever think of leaving him?'

'You know something?'

'What?'

'You haven't told me your name.'

'Jim Hokanson.'

'Oh, the famous Jim Hokanson.'

'Famous?'

'A lot of people in town are wondering who you really are.'

'Just another pilgrim.'

'You still want to know if I ever think of leaving him?'

'Yes.'

'Well, actually, I have left him three times but he always brought me back.'

'He loves you, then.'

'No, but he needs me for a front. I don't make scenes, I really play the part of the dutiful wife whenever I need to, and I don't cost him all that much money when you come right down to it. I've even made him money, me and my cancer.'

'You have cancer?'

'No. Or at least I hope I don't. But he tells people I do. It's one of the ways he raises money.'

'He seems to be awfully successful. I saw his matching white Lincolns – one of which you're driving tonight, I believe.'

'Yes, luckily I was able to get to it before Mindy was.' A lurid smile this time. 'I shouldn't be saying all this, but I'm a little drunky-poo and right now I don't care.'

I wasn't sure what she was talking about but before I could answer, the bartender had come over.

'There's a phone call for you, Mrs Roberts.'

'Tell him I'm not here.'

'I already told him you were.'

'I thought we had an understanding, you and me.'

'Mrs Roberts, I don't want to get in the middle of somebody's family argument. Now why don't you come over and get the phone?'

He walked away.

'This place is really a pit, isn't it?'

'I guess I could agree with that notion,' I said.

'This is the kind of place I used to drink in before we came into money.'

'And when was that?'

194

She thought a moment. 'Four years ago.'

'Is that when his ministry really took off?'

'His ministry? Honey, his ministry has never taken off.'

Then where did he suddenly get money, I wanted to ask.

But the bartender was shouting above the jukebox for her.

She put down her drink and walked over to the bar, still a good-looking woman as all the appreciative male eyes indicated.

She didn't do much talking, just held the phone to her ear for a minute or so and then handed the receiver back to the bartender.

Sliding into the booth again, she said, 'I'm not supposed to talk to you. I'm supposed to get my fucking ass out of this fucking dive and get the fuck home. You know, I've never gotten used to saying the F word. Still think in the back of my mind that it's very unladylike. But the Reverend, he uses it all the time.' She looked at her watch. 'I really better go.'

'I was hoping we could talk a little more.'

'He knows you're here and he knows we're talking. And that's what he's so upset about.'

'How'd he find out I was here?'

'Lou.'

'The bartender.'

'Uh-huh. Lou keeps the Reverend clued in and the Reverend gives him money.'

'You going to be all right to drive?'

'I'll be fine.'

'You were going to tell me about your husband coming into money suddenly.'

She stood up, grabbed her purse. 'Call me some other time and we'll talk. Right now I just want to get home and get all his yelling and swearing over with, and just go to bed.' The killer smile again, the one that broke all those hearts in those misty days of yesteryear when we were young and optimistic and immortal. 'Dream about me tonight, Mr Hokanson, because I'm sure going to dream about you.'

Then she was gone.

# 11

The escape didn't go so well.

Number one, the getaway car, a new rental Chevy, had an overheating problem, which made the three hoods Rosamund had hired fifteen minutes late in getting to the road that ran parallel to the soybean field.

Number two, he himself had come down with a cold and sore throat that made him miserably ill the night before the planned escape. Even worse, he'd had an impossible time sleeping, waking up every fifteen minutes with an image of the guards shooting him dead. He was scared. So many things could go wrong with this kind of set-up.

Number three, one of the guards was a new guy and a real cowboy to boot, all chewing tobacco and bullshit drawl and mean pecker bronc-buster soul, eager as hell to kill somebody so he'd have a good story when he played bumper pool down at one of the nearby taverns.

Given all these problems, the escape went about as you'd expect.

The Chevy appeared, driving slow.

He sees it, starts drifting toward the highway.

The cowboy's way the hell down the row, shouldn't be any trouble.

But as soon as he cuts and runs, ass-over-appetite heading for the highway, the cowboy sees him and comes running.

The cowboy starts shooting.

Sounds like fucking World War III.

All he can do, running toward the highway, is weave left and weave right as he runs, hoping he's eluding the bullets.

Reaches the highway and trips.

Trips.

196

*Down on his hands and knees.*

*Three guys in ski-masks are now standing in the middle of the highway, returning the cowboy's fire.*

*He's a little out-gunned, the cowboy, with his CAR 15. They've got semi-automatic weapons.*

*Not until he crawls halfway across the highway, the air exploding with gunfire and gunsmoke and cursing, does he realize he's been wounded.*

*That's why he tripped.*

*He's bleeding badly.*

*Shit, is he going to make it?*

*Has all this been in vain?*

*Motherfucking cowboy, anyway. Why do they have to hire goons like that for prison guards?*

*And then he smiles: yeah, why don't they hire some real nice understanding liberal hand-wringers as prison guards?*

*Wouldn't that be nice?*

*He's in the back seat now, thinking all these things, blood all over him now, consciousness waning quickly, laughing to himself about his notion of hiring liberal hand-wringers.*

*And then he's pissing his pants.*

*And then he's crying.*

*And then he's freezing his ass off.*

*Never actually heard his teeth chatter before but that's exactly what they're doing now.*

*In prison one day, a would-be intellectual inmate said to him, 'You know, we're nothing more than blood and bones and shit and piss and come. Not one thing more.'*

*He never understood what the hell the guy was talking about.*

*Till now.*

*When he could feel various parts of his system shutting down, as if he were some vast complex engine that was ceasing to function.*

*Aw, shit. Please not now. Not after Rosamund worked so hard to put this together.*

*The three guys pile into the car, then.*

*Chevy hauls-ass away, squealing rubber and two or three metal-bang shots into the trunk of the car.*

*'You fucking asshole,' one of the guys says. He's hysterical.*

*'You killed two guards. All we was supposed to do was cover him so he could make a break for it.'*

*'We just gotta stay cool,' one of the other three in the front seat said.*

*'Yeah,' said a third voice, 'stay cool. Use our fucking heads and not panic.'*

*'They're gonna fry our ass for killin' a guard like that,' the hysterical one said. 'You just wait and see.'*

*But the talk fades as he plummets deeper into the darkness of pain and blood-loss and the breakdown of his human engine.*

*Deeper . . .*

# 12

'Are you sure you're up?'
  'I'm sure.'
  'I can always call back.'
  'No, Sheila, really, this is fine.'
  'I found out some things about Tolliver.'
  'I'm listening.'
Sunlight traced the edge of the motel room curtains. I'd set my travel alarm but dimly remembered stomping it into silence with the heel of my hand and then going back to sleep.
  But the intrepid Sheila Kelly was now going to make sure that I was awake.
  'You ready?'
  'I'm ready.'
  'He nearly went broke in 1963. He had been CEO of his father's trucking business for three years and the whole thing came tumbling down.'
  'But he made it?'
  'He'd fired a man named Farraday, a man who'd always been his father's right-hand man. You know how it is with young CEOs – they don't want any reminder of the previous regime.'
  'You think Farraday being fired hurt the company?'
  'No doubt about it. Farraday went all the way back to the beginning of the trucking industry, back when the Teamsters were still blowing up trucks that weren't registered to union members. This Farraday knew all the routes and all the federal regulations, and how to make money on what they call short hauls. In other words, he was a very important guy.'
  'And Junior fired him?'
  'Right. But then Junior must have had a religious conversion

199

because he hired him back at three times the salary.'

'Wow.'

'He also gave him ten percent of the net profits per annum.'

'Sounds like Farraday had really been mad about being canned.'

'Very, very angry. But since he now had ten percent of the company, he made it work again. He stayed there until he died of lymphatic cancer in 1979. By then, Junior had figured out how to run things himself. He was making a lot of money again.'

'How about his personal life?'

'A widower. His wife died in a sanitarium in 1983.'

'A mental hospital?'

'No. Some kind of fancy drying-out place for the idle rich. You know, people like you.'

'What was her name?'

'Kendra. She was a runway model in Chicago when Tolliver married her in 1958.'

'Any children?'

'One. A boy named Craig.'

'Tolliver said he's dead.'

'He is. And guess how he died?'

'How?'

'In a prison escape.'

'Tolliver had a son who was in prison?'

'Second-degree murder. Really cut up this sixteen-year-old girl. They found what was left of her in chunks and pieces buried next to a river. Tolliver had to use all his money and influence to get the charge reduced to second-degree.'

'He didn't try insanity?'

'Oh, he tried, but the district attorney wouldn't go for it. Or did I mention this wasn't Tolliver's home state? He might be important in Iowa but not in Illinois. Anyway, Tolliver tried to get Craig declared insane and put in a state mental hospital but the DA wasn't buying and neither was the judge nor jury. Tolliver's people finally had to plead him guilty of second-degree.'

'How long was he in before he escaped?'

'Three and a half years. But there's something else.'

'What?'

'You remember that word you asked me about, "Conmarck?" '

'Right.'

'That's the name of the town where the prison is located. It's in Illinois.'

'Wow. Then Vic knew something about the escape.'

'Vic?'

'Remember the Nora I told you about?'

'The one who claimed to be Tolliver's daughter, right?'

'Right. She had this assistant named Vic. He's the one who used the word.'

'Well, Conmarck was where Craig died, anyway. Three guys were supposed to cover him while he ran from a soybean field but one of them killed a guard. Craig was shot in the crossfire, and he died in the back seat of the getaway car. His three friends died a few miles further on in a shootout with a Highway Patrol helicopter.'

'So there's a connection between Nora and Vic and Tolliver after all . . .'

'What?'

'Just thinking out loud, Sheila. Sorry. You've really earned your money.'

'I just hope it helps.'

'It helps a lot. Send the bill to my Charlesville address.'

'If you need something else, let me know.'

'I will, Sheila, and thanks again.'

# 13

'And here's the old biplane that Curtis Lefler built,' Herb Carson said an hour and a half later, as he finished giving us the tour of his aviation museum.

Curtis Lefler was another Iowa flying legend, having built this and half a dozen other pioneering airplanes in his father's garage.

So far this morning, we'd seen several planes, including a very rare Whitey Sport with its 55-horsepower LeBlond engine, but this was the one I fancied.

Seeing it there in the sparkling sunlight, with a cloudless blue sky like this one, recalled the days of the barnstormers, men and women (there were a lot more female barnstormers than is commonly believed) who bought used WWI planes from the US Government then went all over the countryside setting up air shows at carnivals and county fairs, or putting down in a field and taking people for a ride for $3.75 a head.

'She's a beauty, isn't she?' Herb said. He looked older than the last time I'd seen him and that was a sad realization. I was at the age when most of my heroes were dying on me, Herb among them. In his blue turtleneck and jeans, his white hair burred military-style, his skinny frame bent now with age, he looked like the last of the barnstormers surveying a world that no longer knew what to do with him.

'She sure is a beauty,' Jane Avery said, then turned back to me. 'Is this the biplane we're going up in?'

'It sure is.'

The plane before us was an old Travel Air, one of the first biplanes used by adventurous businessmen back in the 1920s. With a double cockpit and red paint, it still looked jaunty all these years later.

'Great,' she said.

Herb grinned. 'Always like to see somebody respond to a baby like this one. Does my old heart good. You get ready. I'll go prop her.'

I looked at Jane. 'You all right?'

She shrugged. 'Just a little nervous.'

'We'll be fine.'

'I know. It's just—'

I smiled, leaned in and touched her hand. 'Everybody gets nervous. That's part of the whole process.'

She grinned. 'You're really a damn nice guy, you know that? Most of the time, anyway.'

We stood next to the plane, which smelled of sunlight and oil and the worn leather interior.

'Bet you wish you lived back then,' Jane said, 'with the barnstormers.'

'I sure do.'

'I can see you doing that, actually. There's something old-fashioned about you.' She squinted at me in the sunlight. 'That's why it's so hard to imagine you working for the FBI. All that cloak and dagger.'

'And yet it's something I believe in. That's why I did it.'

We walked around the plane, taking another close look, two people in a farmfield in the middle of Iowa on a lovely spring day.

For the next twenty minutes, we gave her a complete mechanical check-up, Herb and I, and then the three of us pushed her out to the small patch of runway and Jane and I climbed in.

'Wish I was going along,' Herb shouted, just before he took the propeller and rotated it so that we could get the oil circulated through the engine.

While he was doing that, I was turning on the magneto, which is similar to popping the clutch in a car. Then Jane and I pulled down our goggles.

The plane roared into being, Jane and I waved goodbye, and then I proceeded to do all the subtle things an old craft like this demands.

Then we were airborne.

Only from the air can you appreciate how right Grant Wood

was, in the way he painted Iowa, the rolling countryside, the checkerboard topography.

'This is great!' Jane shouted.

'Not scared?'

'Not at all!'

I gave her the grand tour, skimming low along a winding blue river, tracking between two looming clay cliffs, doing a modified roll and then following a forest of pine and hardwood that stretched for miles.

We were up high enough – but not too high – to enjoy the benefits of temperature inversions which, on a day like this one, kept the mercury at 60 degrees.

'Do another roll!' she shouted. 'That was great!'

I'd made a convert and to celebrate that fact, I did another roll. People always worry about falling out but between the strap you wear and centrifugal force, you're actually pretty safe.

I was just taking the plane down lower when I noticed where we were at, just above the Brindle farm where the bodies of Nora and Vic had been discovered.

I also noticed something else.

A blue four-door Toyota sedan was just pulling out of the barn at the rear.

It moved quickly down the gravel drive and out to the gravel road, and then headed swiftly back to town.

I recognized the car, of course. It once belonged to Sam Lodge.

I had a good idea who was driving it now.

'How about one more roll?' Jane shouted, seeming not to make anything special of the blue Toyota.

'You're crazy!' I laughed.

And then decided to put the plane into the kind of roll that both of us would remember for a long, long time.

This time, Jane even screamed a little bit, the way boys and girls do at county fairs their first time up on the Ferris wheel.

After we'd said goodbye to Herb and were walking back to our respective cars, Jane said, 'Did you see that blue Toyota at the Brindle farm?'

I smiled. 'I was hoping you didn't.'

'Are we competing on this case?' She sounded angry.

I wanted to tell her everything, especially about Melissa McNally being kidnapped, but I knew better.

'No,' I said. 'We're not competing.'

She stared at me for a long time. 'This is kind of a confusing situation. And it's my fault, because I'm the one who's let it become confusing.'

'What's confusing about it?'

'I want to take you down to the station and make you tell me everything you know.'

'That's natural enough. You're the Chief of Police.'

'But I also want to invite you over for another meal tonight. Maybe some tacos or something. On me.'

'Well, why don't I come over about eight and we'll talk about how confusing everything is.'

'I don't know, Robert. I just don't know.'

We stood there and looked at each other for a time. There was nothing to say and I knew better than to try and touch her in any way.

I gave her a little nod, got in my car, and drove away.

# 14

The historians of Cedar Rapids love to tell the story of the man who built the town's first log cabin back in 1838.

His name was Osgood Sheperd. While most town histories love to extol the noble virtues of their first citizens, the folks in Cedar Rapids delight in revealing that Osgood was, among things, the town's first tavern-owner and a horse-thief.

In the early 1840s, the enterprising Osgood converted his cabin on the river's edge to a drinking establishment, which was perfect for those people who wanted to get drunk before they forded the river.

As with most such places, the tavern soon attracted its own group of cronies, among whom were several horse-thieves.

Apparently, old Osgood became a part of the gang himself after the tavern was closed down thanks to pressure from responsible civic leaders. He subsequently drifted to another state and took up the noble calling of horse-stealing.

Unfortunately, Osgood wasn't nearly as good at it as his cronies were. He was caught, and hanged by the neck until dead.

From the northernmost bluffs, Cedar Rapids looks like a picture-book city. The downtown area, abandoned by merchants who could no longer fight the fight with the shopping malls on either edge of the city, is now home to several new buildings. After complete refurbishment, it is now a business center, with stocks and bonds developments, insurance and law offices, fund raisers and research companies. And enough BMWs to make you think that Ronald Reagan is still in office.

I drove right on through, the place I was looking for being in a somewhat less pricey neighborhood, one of those that the Chamber of Commerce keeps trying to will out of existence.

325 River Street was an aged concrete block building that had probably started life as a corner grocery store. It was now boarded up, covered with some rather uninspired graffiti, and surrounded by a sidewalk that was littered with so much broken glass and dog shit it looked like an obstacle course.

I parked and got out.

Except for 325, this half of the block was nothing but a large grassy vacant lot. Down on the far corner, two young black men stood watching me. They were probably wondering why anybody who didn't absolutely need to, would enter a neighborhood like this.

I walked around 325 twice, looking for some kind of peek-hole for a glimpse inside. Nothing.

I walked down to the end of the block and the two young men. The closer I got, the older they looked. By the time I reached them, they looked a lot older, mid-twenties probably, which made their worn-backwards baseball caps seem like a wistful affectation meant to bring back their youth.

'Morning,' I said.

They were a perfect Mutt and Jeff, one tall and rangy, one short and squat. Or Bud and Lou, if you prefer.

They nodded, said nothing.

'You live around here?'

The squat one grinned. 'No, man, we live down to those penthouses along the river. We jus' come over here 'cause the scenery's so beautiful.'

'I guess it was a dumb question,' I said, grinning back.

'You a cop?' said the tall one.

'Nope.'

'You look like a cop. The new kind.'

'There's a new kind?'

'Sure. Them college boys. They's real polite, man, till they gets you in the back seat. Then they kick the shit out of you jus' like the old kind.'

'They fuckin' busted us for no fuckin' reason last Saturday night,' said the squat one. 'They jus' had a hard-on to bust them some niggers and we happened to be the ones they found. All we was doin' was walkin' down the street. Tha's all we was doin'.'

'An' this'z what I got for it,' said the short one. He took off his ball cap and showed me a half-inch cut on the left side of his forehead. It was red and blue, the wound, against copper-colored skin.

'Like we don't have no fuckin' right to walk down the street, man,' said his friend.

Hard to tell. Two sides to everything. You sit down with the police officers who busted them and you'd likely hear that these two guys looked suspicious, late at night, shambling down the street, possibly drunk, possibly doped up, and who knew what they were up to? Better to be safe than sorry and all that. So they busted them. And the short one got mouthy. And one of the cops hit him, nothing serious because if it had been anything serious these two would have gotten themselves a lawyer by now and instituted some giant-ass suit against the city. Just doing their jobs, the cops were, at least that's how they'd see it, and tell you about it.

While, of course, these two young men had a very different version of what had happened.

'You know much about that place?' I said to the short one.

'What place? That building down there?'

'Yes. 325.'

He shrugged. Glanced at his friend. Grinned. 'Used to be like the place to go when we was kids and wanted some grass or beer or somethin'. Real good hidin' place.'

'Have you seen people go in and out lately?'

Another glance, another grin.

'You sure you ain't a cop?' the short one said.

'I'm not. Honest.'

The tall one shrugged. 'The white Lincoln.'

'What?'

'White Lincoln. Guy always wheels in here real early in the morning, two, three in the morning, but I ain't seen him for a long time.'

'Did you ever get a look at the guy driving the Lincoln?'

'Not a good one.'

'So you're not even sure it is a guy?'

'Huh?'

'Could be a woman.'

He shrugged again.

'Could be,' said the short one.

'And he goes inside?'

'Right.'

'How long does he stay?'

The tall one shrugged. 'Man, we're usually asleep by then. Our wives, man, they kick our butts if we stayed out that late.'

'So the guy in the Lincoln could stay all night.'

'Could be,' the tall one said.

'Thanks,' I said, nodding to them.

'That's all you wanted?' the short one said.

I smiled. 'That's all I wanted. See, I told you I wasn't a cop.'

The padlock was a bitch to get open. Took fifteen minutes.

I got the back door free and stood in the dark doorway. I wrinkled up my nose as the odors hit me. The high tart tang of blood; the sour-sweet smell of bodily waste.

With great reluctance, I went inside, remembering a Cairo garage I'd entered one day looking for an informant that the Agency wanted to protect. I found him, all right, along with three or four of his friends, chopped up and piled inside a closet. It took several weeks of showers before I felt clean again.

I got the light on. The place was one big room with three smaller rooms off to the right. The big room had an auxiliary battery and video equipment and a large cardboard box shoved into one corner.

I went over and looked into the box. I found wigs and black leather sex masks and handcuffs and women's panties. I also found spiked belts and chains. The chains were dark and sticky with blood. There were also pieces of wound cloth that had obviously been used as gags.

I didn't have to wonder what kind of videos were being shot here.

Two of the three small rooms looked to have been storage areas at one time. Now they held small cots and an impromptu make-up table complete with round theatrical mirror. Somebody had written 'Pussy' in the middle of it with red lipstick long ago dried out. A lone Polaroid lay on the table, shriveled like an autumn leaf. I picked it up and stared at it. There was a girl, no more than eight, naked and with her legs parted wide, spreading her sex for the camera. It was going to take an awful lot of showers to make me feel clean this time.

The third of the rooms was where I found the blood and the excrement, the blood splashed all over the walls, the way slaughter houses sometimes look, the floor covered with large feces of the human variety. This is the way a lot of jail cells look in Latin America, after prisoners have been held there for a month, and have been beaten regularly during the process.

Somebody had been held prisoner here. No doubt about it.

The air was dead and stifling in the small dusty room; cobwebs sticky to touch. The lone window high on the wall was pebbled glass to begin with. Filth made it even more opaque. You could hear screams echoing in here, what it must have been like for whomever had been kept here, shitting on the floor, clawing at the door like a sick animal. About knee-high on the door you could see fingernail scratches. She'd probably pleaded with them. *Please please please*. I wondered how old she'd been, or rather they'd been. Plural. There'd surely been many more than one here over the months designated on the rent receipts. Somebody's little daughter; somebody's little sister.

I went back out to the main room and looked around again. A few dozen businesses had probably been housed in this place over the past forty or fifty years – a few dozen dashed hopes of the small business person – until it had spiraled ignominiously down to this, a place where children were exploited for reasons of greed and some dark and unimaginable predilection of the human spirit.

A white Lincoln, I thought. A white Lincoln.

# 15

When I stopped by the motel office to check for any messages, a woman I hadn't seen before said, 'You've got a visitor.'

'Oh?'

'He said he wanted to surprise you.'

'He did? I see.'

'It's your father.'

'My father?' My father had died fourteen years ago.

'He's in your room. Waiting.'

'Thanks.'

At the door, I put my ear to the wood and listened. No sound. I pushed the door open and went inside.

He sat in the same chair he'd been in the other day. He wore a blue sport coat and gray slacks and a white button-down shirt without a tie. His white hair almost glowed in the sunlight streaming through the door.

'I hope you don't mind,' he said.

I closed the door behind me.

'I've decided to tell you the truth,' he said.

'I see.'

'Or aren't you interested?'

'Oh, I'm interested. If that's what I'm going to hear. The truth, I mean.'

He smiled. 'I don't blame you for being cynical. In your line of work, I don't imagine you hear the truth very often.'

'Are you going to start by telling me about your son being in prison?'

The smile again. 'I should have figured that a resourceful man like you would have done some checking on me.'

'He died in a prison escape.'

211

This time the smile was bleak. 'He died a long time before that, Mr Hokanson. A very long time before that.'

'I don't understand.'

'I'm speaking spiritually, Mr Hokanson. Spiritually, he died a long time before that.' His fingers touched a manilla envelope placed across his lap and he leaned forward, fixed me with a painful gaze and began the following story . . .

'One day I came home from work – this would have been back in the early sixties when my son was probably nine or ten – and I saw my wife in the kitchen with our Mexican maid. They were arguing. I'd never seen my wife, who had always been a frail and quiet woman, this angry before. Then my wife slapped the maid. I couldn't believe it. My wife just wasn't a physical person. She hated *machismo* in particular – you know, settling arguments with physical force.

'The maid was in tears and ran out of the kitchen. I went over to my wife. She seemed to be in some kind of trance. I wasn't even sure that she knew I was standing next to her. I tried to touch her but she jerked away from me. Upstairs, I could hear the maid opening and slamming doors. Then she came downstairs carrying her bags and went out the side door to her car. She had a little VW Bug of which she was very proud.

'I asked my wife why they'd been arguing but she wouldn't even look at me. I really did wonder if she was in some kind of trance.

'And then without a word, she left the kitchen and went upstairs to her room.

'I just stood there looking out the window at Maria, the maid, backing her VW out, and then pulling away. I never saw her again.

'I was just about to go upstairs, and try to get my wife to talk to me, when I noticed the blood on the top of the stairs leading to the basement.

'It was very dark, and there was this iron-y odor to it.

'I knew enough to be afraid – knew enough to sense that I was about to find something that I would be better off not knowing – but I couldn't help myself.

'I went over and turned the basement lights on and followed

the blood all the way downstairs.

'Six months earlier, we'd had new floor tiles laid, the same kind that we had on the stairs, an amber color, and the blood was very stark against them. There was a lot of it, the blood I mean.

'The basement had been turned into several rooms, one of which was my son's "den" as we called it. He had his TV, his stereo and all his comic books down there. He was a great comic book collector.

'That was when I saw the first piece of flesh, just outside his door, flesh and white hair soaked with blood.

'I knew right away what I was looking at. A few weeks previously, my son had stopped by a pet shop and found these two rabbits he really liked. He called them Dean and Jerry. He loved Jerry Lewis movies. He kept the rabbits in a large cage in his den.

'You can guess what had happened.

'Craig had killed the rabbits. And not cleanly. He didn't just shoot them, or put a blade into their hearts. From the pieces I saw, and especially from the way their eyes gaped when I found their decapitated heads, I realized that he had tortured them first and then started cutting them up into chunks while they were still alive.

'Later that night, I learned what the argument between my wife and Maria had been about. Maria had found the rabbits and gone to my wife and told her that Craig had killed them. My wife absolutely refused to believe this. Of course, this wasn't the first time we'd had troubles with Craig. When he was eight, he'd been playing with a little girl he'd invited home from school. He was out in the old barn – this was when we lived outside of Des Moines – and he'd taken a hammer and nail and nailed her to the ground. Even at that age, he was smart enough to gag her so we wouldn't hear her cries.

'We sent him away to a school where he spent half his time with psychiatrists and the other half on his school work. But even then my wife wouldn't admit that there was anything fundamentally wrong with Craig. She always said it was just a "stage" he was going through. She also clung to the idea that Craig didn't fit the general profile of disturbed young boys. We'd never brutalized him – we were very obedient disciples of Dr Spock and didn't even spank him – and we certainly expressed our love to him. I spent at least a dozen hours a week doing all the things you see fathers in movies do – we played baseball, we went fishing, we rode horses.

'But Craig was never much interested in anything I suggested. He didn't hate us exactly, but he certainly didn't love us either, not in any way we understood.

'When he was sixteen and home for the summer and adamant about us letting him get his driver's license and giving him a car, he brought a girl home to walk down by the lake on the east end of our property.

'I woke up in the middle of the night. I heard somebody screaming and I threw on some clothes and ran out of the house. I knew I shouldn't call the police; I don't know how I knew, I just did.

'He had her tied to a tree and stripped completely naked. He was cutting her with a switchblade. She had a gag on but it must have slipped off for a few moments and that's how I heard her scream.

'He wasn't killing her; he was marking her up for life.

'I knocked him out. It took a rock to do it – he was a very slight boy but he had incredible strength and energy – and I got both of them up to the house.

'After that, my wife didn't have any choice but to see Craig for what he was. We were able to settle a great deal of money on the girl and her parents to keep them quiet but we had Craig committed to a sanitarium right after that.

'He stayed four months, and then escaped. Believe me, people had been trying for twenty years to escape from that place but nobody before or since Craig had been able to.

'We had no idea where he went but about eight months after he escaped – and by this time, his mother herself was in very serious therapy, and she was also drinking a lot – about eight months afterward, we started getting Polaroid photos of girls who were eight to twelve years old . . . and they were cut up and sexually mutilated beyond belief.

'There was never any note. Just the photos.

'After the sixth photograph, each of a different girl – and we always knew who was sending them – his mother overdosed on gin and barbiturates.

214

'I was in Phoenix at the time.

'Craig didn't come back for the funeral.

'In fact, I didn't hear from him again for two years.

'You know the way I heard from him again?

'More Polaroid photos started arriving.

'Very young girls again. Tortured and maimed in ways I can't ever quite get out of my mind.

'He was going all over the country – just the way Ted Bundy did – slaughtering young girls.

'I wanted to stop him – I wanted to tell the police what was going on, but I . . . couldn't. I came very close, but then I . . . couldn't.

'Pride, I suppose, though I hate to think I'm that selfish and venal.

'Anyway, one day I got a letter from a law firm I'd never heard of. Out-of-state.

'Craig was being tried for several crimes unrelated to the murders. I flew up to see him. I hardly recognized my son. There was such a . . . strange . . . aspect to his face. If I said diabolical, that would sound very melodramatic, wouldn't it? But that's the only way I can describe it. He was handsome – very handsome, yet even being around him made me nervous.

'He asked me for help but I turned him down. I told him that he was going where be belonged. He was very angry. He cursed me.

'I didn't see him for years after that. He wrote me a few letters but I burned them. His lawyers would call from time to time and ask me if I'd go visit him but I said no. I no longer wanted to see him.

'Some time later, his lawyers wrote me and told me about his relationship with this woman who had apparently fallen in love with him in prison. They told me she was planning to marry Craig.

'I checked her out. She'd been in and out of mental hospitals most of her life. Ravishingly beautiful but totally unable to deal with life. She lived on a huge trust fund from an old San Francisco banking family. This wasn't the first time she'd married inmates. She'd done it twice before Craig.

'Then came the escape, when Craig was killed.

'I brought him back to Iowa and buried him. And that was that. Or so I thought, anyway.'

'So you thought?' I said.

'So I thought.'

'Other things happened?'

He sat in his chair, a prim, composed man who looked uncomfortable sharing secrets.

'The photos,' he said eventually.

'The dead girls?'

'Yes.'

'They started arriving again?'

'Yes. I burned each one right after it arrived, but there were always more coming.'

'Who was sending them?'

'I assumed this woman, the one you met as Nora.'

'You assumed?'

'Who else would be sending them? Who else would have known what my son was doing?'

'I guess that's a good point.'

'And then someone broke into my house and stole some things from my office. Nothing very valuable – just some records relating to Craig.'

'And you assumed the thief was Nora, too?'

'At first, but I hired an investigator, one recommended to me by a judge on the California supreme court.'

'And he learned what?'

'He learned that Craig hadn't died.'

'*What?*'

'I know – that's how I reacted at first, too. With total disbelief. Oh, he'd been badly injured, but then this woman decided to take advantage of the situation. She paid off all the right people – remember, she had a great deal of wealth to draw on – and his death was faked with the help of the prison doctor. The investigator secretly had Craig's grave opened up and found that it was empty except for a few heavy sacks of feed.'

'Was Craig with Nora?'

He shook his head. 'No. The investigator learned that they'd spent eight months in Mexico together where Craig had had a

216

series of operations involving plastic surgery. He bore no resemblance to the old Craig.'

'Did the investigator get a photo of the new Craig?'

'No. He didn't have time. Right after returning from Mexico, the investigator was murdered.'

'By Craig, you think?'

'Who else?'

'Why did Nora contact me?'

He shrugged. 'According to my investigators, Craig was tired of her. He wanted to get as far away as possible from her. So he came back to Iowa.'

'And where is he now?'

'Here.'

'In town?'

He nodded. 'In town.' He took the manilla envelope from his lap and held it up to me. 'The last investigator found three men who could possibly be Craig – men who showed up here four years ago, just about the time when Craig was running from his lady friend, men who have very hazy pasts.'

'What's in the envelope?'

'Background on the three men.'

'Who are they?'

'Reverend Roberts, Kenny Deihl, and Richard McNally.'

'You're sure one of them is your son?'

'Positive. The last three letters I got from him were postmarked from here. And that's very like Craig. To taunt me like this: dare me to come and get him.' The bleak smile again. 'Find him, Mr Hokanson. For everybody's sake – *find him*.'

217

# Five

# 1

An hour later, I was driving past the New Hope town square. The temperature had dropped several degrees since I'd left, and the sun had vanished completely, leaving a gray sky that was boiling with storm clouds to the west.

Even though all I could think of was the white Lincoln the two black men had described, I needed to stop by and see Eve McNally first. I wanted to know about her daughter and if she'd heard anything from her husband. I was beginning to suspect how McNally and Sam Lodge fitted in with the good Reverend.

After leaving the small shopping area, I swung left to pick up an asphalt drive that would take me straight to the north-east edge of town, where Eve McNally lived.

The sky was getting so dark, several oncoming cars turned on their headlights. Then the rain came, spits and fits at first, increasing to a rumbling grumbling downpour.

I heard the siren before I saw the spinning red cherry, then I noticed my speedometer: I was traveling at 46 mph in a 35 mph zone.

I pulled over on the shoulder of the road, set the gear in neutral, heeled on the hand brake.

It was a long minute before anybody got out of the squad car behind me. In the downpour, it was hard to make out any face, just a person with a campaign hat and a fold-up plastic raincoat on.

I watched the cop approach in my rearview mirror. Then the mirror was empty.

Where had the cop gone?

Knuckles rapped the window on the passenger side. A finger pointed to the door lock. I leaned over and unlocked it.

The cop got in, smelling of rain and chilly but very fresh air.

'You were speeding.'

'I'll say one thing, getting stopped by a cop as pretty as you is a real pleasure.'

'Yeah, I look great in this campaign hat,' Jane Avery grinned. 'Like Smokey the Bear's daughter.'

'You look fine to me.'

'I saw you coming in from the highway.'

'Yeah.'

'So you were out of town?'

'Uh-huh.'

'You going to tell me about it?'

'Boy, you're really relentless.'

'Your friend Karl in the hospital?'

'Yeah?'

'He died this morning.'

I looked through the steamy window at the rain. It danced like bouncing nail-heads on the asphalt. Headlights appeared and faded, appeared and faded, in fog and rain.

'Something terrible's happening to me,' she said after our mutual silence.

'Yeah? What?'

'I'm starting to like you.'

'Well, for what it's worth, I'm starting to like you, too.'

'But I can't trust you and that scares me.'

'Of course you can trust me.'

'Then you'll tell me what's going on? Who Eleanor Saunders was, and who Karl was, and what's the matter with Eve McNally?'

'This doesn't have anything to do with trust – not in the way you mean it.' I turned toward her in the seat. Her eyes looked more hurt than angry – she really was taking this personally, as perhaps I would, too – and her otherwise full mouth was pursed tight. 'This isn't personal, the reason why I'm not confiding in you. It's professional – and there's a difference.'

Now it was her turn to stare silently out the window.

'I saw Joanna Lodge,' she said after a while.

'Did you ask her why she was out at the Brindle farm this morning?'

'She gave me a reason but not a very believable one. She said she felt like going for a walk in the country and that the Brindle place was nice because it was deserted.'

'You're right. Not very believable.'

'She wasn't any more cooperative than you've been. She knows what's really going on, too. That's you and Eve McNally and now Joanna Lodge. Who else knows except me?'

I sighed. 'You're making this harder than it has to be.'

'I'm a cop. A good one, I think, at least a dedicated one. I need to know what's happening in my town. And you can tell me.'

I shook my head and said, in barely a whisper: 'No, I can't, Jane. No, I can't.'

She stared at me silently for a moment and then announced, 'I think we'd better skip tonight.'

'I was afraid you were going to say that.'

'Do you blame me?'

'I guess not.'

She put her hand on the door handle, opened it up a few inches. Rain hissed. The air was cold. 'I had some real hope for us. I really did.'

I was going to say something soothing but she was gone, slamming the door before I could form the right words.

If there were any right words.

# 2

*The plain pure smell of it, of human flesh as it rotted . . . Sometimes he would dip his head down into the darkness below and let his entire consciousness be suffused with the odors. And in the frenzy of it he would touch himself, that was all it took at moments such as these, he'd touch himself and know an orgasmic ecstasy none of the women, not even the dead ones, had been able to give him. Nor was there any pity or scorn or smirk in the air because he had failed them and failed himself – the charge of orgasm was perfect, blinding, all-encompassing emotionally as well as sexually.*

*He watched as they scrambled and scurried below. Sometimes they even climbed high up on the ladder, their claws digging into the wood . . .*

*He felt a oneness with the universe, a calmness, tranquility, wholeness – feelings he had never known before until the past few years.*

*But now somebody was threatening this. Nobody had known anything until the man who called himself Hokanson had shown up here a few days ago. And didn't the ladies all love him, the sonofabitch. And you could bet that he didn't have any problems in bed, putting the hard cock right to them and riding them for hours if he wanted to.*

*This was all he had, the corpses and their smells, and now it was in serious jeopardy.*

*Hokanson had everything he wanted . . .*

*Just now he caught a glimpse of himself reflected in a window.*

*And smiled.*

*Weren't appearances deceiving?*

*Somebody looked like one thing but they were actually quite another.*

224

*'Boys will be girls, and girls will be boys'*

*God, he hadn't heard 'Lola' in years . . .*

*He had to do what was necessary with Hokanson. Had to – and right away. Before Hokanson figured everything out and destroyed this little paradise . . .*

*He walked out into the rain, liking the cold clean bite of it, liking the way it cleared his senses, liking the contrast of its chills with the hot jism in his underwear . . .*

*Fucking Hokanson, anyway.*

*Things had been going so well . . .*

*He got his car started and went in search of the only man standing between himself and his continued happiness.*

# 3

'Joanna?'

'Yes?'

'It's Jim Hokanson.'

Pause. 'I really don't want to talk to you any more. I shouldn't have flirted with you yesterday. Now Sam's dead and what kind of memories do I have? That I wanted to go to bed with somebody else on the very day my husband is murdered.'

'I think I know who killed him.'

'Are you serious?'

'Yes.'

'Jane Avery was here. She seems to think that I know something about the murder, but I don't.'

'I'd like to come over there in a little while and look through your husband's office.'

'For what?'

'At this point, I'm not really sure. But I'll know it if I see it.'

'I haven't been a very good wife,' she said suddenly.

And of course I thought of Eve McNally, and her notion that she hadn't been a very good mother.

But all I said was, 'I'll see you in a little while.'

No white Lincolns in the drive. No lights on in the windows of the house on the hill behind.

I pulled up in front of the church, left my car running, and ran up to the double front doors. Locked. I stood for a moment under the porch roof watching the rain in all its drab fury. I didn't especially want to run back out into it. I hadn't been a good boy. I'd brought neither my rubbers nor my raincoat. But finally I had no choice.

I ran back to my car, feeling the rain pound and soak my back.

There were a few puddles already formed, and these soaked my shoes. I'm one of those people who can stay calm about having an arm broken but let me sense a head cold coming on and I get very uptight, even surly. I hate being unwell in any way.

I got inside the car and aimed it up the hill to the house. The gravel was chunky. I kept fish-tailing.

This time I shut off my engine. Before getting out, I opened the glove compartment and removed my Ruger, dropping it into my jacket pocket.

Even in the hard cold rain, the two-story Spanish-style house was imposing and attractive, the smooth texture of the white stucco exterior contrasting nicely with the roughness of the red tile on the various planes of the roof. It was a *nouveau riche* dwelling, and one with no apologies to the more modest standards of the community.

Nobody answered my knock.

I walked down the side steps to the double garage and peered inside. Both white Lincolns were gone.

I went back to the front door and tried knocking again. Nothing happened this time, either, except that I got a little wetter.

I made my way back to my car and was just opening the door when the first bullet shattered the glass of the driver's window.

I haven't been shot at many times in my life. Despite a few feats of derring-do, most of my Agency work was conducted at a desk in the wilds of Virginia, where the most murderous people you'll find are reporters in search of another Agency scandal.

My first reaction was that I must somehow be wrong. A shot? No. Something else.

Then the second shot came and I knew I wasn't wrong at all.

I dove into the car, slamming my knee hard against the steering wheel as I did so, and lay flat on the front seat.

Two, three more bullets came in quick succession. Windows imploded into dense spider webs.

Whoever he was, he was a good shot. He had to be hiding down behind a corner of the church. He also had to have a pretty high-powered rifle.

I was huddled inside a cocoon of myself – all bad nerves and fear and anger and sudden heavy sweat.

227

Oh yes – and panting. I sounded like a big old sheepdog on a very hot day.

Then, nothing. I lay there rubbing my sore knee, listening to the tinny sound of the rain on my car roof and hood.

I don't know how long it was before I heard an aged truck grinding up the gravel hill to the house.

I very cautiously sat up, peered down the hill.

The killer was long gone, of course. No sign of him at all.

The truck had G&H MARKET written on the side of its doors. It was a white Chevy that had to be a quarter-century old. The gear box sounded awful.

A white-haired man pulled it up to the garage and the door to the side, braked noisily and shut off the engine.

He walked slowly over to me in the rain, his watery blue eyes fixed on the bullet webs in the windows. He wore blue and white striped Osh-Kosh overalls and had a pipe stuck in the corner of his mouth. He walked with a slight limp.

'I was right. Them was gunshots I heard,' he said, examining the bullet holes more carefully.

'Yes,' I said. 'You were right.'

'You called the law?'

'Not yet.'

He grinned. 'If I was you, I'd be in taking a good long piss. I was in the South Pacific in World War Two and every time the Jap fire would get close to me, I'd piss my pants. Wasn't ashamed to admit it, either. No, sir, I sure wasn't.' He paused, examined the spider webs again. 'You got any idea who it was?'

'Nope.'

He shook his head then looked at the house. 'They home?'

'I don't think so.'

'Hell, she just called me two hours ago and told me to get her order out here as fast as I could.'

'Sorry.'

'Between you and me, she's kind of a bitch, anyway. High and mighty, you know.' Shook his head. 'I probably shouldn't say that about her, with her cancer and all, but that's how she strikes me.'

I thought of what Mindy had told me, about the good Reverend faking his wife's cancer as a means of raising money.

I decided not to disillusion the old guy.

I leaned forward and started my car. 'Guess I better head back to town.'

'Good thing the rain's let up.'

As, suddenly, it had, not much more than a sprinkle now.

'Yeah,' I said, 'good thing.'

I waved goodbye to him and drove off.

# 4

Eve came to the door after three knocks and peered out through the screening. This afternoon her facial bruises looked even worse, discolored streaks of purple and yellow on left forehead, right cheek, left jawline.

'Have you heard anything about your daughter?'

She shook her head. 'I think she's dead.'

She needed somebody to talk to. I felt guilty for not having more time.

'I found out some things this morning, Eve. I think I'm finally figuring out what's going on. I also think that I know who may have kidnapped her, and why.'

She touched a trembling hand to her face and started bitterly crying. 'You know one time, what I did one time, I mean?'

I couldn't take it. I quietly opened the screen door and stepped inside and took her in my arms and held her. She was very near the edge. Very near.

'I got mad at her one time and I slapped her right across the face. She couldn't've been more'n five years old. And I slapped her right across the face. I just keep thinkin' about that now, how I treated her when she was so little. What a terrible mother I've been to her.'

Her sobs came in small eruptions now and she choked on words the way a small child does who is crying too hard to speak intelligibly.

'You've been a good mother, Eve. You've got to stop thinking that way.'

She had to cry herself out.

I led her over to the couch and plumped up a couple of throw pillows then found the bedroom and dragged out a blanket and got her covered up. In the bathroom, I filled a glass with cold water and snagged the Excedrin bottle. Sara, the sweet golden retriever, followed me back into the living room and gave Eve three affectionate laps with a big pink loving tongue and then went over on the far side of the room and sat and watched all the human stuff going on.

I got three tablets down Eve and said, 'Have you eaten breakfast yet?'

She shook her head, her cheeks red and rough from her tears. Her eyes were watery and forlorn.

'I really have been a terrible mother. You just don't know. Gabbin' on the phone when I should've been spendin' time with her. Bowlin' with the girls when I could've been taking her places.'

I knelt next to her and said, 'We aren't perfect, Eve, and it's too much to expect we ever will be. All we can do is try.'

She looked at me and said, 'Maybe he's dead, too.'

'Your husband?'

'Uh-huh.'

'So you haven't heard from him?'

She shook her head.

I took a washcloth I'd run lukewarm water over and laid it gently across her forehead. She smelled of tears.

'I'll check back with you later this afternoon,' I said.

'I wish my husband was like you.'

I smiled. 'That's a nice compliment but you don't know me very well.'

'I know you enough.'

'Well, I know you enough, too. And you're a very decent woman. And a very good mother.'

I kissed her on the cheek. 'I need to ask you something, Eve. And you've got to tell me the truth.'

She looked at me tearily and nodded.

'Has your husband come into some money over the past few years?'

She nodded.

'A lot of it?'

She paused. 'Well, a lot for us, anyways.' She nodded to the new furnishings and the new TV. 'And then he bought a brand-new Ford and paid cash for it. He's in trouble, isn't he?'

'I'm afraid he could be, Eve.'

'I knew he was. But I was afraid to think it was true.'

She had angled her head away, was getting trapped in her own despair again.

'Did your husband ever work for Reverend Roberts?'

She turned back to me, tried to read my face. 'This has something to do with Reverend Roberts?'

'Not necessarily,' I lied. 'But I'm curious.'

'Well, sure, he used to have a kind of cleaning service on the side.'

'What kind of cleaning service?'

'Oh, you know, clean rich people's houses.'

'But Reverend Roberts has a maid.'

'Richard didn't clean the house. He cleaned the church.'

'I see. How about Sam Lodge?'

The eyes searching my face again. 'How'd you know about him?'

'Lucky guess.'

And it was.

'Well, Richard, he used to clean the Lodges' house, with their antiques and all. Then Lodge started inviting Richard to go along on his antique trips, help carry the heavy stuff. It wasn't too long after this that he started . . . well, being unfaithful. I could smell the other women on him. And now he's gotten Melissa kidnapped.'

She broke again.

I leaned over and put the fresh side of the washcloth on her forehead and held her hands as she gave into her tears, her entire body shaking.

'I was such a shitty mother.'

'C'mon, now, Eve. You know better than that. You really do.'

'You don't know. You just don't know. All the times I could've spent time with her and—'

Then she fell to crying again.

Sara, as if understanding that Eve needed great care and fondness, trotted over and gave her a few more love licks on her teary cheeks.

Eve laughed through her tears. 'Good old Sara.'

'She sure is,' I said.

Eve looked up at me, a sad stricken glance. 'Please find my daughter. Please. You don't know how bad I wanted to call Jane Avery. But I can't. So you're my only hope. My only one.'

'Maybe I'm getting closer,' I said.

She reached up and took my hand. 'I really appreciate all this. Don't think I don't.'

'You'd do the same thing for me.'

And she would, too.

I leaned down, got her pillows straight behind her head, kissed her on the cheek again, got the washcloth straight on her forehead and said, 'I'll try and call you early this evening. Let you know how things are going.'

She gave my hand a squeeze and then sighed deeply and closed her eyes.

Maybe she'd take a little nap, after all.

# 5

I spent the next few hours in the old stone library, the one with the lion and the gargoyle respectively guarding the entrance.

People came through the front doors knocking rain off their hats and shaking out plastic raincoats and smelling of fine chill air.

I sat in the Reading Room looking through back issues of the *New Hope Clarion*, which was the weekly paper. I had dug out the papers from five years ago.

I saw stories that made me feel I was in some kind of time warp. Pleasantly so. No banner headlines about serial rapists or shootouts at drug busts or four-year-olds mysteriously snatched from playgrounds . . . No, here the headlines ran to tractor pulls and VFW picnics, to softball tournaments and concerts in the town square. There was a great old 'Twilight Zone' short story about a commuter who looked out of his train window every day and fancied that he saw a peaceful turn-of-the-century town there just waiting for him to visit. So one night, sickened by a grisly job in advertising and an equally grisly wife, he jumps off the moving train . . . and dies. And when he wakes up, there he is, in the turn-of-the-century town. There are many such towns in Iowa even today, and you don't need to jump from a moving train to find them, either.

After an hour or so, I took a break, ambling down the hall to the restroom and then to a small room where a coffee vending machine stood next to a Frigidaire from the early 1960s, on the face of which was a sign that read *PEPSI 25 cents*. Who could pass up a bargain like that? The room had three small folding tables with a few chairs designated to each table. It was a room for sack lunches and lazy lunch-hour gossip.

While I was sitting there drinking my bottle of pop, a white-haired elderly woman wearing a flowered summery dress and a cute little straw hat bought a Pepsi of her own and sat at the table next to mine.

We smiled at each other in the way of polite strangers, and then I decided that if she was a long-time citizen here, she just might be able to help me.

After introducing myself, I said, 'Have you lived here a long time?'

'Oh my, yes,' she smiled. 'Nearly seventy-five years.'

'It's a wonderful little town.'

She laughed. 'You must be from the city.'

'These days I am.'

'People my age who grew up in towns like these have a lot of great memories but not everything was so wonderful.'

'Oh?'

'Well, we didn't have a hospital here until 1932, for one thing. A lot of people died by the time somebody could get them to Cedar Rapids. And for another thing, if you lived on a farm, the way my folks did, you didn't have running water and electricity until about the same time the hospital was built. And the state didn't get around to building good roads until well into World War Two. But the worst of it was the outhouses. There're a lot of jokes about them these days but believe me, back when you were a young girl trying to be a proper lady, outhouses were no fun at all, especially on winter mornings.'

I laughed. 'You make it sound pretty bad.'

'No. I just make it sound realistic. It was a much better world back then but you sure had a lot of inconveniences.'

I coughed. Getting drenched while ducking bullets was probably going to net me a nice strong head cold.

'Did you ever know a man named Brindle around here?'

'Stan Brindle?'

'Why, yes. Stan Brindle.'

'Sure I knew him. Most folks did. He was a pretty prosperous farmer up until the late eighties,' she said, sipping her Pepsi.

'That's what I'm trying to find out.'

'Oh?'

'What put him out of business, I mean. So suddenly.'

'Well, it's no secret. The same thing that put a lot of other farmers around here out of business. He came out of the seventies looking very good on paper but owing the bank a lot of money. In the old days, a farmer could always borrow against the next year's harvest if he needed to. But credit was drying up everywhere.'

'So he went bankrupt?'

She nodded. 'That and some trouble.'

Which is what I had been looking for in the newspaper stacks, the trouble Stan Brindle had gotten into.

'Drugs,' she said.

'Selling them, you mean?'

She shook her head, looking old lady elegant as she did so.

'Not selling them, but letting drug dealers use his farm to store their drugs and have some of their meetings. Cousin of his from Davenport, I believe, he was the one actually running the drugs.'

'They got caught?'

'Yes, they did.'

'Did Brindle go to prison?'

She frowned. 'He made it as far as county jail. He was in there two nights and he hanged himself with a belt he wasn't supposed to have. It was pretty sad. I knew Stan ever since he'd been a little boy. He was a big dreamer, and sometimes he could be a braggart, but he wasn't really a bad boy. Not really. In fact, he was pretty much straight until he met Reverend Roberts.'

'The same Reverend Roberts who's in town now?'

She smirked. 'The one and only. After he started getting into so much financial trouble, Stan and his wife decided that they needed to start going to church again. You know how people do when they're desperate. "I don't want to hear a peep out of You, God, unless I get in trouble." That sort of attitude. Well, anyway, they started going to church there and then they started socializing with the Reverend and his wife. And the Reverend started spending a lot of his spare time out at the farm, hunting and things like that. That was what he said, anyway. But what really happened was that he started having an affair with Stan's wife, who was one of those very pretty, shy little women who always wound up getting dominated by their men. Rachael, her name was. Anyway, one night things got so bad – apparently he'd caught them in bed – that Stan went over to the Reverend's house with a shotgun. Took a couple of shots, too, but missed. Law got called in and everybody in town pretty much knew what happened and Rachael moved away, went back to Springfield, Illinois, which was where she was from originally. It was after that, that Stan got caught up in the drug thing with his cousin from Davenport.'

'But you say that the Reverend used to spend a lot of time at the farm?'

She nodded. 'A lot.'

If that was the case, the good Reverend had easy access to an ideal place to bury the bodies of young girls he'd molested while filming them performing illegal sex acts. For the first time, I thought of Mike Peary's letter to Nora, Mike detailing how several girls who'd visited New Hope had later been murdered. Traveling around the countryside and killing young girls would be no trouble for a man who was already traveling anyway.

She looked at her watch. 'Oh, heck.'

'What?'

'I wanted to be home in time to watch *Oprah*. She's the only one of those talk show people I can stand. She seems genuinely sincere.' She looked out of the gray window at the dripping rain. 'But I'll never make it in time.'

'Tell me where you live. I'll give you a ride.'

'But don't you want to go back to your newspaper stacks?'

'Thanks to you, I won't need to. You told me everything.'

She beamed. 'Well, it's nice to know that somebody finds me useful at my age.'

# 6

'You lucked out, Robert,' my FBI buddy said on the phone ten minutes after I left the library.

'Yeah?'

'Yeah. Brooklyn, 1956.'

'All right.'

'Guy was into disembowelling women, but he got so bloody doing it he was afraid somebody'd spot him with blood all over his clothes. Killed four women that way.'

'And then?'

'Then he decided that, rather than kill them in parks or alleys as he had been doing, he'd knock them out, put them in his car trunk, and take them back to his garage.'

'I see.'

'After that, he became a much more efficient butcher. He started using a power saw and bought himself a butcher's rubber apron and gloves. He disposed of the bodies by chopping them up and burying the pieces all over his neighborhood. There was only one problem.'

'Oh?'

'Dogs. He was all right in the winter, burying the meat in the snow, but when he buried it under plain dirt, the neighborhood dogs found it.'

'Wow.'

'But, to answer your question, there are forty-three cases where the killer suddenly changed body disposal patterns.'

'How often did burying them show up?'

'In twenty-six of the forty-three.'

'So it's a popular method.'

'It's popular until they get caught.'

'Thanks, I appreciate it.'
'Just send me a new Mercedes.'
'You bet.'

# 7

He didn't want the man at the pet store getting suspicious so he bought most of the puppies in Cedar Rapids or Iowa City.

Look funny, a guy coming in once a month or so and buying himself a puppy. Month in, month out that way.

But today there wasn't time.

Had to buy it right here in town.

Ran into the pet store out of the rain; ran out ten minutes later with a plump, cuddly three-month-old Scottie puppy. Black it was, and cute as a button.

Thing yipped all the way out of town, all the way out to its ultimate destination.

He didn't do this because he hated the puppies or because he was sadistic.

No, he just thought that he owed it to those little friends of his.

They pretty much had the same menu all the time. They'd certainly appreciate a change of pace every once in a while.

That's why he bought the puppies.

He'd tried cats once but they weren't plump enough if they were still in the pet store.

If there was time, he'd probably go out in the woods and do a little hunting.

Boy, he could bag some things that would really make those little friends of his excited and happy.

Very happy.

The ride wasn't all that long.

Took the puppy from the back seat, still yipping of course, and carried him in the cardboard container straight down the hill and inside to where the trap door lay beneath the empty rusty milk cans

240

*that still smelled sour from their long-ago milk.*

*Took the puppy out of the cardboard box.*

*Aw.*

*He really was a cute little shit.*

*Such a sweet face. And those big brown eyes. And that wet black nose.*

*Knelt down, then, the puppy struggling in his grasp, and yanked the trap door open.*

*The odor nearly knocked him backwards. Always did, right at first.*

*But then he began inhaling deeply, purposely suffusing himself with it.*

*God, he loved that smell. Once he got used to it.*

*Puppy started squirming hard then so he really had to belt him across the head and pull sharply on his floppy black ear.*

*'Fucker, you be quiet now. You hear me?'*

*Then he leaned over the square hole in the floor and peered into the cold darkness below.*

*They were down there, oh, yes they were down there, his friends with the red eyes and the fat gray bodies and the knife-sharp teeth that could rip a human body clean to the bone in just a few minutes.*

*Well, maybe not an adult human body.*

*He'd never actually pushed one of those down there.*

*But the little girls, when he was done with them; the little girls he always pushed down there.*

*And one night, he brought a flashlight along so he could see it, see the dozens of them swarming over the naked little body, rending and ripping and chewing and chittering until their mouths shone with blood and the smell of the kill was enough to make him come without even touching himself.*

*Oh yes; oh yes.*

*And when there wasn't a little girl to give to his red-eyed friends, well, that was when he brought them a nice new puppy.*

*As now.*

*'Bye-bye, little friend,' he said.*

*The puppy wrestled, protested, as if it well knew what was about to happen.*

241

'Nothing personal,' he said.

And dropped the sweet little thing through the deep dark opening in the dirt.

There was a distant thwump when the puppy hit the far dark ground. And then a curious silence, as if the red-eyed things didn't know what to make of his gift.

But then reason prevailed.

And they knew very, very well what to make of his gift.

And what to do with his gift.

The puppy yipped and cried as they swarmed over him, and began the frenzied tearing, the frenzied ripping, the frenzied frantic separation of flesh from bone.

And there he knelt, peering down into the darkness; watching, watching.

# 8

She came up from nowhere, just as I gave the door to my motel room a small push.

I smelled her perfume before I heard her, the cold rain having started again, the six o'clock sky dark as night now.

'I want to show you something,' she said.

I stepped back, letting her walk into the room ahead of me.

She found a lamp, snapped it on, sending faint illumination throughout the shabby room.

'God, this is really a depressing place.'

'That's what I was thinking,' I said.

'Too bad there isn't another motel in town.'

She looked as good as always, Joanna Lodge, in a starched white blouse, blue cardigan and trim jeans flattering her slender body, her tumbling golden hair drawn up into a loose chignon.

I went over, grabbed a warm diet Pepsi, filled two plastic glasses half-full and then handed her one of them.

She smiled. 'I'm not sure I should thank you for this.'

'I'm a jet-setter,' I said. 'I live large.'

She looked around. 'I really do feel sorry for anybody who would have to stay here for any length of time. Rooms really affect my moods.'

'Which chair do you want? The blue uncomfortable one or the red uncomfortable one?'

'How about the blue uncomfortable one?'

'It's yours.'

We spent a few minutes talking about her grief, or lack thereof. 'I keep wanting to cry.'

'You will.'

'Maybe not. Maybe – well, I had been sort of psyching myself

243

up for a divorce, anyway. I just couldn't deal with all the women he had. Maybe I just closed myself off to him. Permanently, I mean.'

'Possible, I suppose.'

'When I talked to his parents last night, I really hurt their feelings.'

'Because of how you sounded?'

She sat there in her blue uncomfortable chair sipping her warm diet Pepsi. 'I wanted to sound dutiful. You know, properly bereaved. I gave it a good try but I don't think I was very convincing. And I know I hurt them. They're very decent people. I always wondered if Sam hadn't been adopted. Emotionally, he was their total opposite.'

'You really think he was adopted?'

She shook her head. 'No, he looked very much like both of them. But in every other way, he was unlike them.'

'You said you had something you wanted to show me.'

She opened her purse, took one white number ten envelope from it, and then a manilla envelope.

'I didn't tell you this the other day because I wasn't sure about you. Sam had been acting very strange lately. Upset – or frightened may be a better word. Jumpy when the phone rang; always looking out the window when he heard a car go by.'

'Do you know why?'

'No. But last week, I followed him a couple of times.'

'Followed him where?'

'To the old Brindle farm. I went there the morning after his death, too. Jane Avery stopped over earlier this afternoon and all but accused me of knowing something about his murder. She also said that she'd seen me drive out to the Brindle farm this morning.'

'Did you?' I said, knowing the answer because, like Jane, I'd seen her blue Toyota sedan go into the main barn on the Brindle farm.

'Yes. I was trying to figure out why Sam kept going out there.'

'And did you?'

'No. I mean, I walked around but I couldn't find anything. Anything at all.'

'But you must have found something.' I nodded at the two envelopes in her lap.

'Oh, right. These.'

She got out of the blue uncomfortable chair and walked the envelopes over to me.

I opened the first manilla envelope and knocked out a piece of heavy official paper from inside. It was a birth certificate.

'Craig Tolliver,' I said slowly.

'Who?'

'Craig Tolliver.' The son that the rich man Tolliver had told me had 'died' but who was still alive and somewhere in town. 'You never heard your husband mention him?'

'No.'

'June 23, 1958,' I said. 'That's the birth-date given here.'

'I wonder what Sam was doing with that.'

I set the birth certificate down and opened up the flap of the white number ten envelope.

Inside was a piece of letterhead from the First National Trust Bank – 'Your Friend In Deed Since 1926' – thanking Sam Lodge for renting a safe deposit box and saying that he was sure to find many of their other services to his liking, too.

'He ever mention a safe deposit box to you?'

'Not this one. Where we do the rest of our banking, in Iowa City, we have a safe deposit box there.'

'When can you get this opened?'

'I called my attorney. He said that if I take in proper ID, along with this letter, the bank will probably let me open it up tomorrow.'

'You going to do that?'

She nodded. 'Maybe when I get it open, I'll find out who killed him.' She smiled sadly. 'Maybe by then I'll be able to cry.'

'You mind if I keep this birth certificate?'

'That's fine.'

We were silent for a moment. She looked around the room. The rain pounded and bounced on the roof.

'This room really does depress me,' she said.

I was the same way after my wife died, so I recognized the feeling, fleeing any room where my memories of her grew too painful. It could be any room at all, one I'd never even been in before. But when the memories overtook me, I had to get out.

She was up, at the door.

I walked over to her.

'Thanks for bringing me these.'

She looked up at me. 'Maybe I'll drive to Iowa City and go to a movie.'

She wanted my permission. 'That sounds like a good idea. See something light.'

That was another thing I'd learned about mourning. Comedies can help you a lot.

She stepped forward and gave me a hug, not because I was me, but because I was another warm sensate human animal, and she badly needed contact with a like creature. It was a sisterly hug and I gave her a brotherly one right back.

After she left, taking her soft intelligent voice with her, there was just the thrumming sound of the rain.

# 9

The house where Tolliver was staying was three blocks east of my motel. The walk felt good. My middle-ageing body was in bad need of exercise. In the fresh wet air you could smell the summer flowers struggling for birth in the damp dark mud. You don't know what rich black soil is till you've held Iowa earth.

Tolliver was staying in a stone mock-Tudor house that looked as if it might be more comfortable in Beverly Hills. Lights shone in the mullioned windows.

He answered the door on the second knock, wearing a denim work shirt and a pair of chinos. He loked like a rich man trying hard to appear ordinary.

'You look kind of stressed out,' he said.

'I am.'

He stepped aside and let me walk through the vestibule and into the living room with its massive open fireplace and Edwardian antiques. G. K. Chesterton had probably sat in just such a room while he wrote his Father Brown stories.

'Some sherry?'

'No, thanks,' I said.

He pointed to a morris sofa. 'Why don't you sit down?'

'I need to keep moving. But I wanted you to see this.'

I handed him the manilla envelope. He opened it up and took out the birth certificate, which he carried over to a lamp with a baroque shade.

'Is it authentic?' I said.

'From what I can see of it here, yes.' He moved it around in the light under the shade. 'Where did you get it?'

'Sam Lodge's wife found it in their house.'

'Does she know how Lodge got it?'

'No. But that's not too hard to figure out.'

'It isn't?'

He brought the certificate back to me.

'Lodge found this somehow and then started blackmailing your son. Eve McNally told me that her husband suddenly came into a lot of money. Joanna Lodge said the same thing about Sam.'

'So they figured out who Craig is.'

'Yes, and Craig returned the favor by killing Lodge.' I didn't mention that he'd also kidnapped McNally's daughter.

He looked at me with great weariness and sorrow. 'We're getting close to him, aren't we?'

'Very close.'

He grabbed the sleeve of my jacket. 'We've got to stop him.'

'I know. And I plan to.'

He looked longingly at the birth certificate, the way a man would look at a baby picture of his son. 'I've read a lot about genetics these past few years. I suppose he was always a monster – just born that way, you know? But I don't want to absolve myself of the part I played in it. I should have stopped him a long time ago.' He made no effort to hide his tears. 'He really is a monster, isn't he?'

'I'm afraid he is.'

I glanced around the room. What a perfect night for a place such as this, and all the better if you had Jane Avery for company. You could make her some hot cocoa and put on one of the old Basil Rathbone Sherlock Holmes movies, set in foggy and mysterious London, but the fog and mystery of fiction, not the gore and grief of real murder.

'I'll keep you posted,' I said.

The last thing he said was, 'Do what you need to, Mr Hokanson. Anything at all you need to.'

I nodded and went back out into the night.

In my room, I grabbed a box of ammunition, a flashlight and my small leather bag of burglary tools. I sensed it was going to be a long night.

In my car, I laid my Ruger on the passenger seat, put the ammunition neatly next to it, and reversed out of the parking lot.

I needed to go back to the church. It was time to confront the good Reverend and tell him everything I knew; then it would be time for him to give Melissa McNally back to her mother.

Condensation covered the windows. The defroster didn't seem to help much. By the time I had rubbed the window clean, I was pulling up next to Jane Avery's empty patrol car in the parking lot of her apartment complex.

She answered on the first knock. Whatever it was she really wanted to say, she restrained herself and said simply, 'Oh.'

'I figured you'd be happy to see me.'

'I've got a headache, Robert, and I'm really not up for this.'

I sighed. 'Look, I know you're taking all this very personally but you shouldn't.'

'That's what you drove out here to say?'

'I drove out here to say that I like you. A lot.'

'I wish you'd leave.'

'Goddammit—' I shook my head. 'Sorry. I'm a little strung out at the moment.' I looked inside her decidedly untidy apartment. 'You're getting better. I don't see any panties hanging on any doorknobs.'

She didn't laugh. She didn't even smile.

'Are you going to invite me in?'

'No.'

'Just like that? "No." You didn't even have to think it over.'

'You're obstructing justice, for one thing. You could be arrested.'

I reached out and touched her shoulder. At least she didn't wince away. 'When it's all over, you'll understand why I couldn't tell you anything.'

She turned her fetching head sideways, looking over her shoulder. 'I've got some vegetable soup on. I'd better go eat it.'

'You make it yourself?'

'Right.'

'I forgot. That you're a lousy cook, I mean.'

She looked at me a long time and said in a voice husky with pain, 'Robert, just get the hell out of here, will you? I really don't appreciate this.'

There wasn't much I could say to that.

I leaned forward and kissed her on the cheek and said, 'I meant what I said. About liking you a lot.'

'Goodbye, Robert,' she said, and quietly closed the door, leaving me, in more ways than one, in the darkness.

I felt banished, cast out. I'd started thinking about Jane more seriously than I'd ever intended. Maybe it was her freckles or that stupid little nose of hers; more likely it was her wonderful combination of competence and tenderness I found so alluring.

A faint mist was in the air. The night smelled of the rain that had just quit falling. The parking lot was half-full and lonely looking in the mercury vapor lights.

I was thinking about Jane, and about how I might square things, so I didn't see him until I was a few feet away. In his cheap brown leatherette jacket and dirty jeans, I didn't recognize him at first.

He leaned against the trunk of my car, smoking a cigarette, watching me walk toward him.

He was a lone figure in the rolling Midwestern night, just like the apartment house itself, which was surrounded by woods on three sides.

'I need to talk to you.'

'You should talk to your wife first, McNally. Give her a little peace of mind. She's a good woman.'

'You don't need to tell me that.'

'You ever lay a hand on her again, I'll break your fucking arms, and that's a promise.'

'You supposed to be a tough guy?'

'No. Just a guy who doesn't think men should beat up women.'

His eyes were animal bright and animal quick.

'I want to get my daughter back,' he said, anger gone suddenly. He sounded weary, scared. 'Me and Sam Lodge – we got in way over our heads.'

'Tell me everything. Maybe I can help you figure something out.'

'I'm scared for her, for Melissa, I mean.'

He brought his cigarette to his mouth. His entire hand was shaking. 'I really went and fucked things up this time.'

'Just tell me what you know, McNally. You can beat up on yourself later.'

He pushed away from the car, and was just starting to stand up

250

straight as he flipped his cigarette somewhere on the lawn, when I heard the report of a rifle – then two, three reports.

The odd thing was, McNally didn't jerk when the bullets hit him, not at first. He only slumped back against the trunk as if he were weary beyond measure.

Then he crumpled, and it was quick and bloody and there was the frantic cry of a man who learns in a single instant that life is leaving him, that cold rushing eternal darkness is about to take him forever.

I caught him just as his fedora was tumbling from his head, just before his head cracked the pavement.

As I laid him out on the cold driveway, he fouled himself, the stench hot and sour.

And then the apartment-house door was bursting open. And Jane was coming quickly down the stairs, having obviously heard the rifle shots, and she was saying, 'Are you hurt, Payne? Are you hurt?'

'Over here!'

By the time she reached me, McNally was gripping my hand and sobbing. He was saying things but they were the incoherent rush and jumble of last words.

When she knelt down next to me, she shook her head sadly, seeing at once that McNally would soon be dead.

And before she could object, I slipped my hand from McNally's, got quickly to my feet and started running in the direction from where the rifle shots had come.

By the time I was twenty feet on the wet grass, I had my Ruger in my hand.

On the far side of the woods, I could see headlights from the two-lane highway leading out of town. The woods were no more than a quarter-mile deep and maybe the same across. But they gave a person plenty of places to hide.

The trail through the woods was all slippery mud and splashing puddle. I slipped and fell several times, skinning my knee once, cracking my head against a rather unyielding birch tree another time. The soggy brown leaves of autumns past covered trail and forest like a grimy parasite with a shiny wet shell.

I heard him ahead of me. He had deserted the trail and was crashing through the undergrowth that lay westward. He was the same man who'd shot at me earlier, I knew. And I also knew who he was.

I plunged into the undergrowth, keeping my Ruger held high above the bramble that snapped at my hand like an angry serpent, and the rocks that seemed to jump at my feet in order to trip me.

I was in bramble so deep I had to keep shifting my hips left and right to stop it from clinging to me. The trees changed abruptly from birch to pine, the boughs slapping my face with their scratchy fingers and high sweet perfume.

Horns sounded from the road to the east. Angry horns chastising somebody for nearly causing an accident.

He'd escaped, down the hill from the woods, straight across the highway where he'd likely parked his car.

I stood on the edge of the highway inside the glaze of my own chilly sweat, breath coming in hot rushing gasps, as I watched cars and trucks resume their normal course into and out of town.

He was nowhere to be seen, the man I'd been chasing. Nowhere.

The ambulance siren was still a few blocks away by the time I got back to the parking lot. The night was dark and windy with drops of rain being blown on the breeze. The exterior lights of the brick apartment house gave it the stark imposing qualities of a prison.

A small crowd encircled McNally's now-dead body. A few of the less optimistic ones had brought umbrellas, apparently planning to stay here for some time. As usual with people who show up for murders, they seemed both somber and excited, and maybe just a little bit ashamed of the latter.

Jane was talking on a portable phone, giving orders to her troops about how to handle murder scenes. At least they'd had enough practice lately.

I went up to her and said, 'He got away.'

She snapped down the antenna on the black portable phone. 'Did he tell you anything before he died?'

'He was going to. But he was shot before he could get it out.'

I looked down at McNally. Jane had draped her jacket over his face and the upper part of his chest.

'You didn't get a look at the person who shot him?'

252

'Not really.'

She frowned. 'Even if you did, I'm sure you wouldn't tell me, anyway.'

I wasn't sure how I was going to sneak away from here and go out to the church.

But then Jane went and made it easy for me.

'Why don't you get out of here, Payne? I don't need any more aggravation.'

'If that's the way you want it,' I said.

Just then the ambulance, full of wailing grief, pulled into the parking lot, a hero too late to matter.

# 10

By the time I reached the church, the rain started again in earnest, cold and drab and relentless.

I parked in the U-shaped gravel drive then ran up to the front door. I heard guitar music. Except it wasn't of the churchly sort, those 'born again' ditties that seem to be about romantic love but are really about Jesus ('He's the greatest lover the world has ever known/ The only lover who will never leave you on your own' ran a song I'd heard while dialing around on the radio one day) – no, this was bayou blues crossed with some high fine rock licks.

I went inside, stood in the back.

He didn't see me or hear me, apparently, Kenny Deihl; he just sat up on a folding chair by the altar, pausing now to tune his guitar. The church was dark except for the lone narrow beam of a small spotlight that highlighted Kenny's blond hair.

I listened to the rain, hard and cold, and had a moment of simple animal appreciation for my shelter, even if it had been built by a hypocrite minister.

'Kenny.'

I walked down the center aisle. The stained glass images were difficult to pick out with no sunlight streaming through them.

He'd played a few chords, hadn't heard me.

'Kenny.'

This time, he looked up. He wore a green Western-style shirt and jeans and Texas boots.

'Hi, Mr Hokanson.'

'You seen the Reverend?'

'Not in the last hour.'

'Think he's up at the house?'

254

Kenny shrugged, looked back at his guitar. 'Suppose he could be.'

I reached the altar, looked up at him.

'You a part of it, Kenny?'

He didn't raise his eyes, kept pantomiming notes. 'A part of what, Mr Hokanson?'

'Remember I asked you how the Reverend made enough money to keep everything afloat?'

'Uh-huh.'

'Well, I found out how he does it.'

Now he raised his head and looked at me. 'It's like I told you, Mr Hokanson. The Reverend's treated me pretty good, all things considered, so I don't figure it's my business to ask him any questions about where his money comes from.'

'He's the worst kind of man there is, Kenny. He molests little girls and boys.'

He frowned. 'Now I sure don't believe that. Tell me he drinks a little, or cheats on his old lady from time to time – yes, I'd have to say he probably does. But what you said – no way, mister. No way at all.'

'You ever go into Cedar Rapids with him?'

'Not really.'

'How about Mindy? She go in with him?'

The shrug again. 'Sometimes, I guess.'

'They pretty tight, are they, Mindy and the Reverend?'

He picked a chord. The church echoed with its keening power. 'Tight? Yeah, they're tight, I guess you'd say. After the Reverend learned the truth about Mindy and all. He had a hard time with it at first, the Reverend did, but he seems all right about it now.'

'I guess I don't know what you're talking about, Kenny.'

'About Mindy.'

'What about Mindy?'

He looked at me with unfathomable green eyes. Very somberly, he said, 'Then you couldn't tell either, huh?'

'Tell what?'

'Neither could the Reverend.'

'Tell what?'

'A slight smile this time. 'Heck, I couldn't tell either. Not till the Reverend told me.'

'Told you about what?' I said.

'About how Mindy used to be a man.'

He just kind of drawled it out, nothing special now, old news in fact.

But to me it wasn't old news.

If Tolliver was right that his son was still alive and killing people . . . what better disguise to assume than that of a woman?

'You're sure of that?' I said.

'Mindy told him one night. All about it, I mean. Personally, I didn't want to hear it. When she started talking about how – when he was still a man, I mean – they had to cut off his . . . Well, you know what I mean. I just couldn't get that out of my mind. What kind of guy would let somebody cut off his . . . you know, down there.'

'Where did she have the surgery done?'

'Holland, according to the Reverend.'

I thought of what the Reverend's wife had said last night, talking around a smirk, about how she hadn't known her husband was so 'kinky.' She'd been referring to the Reverend and Mindy. Now her remark made sense.

Her husband was sleeping with a woman who had once been a man.

'They're lovers?'

'Guess so. Like I said, it really ain't my business.'

'And you don't have any idea where I could find either of them now?'

'Not unless they're up at the house.'

'Mindy goes to the house?'

'Oh, sometimes. But then they get to squabbling. You know how women like to squabble.'

He played another lick, shrill and obscene in this ersatz house of God.

Then he grinned at me. 'Gotta say one thing for those Dutch doctors.'

'What's that?'

'They sure gave Mindy one fine set of hooters. I mean, her being a guy and all.'

# *11*

I drove up the driveway to the Reverend's house. My car smelled of dampness now. The rain was falling so hard, it sounded as if hail were being mixed in.

I was still trying to make some kind of visceral sense out of what Kenny Deihl had just told me. It's all very well to watch Oprah and Geraldo and Phil interview transsexuals, but it's another matter to realize that you actually met one. My first instinct, of course, was Kenny's. Why would you willingly submit to having your pee-pee removed? You worked hard all your life to keep it from getting injured or damaged in any way – the little thing was pretty vulnerable when you came right down to it – and now here comes a guy who opens up his flasher coat and says, 'Take me, I'm yours.'

Of course, the reason I couldn't understand that was because I didn't have any sense of why transsexuals do what they do. Homosexuality is at least imaginable in many respects – you keep your born-with sexual identity, which means that you prefer lovers of similar identities. Not very mysterious, when you come right down to it. But transsexualism . . .

Both bays of the garage were open. Only one Lincoln was there. The garage was attached to the house so I parked inside the empty bay then walked up to a veranda filled with colorful lawn furniture that looked like children forced to stay inside because of the rain. The veranda smelled of gin and cigarette smoke.

I knocked on the door several times but got no answer so I tried the knob, which was unlocked, and went inside.

The kitchen was what they call farm-style – wide open spaces with lots of shiny pots and pans and cooking utensils dangling

257

from a wooden contraption on the ceiling; a large butcher-block table stood in the center of the big room, and a gleaming white refrigerator and stove and dishwasher were tucked neatly into the east corner.

'Hello!'

But nobody answered.

'Hello!'

Again no answer.

I walked into the dining room. Like the living room and den, which I saw shortly after, it looked like a tribute to an interior decorator rather than a place where real human beings actually lived and laughed and sweated and snored and kissed. A little too-too, if you know what I'm talking about, from a very elegant but obviously uncomfortable Barrymore sofa to an antique china buffet that had to have cost at least half my annual income. But who would dare risk opening it up? I was as intimidated here as I was in a museum, with a little boy's fear of bumping or nudging or backing into some pricey work of art and watching it tumble to the floor and shatter.

I looked for foot-tracks that a man might make who'd been running through the woods tonight but didn't see any.

The noise was faint but had a regular rhythm. Opening and closing; opening and closing . . . opening and closing drawers, I finally realized.

The house was carpeted throughout so it didn't take any great stealth on my part to quietly reach the door of the master bedroom and put my ear to it.

Drawers being opened and closed. Definitely.

I reached inside my jacket pocket, took out my Ruger with my left hand, and then eased the door open with my right. He was packing, getting ready to flee.

When he turned and saw me, and saw the Ruger, he said, 'What the hell're you doing in here? I could have you arrested.'

He was still every bit the suave TV minister, from the carefully moussed hair to the suitably purposeful gray pin-striped suit to the brilliantly shined cordovan loafers. And he looked right standing in a room like this, with its canopied double bed and huge, curtained window. But despite his bluster, his poise was gone.

I took the photo I'd found earlier this morning, walked over to him and tossed it on top of the bureau.

'Pick it up.'

'Why should I?'

I raised the Ruger and aimed it right at his forehead. 'Pick it up.'

He picked it up. Looked at it. His mouth twitched unpleasantly.

He tossed the photo back on the bureau. 'That doesn't have anything to do with me.'

'I've got two witnesses who saw one of your white Lincolns pull up to an old closed-up shop in Cedar Rapids. And I'll be glad to take you down there and show you the video equipment; and the blood from where the girls were beaten doing some bondage tricks.'

He shook his head. 'It's them.'

'Them who?'

'Them,' he said, sounding miserable. 'I told them they were going to get in trouble. And now they have.'

'I still don't know who "them" is.'

'My wife and Mindy, who else?'

'What the hell're you talking about? Why would Mindy and your wife get together?'

He smirked. 'I spent a few nights with Mindy myself – before I learned that she'd once been a man. But it wasn't me Mindy wanted, anyway. It was my wife. And it was their idea for the porno movies. All I did was sell them while I went around the Midwest with my religious program.'

'I suppose that makes you clean?'

'No, it doesn't. But at least I didn't exploit those little girls myself.'

I startled both of us by hitting him hard across the mouth with my Ruger.

He sank to his knees, blood bubbling through his fingers.

He was crying, and somehow the idea of him crying sickened me, and so, again startling myself, I kicked him hard in the ribs.

He fell over on his side and got into a foetal position.

'Why does everybody go out to the old Brindle farm?' I said, standing over him.

He made the mistake of not answering.

My foot sliced into two more of his ribs.

He started blubbering, blood pouring through his fingers again. He was crying again, too. 'That's where they set up the new studio.'

'So McNally and Lodge were blackmailing Mindy and your wife?'

He shook his head. 'Don't know anything about blackmail.' He groaned, holding his ribs.

I remembered the two black men saying that they hadn't seen the white Lincoln in a long time. I cursed with frustration and the Reverend whimpered in terror.

'There's a trap door in the barn floor,' he gasped. Then he looked up at me and said, 'Don't hurt me any more, all right? I really can't take pain. I really can't.'

But I didn't believe him. I raised my foot and kicked him again, this time in the chest.

But I guess he was right after all, the way he started sobbing. He really couldn't take pain. He really couldn't.

I left him there and walked back through the house and out the side door to my car.

I drove down past the church, past Kenny Deihl's pagan guitar licks, and out into the country.

It was time for me to visit the old Brindle farm.

# 12

Fog wrapped round and round the old Brindle farmhouse, a snake squeezing its victim to death, and glowed silver and opaque in my headlights as I glided down the gravel driveway. Distant and unseen, animals on the neighboring farm bayed and cried, like children calling out for help in the blind and smoky night.

I cut the lights when I pulled even with the farmhouse, and coasted several more feet before shutting off the engine, my tires making the gravel crunch and pop loudly in the oppressive and spooky silence.

Fog had swallowed up everything; I couldn't even see the ornament on the hood of my car.

I did a check of my tools – Ruger, flashlight, knife. The rest would stay behind.

I got out of the car, closing the door softly, almost afraid of another sharp noise in the gloom, as if I might awaken some lurking monster.

In the fog, the shape of the near barn was virtually impossible to see, only the gambrel roof having any real form to it.

I stopped, listened.

I'd heard something, or thought I had.

I was sweating again, and trembling. I kept thinking of how vicious I'd been with Roberts. Unlike me, usually; and not a side of myself I wanted to see.

I listened intently. Nothing.

Shoes scuffing gravel, I walked down to the east door of the barn and let myself in.

Barns retain their odors for decades, all the milk and waste and hay and mud and rotting wood like wraiths on the deserted air.

I shone my light around. There was a bullpen and two wide

261

stalls on the west end; and several narrow cow stalls on the east end. On the walls hung old bridles, the leather coarse and cracked; and rusted pitchforks and shovels and rakes; and half a rusty Schwinn bike that had probably been fine and shiny and new about the time John Kennedy was becoming president; the front wheel was missing.

I found a wobbly ladder angled against the upper floor and climbed it, splashing my light around on the hayloft above. Except for a rotting bundle of hay, the loft was empty, stray pieces of the stuff shining like fool's gold in the gleam of my flash.

Downstairs again, I found a small room that had probably been used for storing feed, and a milkhouse just outside the back door.

Raindrops fell through the holes in the roof and made hollow *pocking* sounds as they struck the floor far below.

It took me twenty minutes to locate the trap door, concealed as it was beneath several boards in one of the narrower stalls.

I thought of what Joanna Lodge had told me about how people in this part of Iowa had dug sub-basements and root cellars to hide runaway slaves.

I got down on my knees, set the boards aside, wrapped my hand around the ring bolt, and gave it a yank. It was three feet by three feet, plenty wide enough for carrying things down. I remembered what Peary had said about the killer suddenly disposing of the bodies differently – and about what the FBI had told me about the Brooklyn man who'd started burying his victims.

Cold and fetid air, the air of the grave, rose from the room below, and I was rocked back on my haunches. I sat still a long moment in the dark and damp barn, letting the gaseous odors subside.

I angled the beam of my flashlight into the room below. A ladder that looked much sturdier than the one leading to the hay-loft stretched down into shadow.

I started climbing down.

The air grew colder, the smell more fetid, as I descended the ladder. Just from the air currents, I could tell that this was a much larger room than I had expected. A few times the ladder rocked, threatening to dump me off, but for the most part, I had no trouble.

I reached the floor of hard-packed earth and turned around.

The room was around ten yards long and at least as wide. On the end where I stood, the wall had been clumsily bricked over, but at the opposite end, some trouble had been taken setting up wallboard and pouring a good stretch of concrete floor.

I walked down there, still shuddering from the chill, still trying not to take the unclean odors too deeply into my lungs.

At the far end was where the videos were filmed.

My light played over a bulky black portable generator that would be adequate to run a few lights and a camera. In this same corner was a bed, now mussed. I found streaks of blood on the white satin sheets and splattered across the wall. A pair of handcuffs hung from the brass bed-post. Blood had turned one of the cuffs dark. I touched it. The blood was dry, old.

For Mindy and Betty Roberts, this subterranean room would be much safer than a rented store in Cedar Rapids. There would be nobody here to note the comings and goings of your white Lincoln.

And then I heard it, or thought I did, that faint mewling that had stopped me a few minutes ago when I was walking down to the barn.

What was it? And where was it coming from?

I took a last look around at the room, trying to imagine what it was like for little girls of eight or nine to be dragged down here and forced to perform sex acts. It would scar them, spiritually if not physically.

I went up the ladder, glad to be climbing out of this evil place.

Back on top, I closed everything up, carefully replacing the boards so that no stray cat or dog would hurt itself by falling down the rabbit hole to the very perverted Wonderland below.

And just as I was finishing up, my flashlight lying atop a stall-ledge and giving me sufficient light, I heard it again.

Even above the chill rain and the cold soughing wind – there came that faint cry that I could only liken to the sound of a young animal crying for help. The fog made the sound even fainter.

I took my flashlight and went back outside to see if I could locate the source of the sound.

I got drenched for my trouble, rain even filling my shoes.

Where was it? What was it?

This time, when the tattered solemn plea came again, I turned back and realized that the cry was coming from the barn. Not the main barn I'd just been in but the much smaller and older barn to the east.

I walked down there, stumbling once through the fog on the foundation of some long-gone silo. They were ideal for tripping dumb human beings who didn't take extra care in the fog.

The closer I got, the clearer the sound was, and by now I could recognize it for what it was, a woman screaming and screaming and screaming.

I wanted to hurry but the fog made that unwise. I carefully picked my way down the sloping hill, my head starting to go numb from the steady drilling force of the rain, my sinuses getting themselves ready for a good long siege.

The barn door hung skewed badly left, thanks to the fact that its only support was a lone rusty hinge. I eased it creakingly open and shone my light inside.

No stalls in this one, no rooms for storing feed, no small round milkhouses or high shadowy lofts, just a square storage box, maybe four feet deep and three feet wide, built along the back wall of the aged barn – that and the rolling ancient dust and the smells of axle grease and motor oil. A 1952 Ford fastback, the kind of car small-town high school boys drove well into the seventies, was up on blocks. A long time ago somebody had put a lot of time and care into it. But now, in the harsh eye of my flashlight, it looked abandoned and corroded, rust taking its eternal toll, the giggles of the high school girls seduced in the back seat long ago flown away, like beautiful butterflies on the last day of summer.

The scream came from the back of the barn, past the Ford, past a shadowy stack of firewood.

I drew my Ruger and moved toward it, still trying to figure out how the sound could be so muffled.

And then I thought, if one barn has a basement room, why not both barns? Didn't Joanna Lodge say that a lot of places had such subterranean hidey-holes?

I went to the west corner of the barn, dropped to my knees and began clawing through some bricks and loose hay that looked as if somebody had carefully arranged it to look messy.

I found the trap door and ring bolt in seconds. This door was as wide as the other but was much heavier in appearance. I took the ring bolt in my hand and tugged but it didn't budge. By now, the woman below having heard me, the screaming was constant. She was also sobbing and blubbering and crying out, 'Hurry! Please hurry!'

It took several tries before the door even budged; three more huge efforts before I could get it open.

There on my knees, I clutched my throat and vomited into the scraps of hay next to me. The odor from below was that foul.

The woman continued to scream but I was afraid to lean back toward the opening and shine my light down there, afraid of what I would see. The reeking odors told me it was something beyond comprehension.

But I had no choice; I had to crawl back there and play my light below.

I can't tell you how many of them there were – a hundred at the least, perhaps two hundred at the most – enough to entirely cover the floor of the small basement. Some were the size of small fat puppies, others barely past the infant stage when rats are blind and deaf. As they swarmed over what was left of Mindy, I could hear the mad chittering of their hunger and zeal. She lay on her back on the ground. Half her face had been eaten away so that an eyeball hung on a bloody cheek, and her gnawed and bloody arms shone white with bone. Her stomach was a bloody hole excavated by dozens of hungry rats. She was still screaming but she wouldn't be screaming much longer. She was very near death.

I thought of the few things I knew about black rats, how they'd originally come from the deserts of southern Asia but then stowed away on the ships of the returning Crusaders, to help bring bubonic plague to Europe, which ultimately killed millions. And how rabid rats had been known to rip apart animals as big and formidable as horses.

Next to Mindy lay the remains of Betty Roberts, the Reverend's wife. Her face had been torn away, as had most of her torso, but I recognized the short, frosted hairdo. At the moment, a rat sat on her shoulder bone and picked the last of the flesh from her nose.

And as I trained my light back and forth across the floor, I saw the picked white bones of young girls, no doubt the runaways who'd featured in the porno movies. Done with, they'd been thrown down here as feast for the rats.

I fired two shots straight into the dozens of rats still massing around Mindy. They scattered briefly, the report ear-numbing as it echoed below, but it was too late. They had gotten the top of her head open enough to begin eating her brain.

I leaned to the side and vomited again, this time in great hot splashing chunks. I would never be able to forget what I'd just seen. Never.

And then I sensed somebody standing at the back of the barn, a silhouette in the gloom, and I raised my flashlight and saw Kenny Deihl standing there in his Western get-up, smiling at me.

'Pretty impressive, isn't it?' he drawled. 'How fast they can totally rip somebody apart?'

I didn't need to ask who he really was, the monster who was Tolliver's son, who had sent photos of his victims to his mother and father.

'But then, you're going to find out all about my friends for yourself, Mr Hokanson. I'm going to put you down there with them.'

I had made the mistake of dropping my Ruger while I was vomiting.

Kenny Deihl had made no such mistake at all. He kept a Magnum trained on me all the time he talked.

# 13

He had killed them all, he told me – Mike Peary, Nora and Vic, Lodge and McNally, Mindy and Betty Roberts. They had all uncovered his secret – or he thought they had, at any rate – and so he was forced to kill them. Eve McNally he'd beaten up when she couldn't tell him where the tape was that her husband had.

As he would now be forced to kill me. He'd tried it once already, on that first day. God, it seemed so long ago. After Mike, he'd gotten nervous about how much Nora knew, and followed her for a while.

'How about Melissa? You took her so McNally and Lodge would give you back something they were blackmailing you with, right?'

He nodded.

'Very creative, those two. They hid out here and watched the taping in the barn over there. I always told Mindy and Betty that I'd drive the girls back to Cedar Rapids and drop them off. But I never did. I brought them over here and fed them to the rats.' He smiled his improbably boyish smile. 'You know the funny thing? Those're the only animals I've ever liked, those rats. Hated everything else.' He shrugged and moved in closer to me. My flashlight was on the floor. He bent over, picked it up, shined the beam in my face. 'So good old Lodge and good old McNally videotaped me killing one of the runaways and stuffing her down with the rats. They made me pay them $6,000 a month. I have some money I diverted from Eleanor before I left her – but I just didn't like the principle of paying somebody blackmail money.'

He was silent for a time. Rain plopped from the roof to the ground in front of me. The old hay smelled sour-sweet in the darkness. I avoided looking at my vomit.

267

Suddenly, he turned the flashlight out. 'Don't say anything or I'll kill you on the spot.'

I said nothing, just eased myself quietly to my feet. He could see me with no problem. And could kill me with no difficulty.

At first, I didn't know what he was so agitated about. There was just the hissing rain and wind and the far distant midnight trains.

And then I heard it, an almost inaudible squishing sound. What was it?

I had to strain to listen for a time before I recognized it. Then – footsteps. Yes. Somebody was outside the barn, sneaking up.

In the doorway I saw nothing but the fainter darkness of the night. And then somebody was there, peering inward.

Rain hammered the roof; wind rattled the back door.

Inward came the person; one, two, three cautious steps.

Whoever it was carried a shotgun.

Four, five steps now.

'Watch out!' I called, pitching myself to the right and the hard earthen floor.

As I did so, I saw a yellow eruption of flame and smoke as Kenny's gun fired in the darkness.

He caught the person; there was a thrash of old hay as, wounded, groaning, the intruder fell to the floor.

'You sonofabitch,' Kenny said in the gloom. 'You're going to regret coming in here, believe-you-fucking-me.'

As I scrambled back to my feet, he turned the flashlight on again and shone it at the person he'd wounded.

The blood from her shoulder ruined the nice starchy look of her blue uniform shirt. She lay on her back, holding a bloody hand to the wound. The injury looked serious.

'Stay right where you are!' Kenny shouted at me above the din of rain and wind.

But I didn't pay any attention to him.

I went over to Jane and knelt down beside her.

'Thanks for warning me,' she whispered.

'Least I could do,' I said, touching my fingers to her wound, trying to see how bad it was. Awful bad.

'You shouldn't have followed me,' I said.

She grinned her girly grin. 'Least I could do.'

Kenny came over. 'Help her to the trap door there.'

My reaction was to spring to my feet and start to swing on him but all he did was raise his Magnum and push it into my face.

'Don't worry about being noble, Hokanson. You're both going to die. I'm too much of a gentleman to let her die alone.'

Just before he hit me hard on the side of the head with his Magnum, I heard a kind of faint bleating sound from the storage box near the back, and wondered if an animal had been trapped in there. But then I didn't wonder about much at all because when the gun cracked against my skull, I felt my knees start to buckle.

He brought his knee up between my legs and caught me hard and straight in the groin.

Pain blinded me momentarily; he pushed me to the floor, next to Jane, and grunted, 'Help her up!'

'Do what he says, Robert. C'mon.'

But I must have moved too slow because he took two more steps toward me. This time he hit me so hard, my knees buckled entirely and I dropped to the ground. I was dizzy and everything was becoming faint and fuzzy.

I pitched forward into the deeper darkness of my mind, where pain and fear lay like shameful secrets.

Could I get up? Drag myself over to Jane in time to help her? Somehow get my hands on Kenny?

I wasn't out long, just long enough for him to carry Jane over to the trap door.

She fought him constantly, even using the arm of her wounded shoulder to drive the heel of her hand into his jaw.

But I had recognized the look in his eyes; he was as eager for death as his friends the rats.

He dropped her hard on the floor, so that her shoulder lay directly over the hole.

The response was instant. A kind of chant, a keening cry unlike anything I'd ever heard before in my life, went up in the old barn, louder even than wind and rain combined, the cry and chant of rats as they are teased with just a few drops of blood falling from above, the same cry and chant of the rats that overran medieval European villages and ate infants in the dark impoverished streets of eighteenth-century London.

269

Kenny smiled at me. 'She's really working them up. They love that blood of hers.'

He watched, amused, as I drew myself to my feet once more. But this time I was so wobbly, I thought I was going to pitch back down again.

Jane, who was obviously losing consciousness, tried to push herself away from the trap door but she had almost no strength left.

Kenny dropped to one knee, jerked her around and shoved one of her legs down the hole.

The cries of the rats came up again as did the scent of their carrion.

They were eager for her, waiting.

And then Jane screamed. She looked at me frantically and shouted, 'One of them is on my leg!'

I lunged at Kenny but he sidestepped me and brought the gun down across my head again.

But this time I didn't drop and I didn't let go. I held on to him as if I'd tackled him. He kept pounding and pounding at me with the handle of his weapon but I wouldn't let go, wouldn't let him be free to push Jane down the hole.

Jane screamed again. I turned my head briefly away from Kenny's mid-section and glanced down the hole.

Three fat black rats were ripping her leg with almost desperate joy. More rats were scurrying up the ladder, dozens of them.

The gunshot came out of the darkness with no warning. Jane, Kenny and I had been too preoccupied to hear him come in, too preoccupied to watch him stand on the edge of the flashlight beam, lower his Remington shotgun and take the top of Kenny's left shoulder off.

All I knew to do was dive for Jane, pull her leg up from the hole and then grab the furry slimy rats in my hand and hurl them back down into the fetid darkness.

I carried Jane over to the wall, got her propped up and then had a look at her leg. They'd torn the flesh severely, and in a couple of places you could see where their teeth had literally chewed off chunks of her flesh.

'*No!*' She was looking over my shoulder when she shouted.

I turned around to see what was going on.

Tolliver, looking curiously composed and wearing, as always, his blue blazer and white shirt and gray slacks and black penny loafers, was lifting his son up in his arms and carrying him over to the trap door.

Kenny was sobbing and pleading incoherently, seeming to know exactly what his father was going to do.

Jane cried out again to stop Tolliver but it was too late. Many years too late.

Tolliver dropped his son to the floor then knelt down next to him and started pushing him head first into the hole.

Despite the fact that Kenny's shoulder had been torn away, he was still conscious enough to know what was happening.

And then he vanished, having tumbled into the hole.

Tolliver stood up and quickly closed the trap door.

Kenny's pleas and cries filled the barn.

Jane covered her ears as the keening of the rats overwhelmed Kenny's screams.

At least they made fast work of him, Kenny falling silent no more than a few minutes after his father had slammed the door on him.

And then the rats fell silent, too.

And then there was just the sound of the rain, the incessant rain, and the soft whispers of midnight on the cold wind.

Jane was crying, holding on to me as if she were drowning.

Tolliver came across, looked at us a moment, and stooped to pick up his shotgun. 'It's over now. And I hold myself greatly responsible. I should have dealt with him long ago.' You could hear the tears in his voice suddenly.

'Thanks for saving us,' I said.

But there in the darkness, he didn't seem to hear. There was just the sound of the soughing wind and his whisper. 'It's over.'

He turned, without saying anything more, and walked out of the barn, the shotgun cradled in his arms.

It took me a moment to figure out what he was going to do, but when I did I ran out of the barn, too, out into the rain and the darkness and the wind.

He stood facing the barn, angling the barrel of the shotgun just under his chin.

271

'Don't do it, Mr Tolliver!' I shouted, wind making my voice faint and ragged. 'Don't do it!'

I ran as hard as I could but I slipped in the mud and just as I was getting to my feet, I saw, through the lashing rain, his fingers tense on the trigger.

The roar of the gun, the kick of it in his hands, the explosion of the back of his head – all happened in moments.

And then he fell forward into the mud, fell on the gun that had served its purpose.

I went over and knelt next to him. The only sound was the rain now. I touched his shoulder and said something like a silent prayer. Maybe he'd been right. Maybe he should have dealt with his son a long time ago, before the boy had killed all those people. But that was easy for somebody to say, and much more difficult to do.

I stayed there with him a little while longer and then got up and walked back down the hill to the barn.

Jane had managed to pull herself to her feet and was leaning against the wall. She had the flashlight in her hand.

'God,' she said, 'I feel so sorry for him.'

I nodded. 'Poor bastard. But maybe it was the right thing for him to do.'

'You want to help me out to the car?'

'In a minute,' I said. 'Right now I need you to shine that light at the storage box over there.'

I'd remembered the mewling sound I'd heard earlier.

There was a padlock on the door to the box so I went back and took Jane's service revolver.

I put a clean bullet through the hasp of the lock and moments after I did so, I heard the muffled plaintive cry again.

I opened the door, knowing exactly who I'd find.

Eight-year-old Melissa McNally was in there, bound, gagged, and tied to a chair.

She was dirty and sweaty and bloody where the rough ropes had cut her, and once I took the gag off her she started crying and laughing at the same time, as if she couldn't decide which was the most appropriate.

And then, free of her bonds, I picked her up and held her tight and told her how much her mother loved her and how happy she would be to see her, and then I carried her back to Jane and the three of us set out into the night and the rain and the wind for Jane's police cruiser.

We went on to the hospital where it was quickly decided that Jane's shoulder wound was bloody but not nearly as serious as we'd feared, though the leg needed a lot of work.

After they'd cleaned the wound and bandaged her up, I went where she lay on the gurney and said, 'You look cute lying there like that.'

'Yeah, I'll bet.'

'You do.'

'Well, if you're so sure of that then how about giving me a kiss?'

I smiled. 'I suppose that could be arranged.'

An hour later, I drove her home.

# 14

We followed the river, blue and fast in the July sunlight, and then we followed the clay cliffs for a time, angling eastward to watch a half-dozen horses who were running over some steep pasture-land, their coats shiny and beautiful in the soft afternoon.

I didn't try any fancy stunts today. Four weeks after our night in the barn, Jane's arm was still in a sling and she tired very easily. Flying upside down probably wasn't such a great idea.

We stayed up two hours and then landed in Herb Carson's small field next to his aviation museum.

'You're going to be an addict by the time this guy gets done with you,' Herb said to Jane as he walked us over to my car.

She looked at me and smiled. 'That's what I was thinking.'

I thanked Herb for the use of the plane and told him I'd probably see him again soon.

I drove us back to town.

'You still going to Washington?' Jane said after we'd been driving a few minutes.

'Next Tuesday.'

'For three weeks?'

I watched her a long moment. 'That's not a real long time. Not if people talk on the phone every night or so, anyway.'

She laughed. 'I guess that's right.' Then she shook her head and frowned. 'See, this is why I'm so shitty about liking some-body.'

'You're not shitty.'

'Sure I am. I mean, we don't have anything official between us at all and already I'm complaining about you going on a trip. I'm just too dependent on people. I drove my husband nuts. The poor guy.'

'Well, I sort of drove my wife nuts, too.'

'You did?'

I nodded. 'I'm the same way. Too dependent. She'd go over to Iowa City to take a class and I'd get all bent out of shape. Feel like I was deserted.'

'Hey, you really are dependent. That's just the kind of thing I'd do.'

I laughed. 'Hey, let's go out tonight and celebrate being dependent.'

'You're on.'

We had reached the city limits now, the tidy little Iowa town in the early July sunlight, everything clean and purposeful and timeless against the rolling green countryside. Home.

We were silent for a while, listening to a little rock and roll on the radio, and then she said, 'Robert?'

'Yeah?'

'You think about him much?'

'About Tolliver?' I said.

'Uh-huh.'

'Yeah, I do. Quite a lot, in fact.'

'I wish he wouldn't have killed himself. But I guess for him it really was about honor, wasn't it?'

'Yeah,' I said, 'honor or something very much like it.'

We found a Dairy Queen and pigged out.